Royal Revenge

J. TREY WEEKS

ROYAL REVENGE

Copyright © 2019, J. Trey Weeks
All rights reserved. No part of this book may be reproduced or distributed in any manner, except in the case of brief quotations included in critical articles or reviews.

ISBN-13: 978-1-6875-6981-3

This is a work of fiction. Names, characters and incidents are either the product of the author's imagination or are used fictitiously. Any resemblance to actual businesses, events, locales of persons (living or dead) is entirely coincidental.

Dedication

I have been fortunate to be involved in sourcing products in China and many countries in Europe and South America, and in operating businesses in many states in the US and the Canadian provinces throughout my career. I have truly appreciated the variances in culture, politics, geography, food, language, and religion internationally and throughout our great country and wish everyone in the US could experience the diversity I have enjoyed. I have been especially fascinated with the intricacies of manufacturing, distributing, importing and exporting and the motivations – not always primarily profit – of business people in the countries and cities in which I've worked and visited.

Thanks to those with whom I have shared these experiences, as suppliers, customers, employees, and employers. Special thanks to Jim Gould and Rick Newbern, with whom I have logged more than a few million miles while visiting and working in many different locations, and to Levon Ezell who will always be the greatest mentor a young man could wish for.

Forward

In 1990, the internet, email, texting, and iPhones were all in the future. Fax machines and laptop computers were still novelties. Most large companies had mainframe computers with proprietary software installed in huge and expensive configurations. Many small companies had no computers at all. Google, Facebook, Twitter, and "social media" didn't exist. PC Desktop computers were just becoming prominent. Cellular telephones were a luxury item permanently installed in cars and were generally not portable.

NAFTA, the North Atlantic Free Trade Alliance, which would allow significant reduction of duties on US imports/exports into and from Canada and Mexico, was being avidly negotiated by the governments of Canada, Mexica, and the United States and was finally passed into law in 1994. Many American, Mexican, and Canadian companies began to work much earlier exploring opportunities and locations in adjoining countries for the first time in anticipation of an increase in trade. Imports from the US into Canada carried very heavy duties prior to NAFTA, and the significant reduction of duties was a subject of avid discussion when this story was being developed.

Canada was and is still a bilingual country where every label, sign, and most public announcements are required to be in French and English. In the late 80's and 90's, Canada was very divided between French-speaking Quebec and the other provinces where English was totally dominant. Toronto was the largest city, and Ottawa was the capital of a "united Canada". Quebec City and Montreal were almost exclusively French, and many companies headquartered there found it difficult to manage operations in other provinces due to language issues as well as *Francophone* versus *Anglophone* prejudices. US citizens wishing to work in Canada were subject to rigorous standards requiring proof that their talents could not be readily duplicated by a Canadian worker. Dismissal of even one Canadian management member was often subject to lengthy government scrutiny and usually resulted in months and months of severance pay required. The total elimination of a "Head Office" as depicted in this book probably could not have occurred except in a very unique situation.

In the US, rarely was a Spanish translation given, and only then in South Florida, South Texas, and the most southern parts of New Mexico, Arizona, and California. There was certainly no "press one for English, press two for Spanish" message, if in fact you did not talk to a human receptionist when you called a business.

Miami and Dade County, because of the tremendous influx of Cubans in the late 1950's and early 1960's, was made up of almost 50% Spanish-speaking people and had developed into a center of Cuban and Hispanic culture. Florida had become the door to South America diplomatically, for trade, for banking, and for significant immigration of people from the northern tier of South America countries, like Venezuela, Columbia, Peru, Ecuador, and Chile. Unfortunately, Miami and South Florida also became the epicenter for the import of cocaine and other drugs unto the United States.

Moving drug product into Florida was often the easiest part of drug smuggling because of the many places small planes and boats could land in Florida. Detection was difficult, relying on radar (which was easy to evade) and Coast Guard patrols. The U.S. authorities were completely overwhelmed and lacked sufficient resources to stem the tide. Moving drugs from there to the rest of the U.S. was a much more difficult task requiring secure storage and transportation.

Although Mexican drug trafficking organizations have existed for several decades, their influence only increased as a result of the demise of the Colombian Cali and Medellín Cartels in the 1990s. The Mexican drug trade was in its infancy in the late 1980's.

It is rumored that one of the largest FBI offices in the US was headquartered in Dalton, GA in response to the huge amounts of drugs that were distributed from there in the thousands of trucks emanating from Dalton and traveling to destinations all over the US daily

The Front de libération du Québec (FLQ; "Quebec Liberation Front") was a separatist and Marxist-Leninist paramilitary group in Quebec. Founded in the early 1960s, it was a militant part of the Quebec sovereignty movement. It conducted a number of attacks between 1963 and 1970, which totaled over 160 violent incidents and killed eight people and injured many more. These attacks culminated with the bombing of the Montreal Stock Exchange in 1969, and with the October Crisis in 1970, which began with the kidnapping of British Trade Commissioner James Cross. In the subsequent negotiations, Quebec Labour Minister Pierre Laporte was kidnapped and murdered by a cell of the FLQ. Public outcry and a federal crackdown subsequently ended the crisis and resulted in a drastic loss of support, with a small number of FLQ members being granted refuge in Cuba.

FLQ members practiced propaganda of the deed and issued declarations that called for a socialist insurrection against oppressors identified with "Anglo-Saxon" imperialism, the overthrow of the Quebec government, the independence of Quebec from Canada and the establishment of a French-speaking Quebecer "workers' society". It gained the support of many left-leaning students, teachers and academics up to 1970, who engaged in public strikes in solidarity with FLQ during the October crisis.

After the kidnapping of Cross, nearly 1,000 students at Université de Montréal signed a petition supporting the FLQ manifesto. This public support largely ended after the group announced they had executed Laporte, in a public communique that ended with an insult of the victim from the group. Nonetheless, FLQ continued to receive the support of other far-left organizations such as the Communist Party of Canada and the League for Socialist Action. The KGB, which had established contact with the FLQ before 1970, later forged documents to portray them as a CIA false flag operation, a story that gained limited traction among academic sources before declassified Soviet archives revealed the ruse. By the early 1980s, most of the imprisoned FLQ members had been paroled or released.

J. Trey Weeks

1

Montreal, Quebec, Canada

The package arrived as the very cold and dreary Canadian day turned to dusk. It looked ordinary enough. The light brown paper in which the small oblong box was wrapped was slightly spotted and rumpled from the damp of melting snowflakes as they merged with the overheated air of the hotel.

Outside the hotel, Montreal's busy streets were just now starting to accumulate the huge ugly mounds of frozen brown slush that would line their edges for the entire gray six-month Quebec winter. The first snow of the season had been falling heavily on the city for most of the day, and the snowplows had been out in force.

Jacques Letrec, the Senior Bell Captain of Les Quatre Saissons, had been delighted to interrupt his own inviolate coffee break to deliver this package. Over the past few months the old Bell Captain had come to expect big rewards from the young Americans who had become such frequent guests of the hotel. A small man, he nonetheless had ruled the ranks of bellmen at *Les Quatre Saissons* for many years with an iron fist. Disturbing his break was something of an event.

The delivery was the Concierge's responsibility, but, as usual, the Concierge had been doing things other than the job he was supposed to do. This time he was occupied in some "emergency conference" with the hotel's manager. The Concierge usually had "important" reasons for sloughing off,

Jacques reflected as he ascended in the sparkling elevator to the top floor.

Letrec was quite surprised to have his delivery to the luxurious two-bedroom Ambassador's Suite rudely intercepted by an imposing, portly sergeant of the Montreal police. Jacques' discomfort was compounded exponentially after the sergeant escorted him into the Americans' suite. He found the occupants of the room very tense and out of sorts. This was very unusual for the cheerful Americans. Was all of this because of this delivery?

Jacques soon found himself the object of terse interrogation by the sergeant's supervisor, Inspector Roch. Roch was swarthy, smelled like smoke, was somewhat disheveled, and tall for a French-Canadian. If possible, he bested the Sergeant's arrogance. While Jacque was being virtually impaled in a hard-to-follow litany of Quebecois French and English, the Americans just stared at the floor, plainly upset and distraught. Almost as an afterthought, the Inspector seized the package from Jacques. He had introduced himself with a quick flash of his official identification, and obviously expected Jacques to hang on his every word.

"How did you come to have this package? Who brought it to the hotel?" demanded the Inspector.

"The package was left at the Concierge Desk by a gentleman who immediately left the hotel, *Monsieur* Inspector. Normally it would be the responsibility of the Concierge to take care of it. I brought it up because the Concierge was busy. I was simply trying to be of service to our American guests," Jacques said, nervously, with a pleading look at the downcast Americans, which was not returned by them.

"And get a big tip," thought Inspector Roch. "The man who delivered it. You saw him? What did he look like?"

"Mon Dieu! What a hardass!" thought Jacque. "Like anyone. A small man. He was not as tall as I am, and he had black hair," Jacques replied.

"Shorter than this man must be a midget," thought Inspector Roch. "Long hair or short hair?" he demanded.

"It was quite long. It fell over the back of the collar of his coat."

"*Le manteau.* The coat. What kind of coat? Of what color was it? Of what was it made?"

"*Au Manteau Noir.* It was a black coat that came to here," Jacques indicated a level just below his hips. "I believe it was of leather. The kind that any messenger would wear. He had black jeans and black boots."

"*Et son visage.* And his face. You saw his face?"

"Just for a moment."

"Well, what can you tell me about his face, *Monsieur* Letrec?" Roch asked, the frustration apparent in his voice.

"*Monsieur* Inspector, *sil vous ples*, I only saw him for a moment."

"*Mais qu'avez-vous vu?* But what did you see? You must remember something of his face!"

This was becoming extremely unpleasant, thought Jacques. Glancing nervously around him at the others who continued looking at the floor, obviously preoccupied and disconnected, Jacques replied, "He had a dark face, with a moustache. He looked like he had a problem with his skin. I would say that he was about thirty years old. He seemed to be in a great hurry. He just came into the hotel, left the package at the desk without a word, and rushed out."

"I feel like a fucking dentist, pulling this idiot's teeth one at a time," thought Roch. "Did he speak to you? Did he say anything?" *"Come on, you idiot, think!"* Roch said to himself.

"No, *Monsieur*. He just left the package on the desk and then he left the hotel."

ROYAL REVENGE

"*Il n'a rien dit?* He said nothing?"

"No, *Monsieur* Inspector."

"How did he leave the hotel? Did you see his car?"

"*Monsieur*, I did not notice. I did not know it was so important."

"Is there anything else you can remember about this man?"

"No, *Monsieur* Inspector. I am sorry."

Inspector Roch dismissed the hapless bellman, sans tip, with an indifferent wave of his hand and a glance of frustration. The waiting sergeant escorted Jacques toward the door. "*With a proper tip,*" Roch thought, "*I could deliver a nuclear bomb to this fucking hotel.*"

Before he opened the door, Roch turned to the sergeant and said, "Find out which officer was supposed to monitor the Bell Desk and send him home and replace him with someone who can think! Bring me his name and badge number afterward. Then take a full statement from this man and get every single detail he can remember, no matter how long it takes," Inspector Roch ordered the sergeant, tersely. "Make sure you cover everything – no matter how important either of you think it is. I want everything! Every single detail!"

Roch closed the door abruptly and placed the wrapped box on the marble coffee table. On the paper with blue ink in flowing cursive was written, "M. Royal, Royal Floors." Roch had spent many years in the Montreal Police, the last ten as a Special Investigator. He was noted for his ability to immediately assess and predict situations, and quickly solve crimes, regardless of the complexity. This case baffled him. In addition to virtually no clues, it involved foreigners – Americans to boot. On top of that, they were wealthy Americans, and well-connected in Montreal and with the Canadian government, which meant he would be under even more scrutiny than normal from his officious boss. They were also likable, and his instincts told him no good was going to come out of this, and regardless of how good he was, he wasn't going to solve this case in the short term.

Offering him a pair of latex gloves, Roch asked, "Will you unwrap the package, please, *Monsieur* Royal?"

The largest of the Americans got up and came to the table. He pulled on the gloves, and hands trembling, Jeff Royal carefully removed the string and then the damp brown paper wrapping. Inside was what appeared to be a gift of jewelry, perhaps an expensive necklace or bracelet, from Montreal's best department store. The long, narrow, black padded imitation reptile-skin box was embossed in gold leaf with the name of the store. It was trimmed on the edges with a gold metallic finish. Inside, it was luxuriously lined with dark blue velvet. Held neatly in place on the blue velvet liner by a matching elastic band was the left ring finger of a woman, wedding rings intact, severed with jagged ferocity just above the knuckle that had connected it to her hand. The skin was very white except for dark bruises around the cut end. A miniscule trickle of blood had drained onto the velvet. Her manicured and painted fingernail was broken.

"Oh my God, how could someone do this to her?" Jeff asked no one in particular as he fell to his knees. With tears rolling down his cheeks, he looked with pleading toward the Inspector.

"These are Connie's rings," he sobbed. "We had this set made from her original wedding rings about six years ago when we bought a larger diamond. Who could do something like this?"

Ignoring the rhetorical question and repressing his own rage at the insanity evidenced by the severed finger, Roch said with as much sympathy as he could summon, "I am very sorry, *Monsieur* Royal, I know this must be very painful. But I have to ask a very difficult question. Can you positively identify this ring as belonging to your wife? Are you sure?"

"I ... I think it must be. I'm sure," Royal said. "But why, Jesus, why would someone do this?"

M. Gilles Roch, Senior Inspector of the Montreal Police was at a loss to answer the question. He still didn't see a motive to this whole situation. If the American had anything to do with it, he was the best actor he'd ever encountered! Still ... something just wasn't right with the whole picture.

The Americans seemed to be innocent victims of a madman. But were they? He hoped the note enclosed in the wrapper would help answer some of the questions he had about this case. Touching only a minute portion of the corner with tweezers extracted from his coat pocket, he carefully lifted the note from the discarded papers. In the Gallic script he was now beginning to recognize, it read:

> "A final warning that you must leave. Quebec is for Quebecers. We will not tolerate intrusion by the Americans.
>
> *FLQ"*

2

Tampa – Miami, Florida – Montreal

Jeff Royal was an only child raised by doting parents in Tampa. The Royals lived for their son. Rita worked tirelessly on school projects, and Rita and David attended virtually all of Jeff's after-school and sports activities. His life was idyllic and simple throughout. He did very well in school, had lots of friends, and considered his parents intelligent and respected their wishes in most cases. The Royal's home became the center of the universe for many of his friends in high school. His parents' deaths changed Jeff's life and his view of life drastically.

During his senior year in high school, Jeff's mother died of a rare form of liver cancer after a very short illness. On March first, she noticed a yellowing in her eyes. On March 15th, she checked into Shriner's Hospital for "tests". On Memorial Day, May 28th, three days before Jeff graduated from high school, she died, having never left the hospital. Jeff and his closest friends visited her every day and Jeff and his father spent most of the weekend nights at the hospital with her. They had depended on Rita Royal for virtually everything in their home life. Rita and David Royal had no brothers or sisters. Jeff's grandparents had been dead since before he was born.

"We're all alone now," Jeff said, choking up as they prepared to enter the packed church for Rita's funeral. "We only have each other."

"But that's more than many people have," said Jeff's father. "And your mom would never forgive us if we spent our time worrying about being alone. We must make the most of the time we have together. I have learned something from this. I'll never again take what I have for granted!"

A few months after Rita's death, Jeff entered the University of Miami. His father, a salesman with a flexible territory, soon sold the family's house in Tampa and moved to Miami to be nearer his son, the only family he had left. He had become severely depressed because of losing his wife. His appearance had suffered from too much alcohol and a poor diet. After a few more months, his territory began to go downhill.

Unfortunately, Jeff was a typical self-centered college student. He spent less and less time with his father and after his freshman year decided to live on campus to be closer to his friends. In his junior year, several weeks at a time went by without Jeff seeing his father at all. Tragically, on the third anniversary of Rita's death, Jeff's father, feeling alone and forgotten, committed suicide with an overdose of anti-depressants and vodka.

Jeff found him on Saturday morning when he went to his father's little house to pick up some extra clothes. David Royal was sprawled on the living room floor with a broken glass still in his hand. Jeff staggered to the phone and dialed 911. He stumbled to the stoop in front of the house and sobbed with his head resting on his knees. Now just under the age of twenty, he was completely alone, an orphan. The Miami police who answered the call were very helpful and drove Jeff to his apartment on campus. The rest of the week, making arrangements, the small funeral service, the details of ending his father's time on earth and going on about the process of living, passed in a blur.

"I wasted the most important thing I had," Jeff lamented to his roommate, Giuseppe Portales. "The time with my father should have been the most important thing in my life and I took him for granted. Now he's gone, and I don't have anyone else!"

Jeff had always had an attitude of strong independence and self-confidence, supported by his high intelligence. The loss of his parents, made worse by the guilt he felt over the lack of time spent with his father, took all the strength Jeff could muster to keep himself steady. First, he had to deal with the loss and the guilt he felt. In addition, he had the problems of being an underage orphan with all the legal and procedural problems that entailed. After managing his way through all of that, he was changed, seasoned, bent. Not broken, but closer to the edge than one should have to come at twenty years of age.

Outwardly, Jeff continued to be reasonably easygoing, but much more of an introvert. Formerly the life of every party, he had always made friends easily, and was quite popular on campus. After his father's death, he became much more reserved. Inwardly, he had become mistrustful of life in general, and he had lost much of his energy, direction, and ambition. Consumed by guilt and self-pity, Jeff Royal avoided any attempt at long-term relationships. Now in his world, strong relationships ended with eventual loss. The risk was too great, so he avoided becoming involved in more than superficial relationships.

Fortunately, his father had enough of an estate to pay for the remaining year of Jeff's education. His major in English had resulted from experimentation with virtually every course of study offered at the University. Although he took a full course load every semester and during several of the summers, Jeff arrived at graduation with a potpourri of courses, good grades, and plenty of hours of credit, but just enough hours in English to qualify for a BA degree. Jeff got his degree, but he had no specialty or profession, and he was unsure as to his plans for a career. Unlike several of his friends, he rejected enrolling in graduate school in the hopes of somehow finding a career objective. He was just glad to be out of school and somewhat excited about starting a new life. Hunting for a job took the edge off a bit, however.

***

The screams dwindled into sobs and then into a whimpering, mewing sound of human suffering. The walls of the old warehouse absorbed the sounds. The only other sounds were those of a leaking roof and the creaks and rattles of an old building being tested by the Canadian wind. The woman shivered, twisted in the freezing metal chair, straining the bonds that held her hands behind her back and her ankles to the legs of the chair. Tears streamed down her face and mixed with sweat born of stress and pain. Her face was a mottled maze of bruises, cuts, and welts, none of which could disguise the inherent beauty that was being destroyed by her pain and her tormentor. Her naked body was bruised beyond description, and she had small cuts and burns over most of her breasts and stomach. She screamed for the ten-thousandth time, her voice hoarse now, as the little man sitting on the stool in front of her savagely twisted her nipple with a pair of pliers, until it bled profusely, while laughing at her extreme discomfort, his foul breath making clouds in the cold air. Urine discharged onto the seat of the chair to which she was tied and mixed in a terrible potion with the other fluids pooled there. Off to the side the silhouette of a much larger man was outlined in the dim light of the old warehouse. He exhaled a cloud of sweet-smelling smoke, wiped the end of his penis with his handkerchief, buttoned his pants as he stood up from the chair in which he had been sitting, and said in French, "Get on with it, Jean-Claude. She's beginning to smell."

***

A few months after the death of his father, Jeff met Connie Parker. When he met her, it was love at first sight. For the first time in what seemed a very long time, Jeff Royal wanted a relationship to be more than a biological coupling with overtures of something lasting more than a few weeks. From Connie's viewpoint, Jeff was interesting, but certainly not the man of her dreams. He seemed immature and a little withdrawn at first. In addition, he seemed to have no clue as to what his future would be after college. Connie Parker was not interested in anything serious with Jeff. She wasn't a virgin, but she had no intention in becoming another trophy in what was rumored to be a fairly diverse string of sexual conquests by Jeff Royal.

After a few weeks, Connie set Giuseppe up on a blind double-date with her best friend and roommate, Maritza. After that first date, Connie and Jeff often got together with Giuseppe and Maritza. Giuseppe soon was on his own path to conquest. As best friends and roommates, Jeff and Giuseppe became even more attached to each other as their time with Connie and Maritza increased. The four of them eventually became inseparable.

As the months passed and they saw more and more of each other, Jeff pursued Connie like no other goal he had ever sought. He wrote poetry for her. He bought her gifts and flowers. He arranged sunrise champagne breakfasts, sunset sails, and every romantic situation imaginable. After the first few dates, and a couple of rather terse rejections of his advances by Connie, he began to demonstrate a respect for her he had accorded no woman since he began dating. Soon she took him home to "meet the parents". Eventually, he won over her family, visiting them on every special occasion (often spontaneously), charming them with his wit, his intellect, small and thoughtful gifts, and his independent spirit.

Eventually Connie was unable to resist the onslaught. From mild interest, she had developed a strong love for Jeff. They were married the day they both graduated from the University of Miami. His marriage to Connie, and the total acceptance of him by her family, seemed to help him get over the loss of his own family. He became more outgoing. He developed a truly strong relationship with Connie's father – more than that of a son-in-law – probably more that of a favorite son. Connie's mother considered Jeff "blood", and often bought him the small presents one's own mother buys for her son. Her sister came to adore him.

Soon, Giuseppe and Maritza got married also. The two couples continued their close relationship as all four had found jobs in Miami. Jeff was happy for the first time in years. He had welcomed his graduation from college and he entered the "real world" with the energy and ambition lacking throughout his college years.

***

The Canadian trip was intended to be a business vacation for Jeff and Connie Royal. They had come to Montreal with Jeff's partner and Royal Floors' Chief Financial Officer, Giuseppe Portales, and Giuseppe's girlfriend, Carmen Saez.

The two were a study in contrast. Jeff was six feet four, lanky, blond, with deep blue eyes and an easy outgoing manner. Giuseppe was short and dark, with flashing black eyes. He had a full beard and wiry frame and a slight Spanish accent. He looked a little like a miniature Fidel Castro. He was very serious, short-tempered, and intense.

They had been together a lot in college. Their friends had tagged them with the obvious label of "Mutt and Jeff". It stuck, and they often used it to describe themselves.

Their friendship began at the University of Miami. Giuseppe had just arrived from Ecuador with a two-year business scholarship for Hispanic students. He had graduated from University of Quito with a business degree in Finance.

He met Jeff in their class on International Studies. Soon they discovered they had much in common, not in personal history, but in the quite insular nature of their personalities and their aversion to lasting relationships. Jeff found Giuseppe very interesting, and Giuseppe found in Jeff a sympathetic and empathetic friend with no alternative agenda. Despite the clear gap in interests, background, personality, and language, the two became close friends and roommates. Giuseppe was also a loner with an aversion to strong lasting relationships, but he confided in Jeff, and Jeff found in Giuseppe the friendship so lacking for much of his recent life. Jeff found comfort even as he listened to Giuseppe for hours talking about the horrible poverty and abuse of his early years in Quito. Their friendship became stronger when they married best friends.

In business, their divergent natures and strong trust and friendship meshed into a fine machine. While Jeff was a real innovative genius in marketing and operations and a superb salesman with customers and employees alike, Giuseppe was reserved to the point of shyness and avoided most contact with customers. On the other hand, Giuseppe was very aggressive with asset-based financing, and utterly ruthless in dealing with venders and creditors alike, an area in which Jeff was not at all sophisticated.

***

The small man looked with hatred at the much larger man, but it was the hatred of the hunted to the hunter. He knew the large man represented safety only as long as his orders were followed to the letter. With an incredibly fast movement, he balled his free hand into a fist and hit the woman squarely in the face, breaking her nose. Her head snapped back and then flopped forward as she lost consciousness. The small man dropped the pliers and picked up a pair of heavy-duty wire cutters. He cut the woman's hands loose and grabbed her left wrist. With a savage motion, he severed her fourth and fifth fingers. They dropped from her hand like small branches from a tree. Blood spurted on the floor.

"For God's sake, tie something around her wrist, before she bleeds to death, you ignorant fuck," the larger man roared in French. With another look of hatred, the small man took the rope he had used to secure her hands to the chair and tied it as tightly as he could around her wrist. The bleeding stopped as all circulation to her wrist was cut off. He picked up the two severed fingers from the pool of blood on the floor and handed them to the larger man. "I'll keep the little one as a souvenir. They will get the ring finger," the large man said.

"What about the rest of her jewelry?" asked the small man.

"When we're finished with her, you may have it. Don't take it now and do something stupid. You know what will happen if the police can trace you. Even worse, you know what I can do," the large man said in a very serious tone. "If you fuck this up, Jean-Claude, you'll beg me to do these things to you rather than turn you over to our friends. Now cover her up and keep her alive."

3

Montreal

The takeover of the 140-years-old Dominion Flooring and Distributors was the most complex transaction Jeff and Giuseppe had faced to date. It was the first acquisition they had done in a foreign country, with all the resulting red tape.

There were two other unique problems. First, and least difficult for Royal to deal with, was Dominion's vertical operation of manufacturing and distribution. Dominion was the first maker of linoleum in North America, actually beginning manufacturing of linoleum flooring by treating sail canvass with linseed oil in 1830 in eastern Quebec. Linoleum gave way to sheet vinyl and vinyl tile in the late Nineteen Twenties. Over the years after the booming Sixties the company had failed to adequately invest in new manufacturing and design, content to live on their lucrative patents and their long-standing reputation for quality and innovation and, not incidentally, their protection by the Canadian government. Their products became inferior and outdated as a result. Then the popularity of vinyl flooring began to wane as wood flooring, ceramic tile, and other natural types of hard flooring became popular. Soon Dominion lost market share even in protectionist Canada.

Dominion's carpet manufacturing operation was even worse. At a time when the Canadian customer wanted to have American-type products with many choices of bright new colors, the Canadian carpet industry was spewing out European-type products in limited spectrums of dark European colors. While of high quality, the stuff simply didn't sell. In addition, both plants were very highly unionized with rigid work rules and extremely costly benefits packages. Even if the products were salable, they would be too costly in comparison to American-made products. However, Jeff and Giuseppe knew they could work around these problems.

The other, much more serious problem, was cultural. The combination of the two cultures, Anglophone and French, in any Canadian business was tenuous. The acquisition and management of Canadian properties by outsiders, especially Americans, was bitterly resented. This problem was more pronounced in the primarily French-Canadian province of Quebec where Dominion's "Head Office" and manufacturing plants were located.

Quebec has a unique problem. It is one of only a few places in the world where the majority is the object of discrimination. The French-speaking citizens of Quebec, who represent over two-thirds of the province's population, are often relegated to the lower paying jobs because they speak only French. Outside of Quebec, they face even worse odds. After all, the major international companies in Canada and the U.S. and much of Europe are managed and operated in English.

Scattered violence, work stoppages, and threats of worse to come marred the two months preceding Royal's takeover of Dominion. This was not uncommon at the time. Montreal was the prime target of renewed Separatist activities on the part of the Parizeau-inspired *Parti Quebecois*.

But the current Dominion management couldn't keep the company afloat without reducing the work force, making major investments in equipment, and cutting costs. They knew that the impending North American Free Trade Agreement between the United States and Canada, resulting in stronger, sharper competition, would probably make their company fail. With the labor situation then in place in Canada and their lack of capital, they were unable to make the changes that were needed. Accepting the inevitable, they began to seek refinancing, a partner, or, as a last resort, a buyer.

The failure of Dominion became certain when the Bank of Montreal refused to renew the Company's lines of credit after an unusually large loss in both the manufacturing and distribution operations. Much of the loss was attributable to Royal's sales force selling American-made products in Canada's major cities at prices that Canadian manufacturers could only dream of. Even Dominion's own distribution division preferred to buy and resell the American products over their own. It was at that time that Dominion's Board of Directors contacted Royal.

Shortly after, with the blessing of the Board, Jeff and Giuseppe toured the factories and Dominion's eight branches across Canada, meeting with their management, line employees, and major customers, reviewing their products, and manufacturing facilities and processes. They saw that Free Trade, with its unique interpretation in Canada, offered a strong opportunity for American firms like theirs to expand into Canada. For even as duties dropped or were eliminated, the Canadian government protected its industries with liberal and protectionist interpretations of the dumping laws, restricting American goods from being truly competitive.

They spent nine days touring Dominion's facilities. It took a full day just to get to Halifax from Atlanta. They spent a half day in Halifax, then from there they flew to Montreal, and drove to the Company's manufacturing facilities in Eastern Quebec. After two days there, they returned to Montreal and flew to Ottawa, then Toronto, Winnipeg, Saskatoon, then Calgary and Vancouver. Each day consisted of a branch tour, meetings with the branch manager, the sales force, and a few customer visits. The evenings were spent traveling to the next city. They ended up in Vancouver, excited but exhausted.

ROYAL REVENGE

After a very short night in Vancouver, the Air Canada flight from Vancouver to Montreal droned on for five hours and passed through four time zones and seemed to last forever. Jeff and Giuseppe had the last two first-class seats. They were both exhausted.

"I feel like we've been in four countries in the last few days. I never realized what we'd find up here. Do you think we can manage a business spread across 5,000 miles?" Giuseppe asked, sipping on a glass of scotch and ice.

"It's really not that different from some of our branches in the U.S. except for the four time zones. Vancouver is Seattle, Calgary is Denver, Saskatoon is Billings, Winnipeg is Omaha, Ottawa is Albany, Toronto is Chicago, and Halifax is Bangor," Jeff said.

"And Montreal is...?"

"Montreal is <u>really</u> something different," Jeff said, laughing. "Maybe a combination of San Francisco and New Orleans, with Philadelphia thrown in for good measure."

"The question is, do we do the deal?" he continued, very serious now. "I think there's a great chance for us to be the best in the business here, now that Free Trade's almost certainly a future reality, in spite of the Canadians' resistance to it. Dominion's got a really good, sound business opportunity when Free Trade becomes a reality, because they are so strong across Canada. They just can't manage around their inherent problems and the cultural problems that exist here. There's going to be very significant consolidation of businesses between U.S. and Canadian companies. The first big project will be to make the carpet mill and the vinyl plant either profitable or be allowed to close either or both of them. Next is to convert the Head Office in Montreal to a local branch office and get rid of about 40 excess employees. We're going to have to make some very unpopular changes there. Closing the Head Office will be seen as a death knell to them."

"The death knell is already there! Dominion's totally desperate. The bank's got them by the balls. They've got to sell out, or eventually fold when Free Trade comes in. The Government will have to let us make the cuts if they want us to save Dominion. Let's see if we can get a management contract for ninety days. Then we'll find out where all the bodies are buried. If we don't think we can make the changes we want, or if we find some other things we can't fix, we'll wash our hands and walk away. All we lose is our time," Giuseppe suggested. "They've got a lot more to lose!"

"What about financing? Can we afford this kind of exposure now, with everything else we're doing and what we've done recently?" Jeff asked, concerned.

"Hell yes! Financing is the sweetest part of the whole deal. Leave that to me. Between the Canadian banks and the Government, we won't spend a fucking cent," Giuseppe said, mentally rubbing his hands with glee. "God, what an opportunity. Steal a business and let the government finance it!"

And so, Jeff and Giuseppe decided to expand into Canada. They spent another full week in a marathon of meetings with lawyers, management, interpreters, and Government representatives. Royal agreed to operate the company under a management contract for three months, with compensation of a dollar a day, with an option to purchase. The Government and the company allowed them full control until their purchase of Dominion could be completed and guaranteed the purchase price and the financing.

Two weeks later, Jeff and Giuseppe made the cross-Canada tour again. Jeff's initial meetings as the new Chief Executive with the employees of Dominion all across Canada were cordial. He was especially well received in the Western Provinces, which were as American as Cleveland, where everyone spoke English, and where there would be few changes due to the buy-out that weren't for the benefit of the employees.

The manufacturing facilities crawled with Royal personnel for the entire time Jeff and Giuseppe were in the western provinces. Upon their arrival back in Montreal, the men met with the heads of their U.S. manufacturing facilities.

"It would be a work of charity to close both of them," said Kenny Middlebrooks. They are really inefficient. We progressed beyond them several years ago."

"There must be some good things they do," Jeff argued. "After all, they've been in business for 140 years!"

"Well, actually there are," said Kenny. "Did you notice that the finishing operation is just as good as ours? If we could make carpet in the States, and back it and finish it here, we could cut their costs dramatically. Also, we would save a fortune on duties since the carpet would be considered made in Canada. The question is how we could justify this plant and these people."

"Not only would that process allow us to state that the carpet was made in Canada," said Jeff. "It would mean that we could sell it throughout the Commonwealth Countries with those significant duty advantages, and completely avoid the dumping regulations we'd have to deal with if we imported finished carpet. How much could we increase production in Canada using that scenario?"

"Tom and I did a preliminary study," said Kenny. "We think we could produce enough in the States to double production here, and still reduce the payroll here by 50%."

"We will be allowed only a 20% reduction in labor force here," said Jeff. "Can you increase the Canadian output more?"

"Sure, by keeping 80% of the workers here, we could triple total production. But it would strain us a lot in the States. Do you think you could sell that much?"

"At the margins I'm contemplating, we'll dominate the industry here. A couple of Canadian mills won't survive, but I honestly think they won't survive Free Trade in any event. Let's add capacity in the States, then. Who's up for sale now?" asked Jeff.

"Well, we've been approached by American Rugs. They would add about 10% to our total tufting capacity. But they want stock and cash," said Giuseppe. "And they're really overpriced."

"Any ideas?" Jeff asked.

"Well, the son-in-law and the daughter and the ex-wife own a total of 60%. They really just want an annuity. Why don't we offer something to them and see where it takes us? Better still, let's buy the family out and then go hit the old man. Once he realizes we have control, he'll sell," Giuseppe continued. "Pay them out over 20 years. I'll bet the old man will sell for a song after that – 'cause he wants mostly cash and he sure doesn't want us as partners. Make it all contingent on the Dominion deal. Kenny, how long would it take us to integrate the American Rugs facilities?

"First, do we have the money?" Jeff asked.

"We've got the credit. I believe we can do a deal within a few days. But we'll need to check with the people here to make sure the whole thing works," said Giuseppe. "Shall I have Kenny approach them?"

"Do it. Now's not the time to be cautious!" exclaimed Jeff. "Now, what about the vinyl lines?"

"Another disaster," said Tom Little. "Typical European styles and colors. And, of course, vinyl flooring is dying worldwide. The only real asset is their vinyl tile line. They can make miles of that crap. And they can make it as cheaply as anyone. But no one makes any money in those products. The margins are awful!"

"Well, would we then be the low-cost producer?" asked Jeff.

ROYAL REVENGE

"You would certainly be in Canada. And you would be in the States, without the duty. But that's 8%. How would you absorb that?" asked Tom.

"By exporting unfinished carpet to be finished in Canada, there is no duty into Canada. But we do get export credits from the U.S. Find out whether the credits generated would equal the duties incurred on Canadian tile," suggested Giuseppe.

"Better yet, figure out how the Canadian tile could be considered unfinished when going into the States," exclaimed Jeff. "Then there's no duty either way – it's just inter-company movement of raw materials. I know. We'll finish the edges after we get the stuff into the States."

"That's really stretching it, Jeff. If either government really looked at that arrangement ..." mused Giuseppe. "Besides, why do we want to get into the vinyl tile business, anyway? No one makes money at it. At least none that I know of."

"The two biggest makers of vinyl, which are also big in carpet and ceramic, use tile as a loss leader. The only reason they sell more vinyl than we – I mean Dominion – is because they convince every one of the dealers that since their tile is low priced, so is everything else. We can probably put one of them right on the edge with this stuff! Also, with the cheapest tile, we can steal quite a few of their distributors. Then we can sell through our own distribution channels as well as theirs. This will also allow us to dominate the cheap commercial market, and we'll be in a position to build a solid export presence in Australia, New Zealand, the Bahamas, Bermuda, and every other Commonwealth country by making the stuff in Canada. That's a huge market, eventually. Study these ideas. I want a detailed plan by the weekend on all these projects. And I'm not interested in knowing how difficult it will be, 'cause I know you guys can do it." he concluded with a proud look around the room.

The meeting broke up with a more than a few mumbles about the difficult schedule Jeff was imposing.

The next morning, Jeff and Giuseppe met with the personnel of the Montreal office. It was there that Jeff had to sell Royal's plans for major changes. The changes involved major shifts in work rules and habits, modernizing the offices and equipment, improving customer service, significant downsizing of the presence in Montreal, and total computerization.

Of course, it was also in Montreal that most of the people would lose their jobs, as most of the Head Office functions would be performed in Royal's Atlanta headquarters, with the rest moved to the manufacturing facilities. Part of Royal's plan called for big reductions in the largely redundant work force in Montreal. And while they were to be offered transfers to other locations in Canada, everyone knew that most of the employees could not or would not move.

Speaking through an interpreter to Montreal's workers was very difficult for Jeff. Even his name was an obstacle, somehow connecting him with the Royal Family in England. His approach in every other location was to sell the sales force on the new company, and to have them sell the rest of the employees. He had hoped to inspire those employees who would remain, to make the changes willingly. But it was really hard for him to give an impassioned plea for reason when each phrase he uttered was repeated in French, and every question had to be translated and then repeated, sometimes twice. Jeff soon felt the not-so-subtle disapproval of the Montreal workers since their new Anglophone Chief Executive couldn't even communicate in French.

The proposed expense cuts, which would allow the company to dramatically reduce its losses, were readily accepted in all Dominion locations except Montreal. There the practices of the past, the Separatist atmosphere, and the fact that the majority of the employees would either have to move elsewhere or lose their jobs, combined to create instant distrust and resentment. Basically, the employees rejected Royal Floors and all the changes they proposed. Somewhat predictably, they chose to react with an illegal strike. One day, none of the workforce except for the territory salesmen came to work.

Jeff and Giuseppe knew immediately that the company could not operate effectively, even if the few necessary employees came back to work peacefully. Trying to resolve the differences with the Quebec workers was obviously not going to be productive. Instead, Royal moved very swiftly, even by American standards, to dismiss the entire staff and management in the Montreal facility, keeping only the salesmen. Within hours of the strike, they moved all of the Head Office functions to Atlanta. Then they brought in Canadians from Dominion branches in the other provinces and two of their best (and toughest) American managers in operations and marketing to Montreal.

Their approach made bitter enemies of the fired Montreal workers, but it worked wonders for the company. In just over a month, with the new staff, dramatically reduced expenses, and a sales force that didn't want to be replaced, the Montreal branch showed a slim profit for the first time in years. The other Canadian branches had produced far more than previous sales forecasts with lower expenses. And the profit in Toronto had rivaled that of some of Royal's best U.S. branches. Jeff's plans for the production facilities were being developed and seemed to make sense despite their radical approach. The unions, because of the strong reaction by Royal in Montreal, even began trying to cooperate. Royal's operation of Dominion Flooring and Distributors for three months under their very unique management contract had had positive results. To the surprise of many of the people at Dominion, the operational changes made almost instantaneously by Royal quickly produced small profits, after several years of losses.

J. Trey Weeks

But success made no difference to the displaced Montreal workers. In recent weeks, the violence in Montreal had begun in earnest. First, some of the company trucks had had windshields smashed and parts stolen. Later, a small fire was started on the property. Finally, the fired workers began making threats toward the new Royal personnel. Things escalated to the point that the police were called multiple times per day. However, it soon became apparent that they were ineffective, and the morale of Royal's workers declined rapidly. In desperation, Giuseppe posted private armed guards around the clock.

Many other companies in Montreal experienced similar problems because of work related changes at the time. Lengthy and divisive campaigns for Provincial elections, further exacerbating the Separatist atmosphere, aggravated the situation. The ever-present issue of French versus English, as well as the prominence of the *Parti Quebecois* divided Quebec, and especially, Montreal, more than ever.

Now Jeff and Giuseppe were in Montreal to finalize their purchase of Dominion Flooring and Distributors. With this final formality, Royal Floors would become the first flooring manufacturer/distributor to distribute their products in all areas of North America. Royal would now have branches and local sales forces in all forty-eight contiguous states and the eight Canadian provinces.

Royal Floors was already one of the 500 largest privately-owned companies in North America. It boasted an ultra-modern fleet numbering almost one thousand trucks, over 1,600 sales persons, 15,000 employees, manufacturing facilities throughout Northern Georgia and now Eastern Quebec, and warehousing or sales offices in over seventy cities. It was among the first in its industry to use computers to manage inventories, shipping, sales assignments, and recently, manufacturing. Its high profits were not surprising. The growth of the company had been very fast. In a mature and rather dull industry, their success was quite astonishing. In the eleven years since Jeff Royal had formed the company, starting with one location in Atlanta and over a million dollars in debt, they had reached one billion dollars in sales and corresponding financial stability.

Royal had begun with the purchase of a small distributor in Atlanta. Jeff Royal was an easygoing salesman who never dreamed of creating the size or scope of business Royal Floors had become today. Up to that point, his life had been lacking in firm direction and quite unstructured.

After his graduation from the University of Miami, Jeff interviewed with nearly every newspaper in South Florida whose personnel department would allow him into their offices. After rejections from all of the majors, he landed a job as a cub reporter for The Miami Star, the city's local answer to The Enquirer.

His first few months were rocky. In the first place, his assignments were the lowest of the low. Covering local events and local politicians that no other of the Star's reporters would touch, and trying to make news of them, was hard enough. But he became tremendously frustrated when he had to rewrite almost every article he submitted. The paper demanded a very sensational style of writing, one that came closer to scandalous gossip than factual reporting. However, Jeff was determined and resourceful. Soon he began to develop his own contacts and sources and was placed on a few more important projects.

Jeff's career in journalism ended with a major conflict over the "public's right to know" and the style in which they were to be notified. All the papers carried stories about Miami's popular mayor, Jesse Castillo. It had been rumored for months that the Mayor's marriage was in danger of collapse because of his alleged close relationship with one of his female staff members. Jeff knew the woman in question, having met her on several occasions, and knew there wasn't any truth to the alleged affair.

The major papers mentioned the rumors, giving little credence to the anonymous sources. The Star wanted to elevate this item from simple gossip to "news", with sensational headlines and lots of quotes from secret sources, most of whom didn't exist, accentuated by very misleading pictures from Miami's cadre of paparazzi. Jeff refused to write what amounted to a smear, partly because he objected to the tactic, and partly because he was simply disenchanted with his job.

Even worse, he informed the Mayor's office just prior to the breaking of the story. The Mayor's staff was very grateful to Jeff, as was the Mayor, who was able to mount a campaign to reduce some of the damage. The Star's editor was furious, and Jeff was fired without notice or severance pay.

Eventually, the Star was forced to print a complete retraction. But the result of their misleading coverage was that the Democratic Party dropped the Mayor as their glamour minority candidate, and his potential career as one of the first Hispanics to be a major force in national politics was ruined.

Jeff, of course, became a pariah to the rest of the journalism community in South Florida. Following the end of his newspaper career, Jeff tried writing a novel. He found the task harder than it appeared. Living with their only income as Connie's meager salary at a local department store, they were forced to spend the last of the money from his small inheritance for living expenses. Their economic situation, never flush, became close to impoverished. One of their first arguments was over Jeff's decision to go to work at a regular job.

"I'm living in a dream world. There's no way I'll finish this book. I'm not even sure I like doing this. You know that most books that are started are never finished. Besides, this time we've really run out of money. It's time I found a job that pays something worthwhile. I'm damned tired of being poor," Jeff said.

ROYAL REVENGE

"We can always live on love, honey, and Daddy won't mind loaning us money for a while," whispered Connie, her voice husky as she began unbuttoning Jeff's jeans.

"C'mon Connie, face facts. You know I can't accept help from your family. We need to be on our own. I can write a book when we're independently wealthy," he said as he pushed her away.

"Maybe then will be too late, Jeff!" she cried. "Maybe you'll have lost the urge by then. Are you ever going to let other people help you? There's nothing wrong with taking help now, when we need it, is there?"

"If I've learned anything about life, it's that I need to rely on myself, and no one else. Supporting us is my responsibility. I'm tired of having no money to spend. I want to buy you nice things. Neither of us is used to living like this, from week to week. I need a job and I'm going to get one. Hopefully one that pays well. That's the end of it."

Connie was deeply hurt, and very concerned that Jeff would abandon writing so early, since he had seemed so sure that writing was what he wanted to do. But she was unable to change his mind. Money had never seemed important to him before. But lack of it was clearly a driving force.

That week, he began interviews through the University's Job Placement Office. He soon realized that the best-paying jobs were in sales. He signed up for interviews with all the companies who advertised, "no experience required, for on-the-job training in the exciting world of business".

After only a few interviews, and literally no forethought, he accepted a job as a salesman for a small rug manufacturer. Jeff liked it because they offered full training, company car, and a big potential income. He felt the travel wouldn't be a problem.

Connie was furious. "You took the first damn job you were offered! You didn't even discuss it with me. Don't we both have a stake in this? Did you ever think how I'd feel about you traveling all the time?"

"Honey, it's a job that pays a lot of money. I can do it for a little while and then do something else. Believe me, I don't want to peddle rugs and bath mats for the rest of my life. Besides, we don't have to move for me to do this and you can keep your job and stay near your family," Jeff said. "I just need to get started on something and start earning some money, so we can get on our feet. They'll even train me. It's only temporary."

The "on-the-job training" was no more than a list of the current accounts, an outdated sales manual, two days' orientation at the North Carolina distribution center, and one week's travel with one of the firm's older salesmen, in his own territory in Virginia. After his week with Jeff, the salesman gave him a set of keys and a map to find the company's van, parked at one of the company's accounts in Atlanta, and wished him well. Once Jeff retrieved the van, there was no one around who could introduce him to the accounts, so he began by visiting every one of them.

Jeff's territory was defined as "all distributors and retail stores throughout Florida and Georgia, excluding certain 'national accounts'". In actuality, there were a great number of national accounts, and the territory actually contained very little on-going business. The total commissions generated by the accounts Jeff inherited were slightly less than the meager pay he had earned at the <u>Star</u>.

But Jeff found that he really enjoyed selling. The hard part for him was managing his time well. He spent too much time on details and travel, and not enough with the customer. The product lines he sold were stylish, profitable, and after being presented well, had strong appeal to his customers. Since the man he replaced was totally inept, Jeff's clients responded eagerly to his honesty and boyish enthusiasm. He didn't like the travel or being away from Connie, but he had a natural ability to relate to customers. He became one of the company's most successful salesmen in a short period of time.

Connie was surprised to find that Jeff liked his job so much. He often got very excited as he talked about ways to streamline and improve things so that he could make more money.

"Look at this commission check," he said one day. "$3,500 just for showing people things that they already want to buy. If I had more time, I could make three times this much."

"So, find ways to save time. The salesmen who call on us at the store spend more time waiting to see my boss and drinking coffee than they do selling," Connie said. "You could travel less if you had a smaller territory. Half the time you're chasing your own tail. Maybe you should hire an assistant. You know, I'm available," she said through half-lidded eyes as she stuck her tongue in his ear.

Jeff became quite creative. He purchased one of the first car phones and hired a part time assistant at his own expense. He bought a personal computer and a fax machine. He used them to minimize his paperwork and to promote new products to his customers by mail, and some even by fax, when fax machines were first becoming popular. His sales and income shot up dramatically. Sometimes Connie would travel with him when he went out of town overnight, if her work schedule permitted.

To his and to Connie's pleasant surprise, Jeff also found that some of his customers became good friends, in addition to buying more of his products. He and Connie became quite close to several of them.

Albert Henry, the owner of Henry Distributors in Atlanta, was one of the best of those friends. At seventy years old, tall, balding, profane, and gruff to the point of rudeness, it was hard to imagine that Henry had any good friends. He had built his business from scratch and was a very tough customer. Jeff inherited Henry as his primary client in Atlanta. Albert liked Jeff instantly, and they soon developed a close relationship.

Albert Henry knew everyone in the business. He was always free with help and direction about which new customers Jeff should pursue. His referrals, phone calls, and letters of introduction were a major reason Jeff became a top earner in the company so quickly.

It was plain that Jeff was exactly the person Albert's own son could never become. Milton Henry, Albert's only child, was lazy, shiftless and had repeatedly shown a total lack of business ability. He worked in the business only because his father paid him three or four times what he was worth.

But their friendship and his fondness for Jeff didn't affect Henry's toughness as a customer. Jeff found it very hard to sell Henry new products. After two years of putting up with repeated rejection of his hottest new items, Jeff lost his temper at lunch one day.

"Albert, why don't you ever want to try something new and fresh?" Jeff blasted. "Don't you get tired of selling the same old shit to the same old customers? Don't you want your business to grow? I can't believe you're passing on all these new products," he said. "Your competitors will run over you unless you start expanding your lines."

"Expand? Bullshit! Listen, *Boychik*, if you had to run this fucking business, and meet the payroll every Friday at my age, you'd buy only the best sellers, too!" Henry grumbled. "Remember that I've been in this business for a long time without your fancy new products. Besides, why expand a business like mine when there's only that worthless son of mine and his *Shiksa* wife to carry it on?" he asked.

"Then why don't you fucking sell it?" Jeff said, totally exasperated.

"Then why don't you fucking buy it?" Henry retorted, mockingly.

ROYAL REVENGE

"Maybe I should," Jeff said. "But there's no way I could come up with what you'd want for it."

"In those words, *Boychik*, are the beginnings of a deal," Albert laughed.

Albert Henry was worn down from the grind of being an entrepreneur. He was tired of the business and wanted to retire. Selling it would turn his years of hard work into an annuity. He realized Jeff was an individual that he would like to help succeed. Even better, Albert was convinced that Jeff could succeed. He offered to sell Jeff his company, and even better, to "tote the note."

After the first blush of excitement when faced with the chance to own his own business, Jeff's thrill turned to near panic. He lacked the financial expertise to run even a small business like Henry's. He was loath to assume the risk on his own. He was also unsure of Connie's reaction and wanted to make sure that she was behind him.

But he knew the venture was sound and felt the company could be expanded successfully. Armed with Henry's financial reports, Jeff met with his best friend, Giuseppe Portales. Giuseppe had become an accountant with Intercontinental Airlines after college. Jeff wanted Giuseppe to run the financial part of the new business and be a minority partner. After looking over the numbers, he jumped at the chance Jeff offered him.

"Risk? Screw the risk! So we lose everything!" he exclaimed. "Neither of us have anything to lose anyway! This is a great deal! We can make a potful of money! Where do I sign?"

Connie was hesitant. "What about your book? I thought you didn't want to peddle rugs for the rest of your life. Aren't you signing on for more than you want to do? Besides, is Atlanta really where we want to live?"

Jeff answered smoothly, "Owning your own business is a little like writing, Connie. You start with an idea, then you improve it. You keep improving it until it really works well. It's risky and we could fall flat on our asses, but as Giuseppe says, 'we have nothing to lose'. I want you to help in the business, too. I think we can be very, very successful."

"If that's what you want, then do it," she said with a smile. "If we lose everything, we just start over from scratch. But, you'll have to pay me a lot of money if you want me to work there."

"I'll even give you regular raises," Jeff said, laughing, as he pushed her down on the bed.

"Just make sure they're all as big as this one," she giggled.

Within two weeks, Royal Distributors, a newly formed Delaware corporation, became the proud owner of all of the assets and liabilities of Henry Distributors. The new company also became co-guarantor, along with its new officers, of a note for $1,200,000, payable over the next six years, to Albert Henry. Jeff Royal became President, and Giuseppe Portales, Executive Vice President.

From the beginning, Royal Distributors was quite profitable. Jeff and Giuseppe reorganized the operation from top to bottom and installed a computer system. They made customer service their credo. They expanded, trained, and motivated the sales force. They added new products and new customers, and in the process became highly visible and responsive to their clientele. In seven months of operation, the company exceeded their first two years' profit forecasts.

After they had paid off Albert Henry three years early, Jeff was content to allow Giuseppe free rein in the areas of cash flow, operations, and finance. Despite his concern about Giuseppe's newly revealed streak of pure greed, and the disagreements this sometimes caused, Jeff realized that Giuseppe was very good at what he did. Jeff readily accepted this arrangement since it allowed him to pour all of his energies into the sales, marketing, and expansion of the new company. They both thrived on the challenge and worked harder than ever before. They began to expand dramatically as the months wore on.

One daring expansion was to purchase a small manufacturer of carpet in Dalton, Georgia. Royal found that they could not only make money distributing merchandise, but they could make more by manufacturing the product and then distributing it. At the time the carpet manufacturers numbered in the hundreds and sold their wares through distributors like Royal. Most of the mills were only marginally profitable because of the fierce competition for distributors. Jeff and Giuseppe were among the first in the industry to begin consolidation by buying up small manufacturers. Within a few years, Royal Distributors became Royal Floors, and became one of the largest carpet manufacturers in the world. Through repeated and risky investments in the newest manufacturing processes, and eventually with a staff of designers and stylists that were the best in the business, Royal led the way in introducing the hottest new styles and colors and manufacturing them as the lowest-cost producer. Immediately after purchasing one of the oldest and least profitable mills, it occurred to them that not only could they make the carpet, they could make the yarn from which the carpet was manufactured. By concentrating on the least expensive, easily manufactured yarns, they became, again, one of the largest suppliers in the industry. Jeff put never-ceasing pressure on his design team to come up with products the consumer would accept made from these fibers. As a result, fashion in the carpet industry became a function of what could be manufactured and sold at the highest margins. And Royal led the way.

The two made an awesome management team and the Company grew, geometrically. The expansion into Canada was the last in a series of bold tactical moves for Royal. In the last few years, they had made several such purchases but never before involving a hostile takeover in a foreign country. Royal Floors' reputation for super marketing, lowest cost production, and a highly-driven sales force, coupled with their appetite for expansion, made them the envy of similar companies across the United States. Often competitive distributors and manufacturers (or their creditors) offered themselves to Royal for sale. Royal also had purchased several smaller, less-dynamic companies in other areas, such as hardwood floor manufacturing, a vinyl tile and sheet vinyl manufacturer, and formed joint ventures with manufacturers in the two hottest product areas, laminate and ceramic flooring. Within five years of the purchase of the company, Royal Floors manufactured and/or distributed every type of flooring sold in the United States and made the raw fiber for almost 50% of their manufactured carpet production. They were also the largest U.S. importer of ceramic tile.

Royal was noted for risky, huge expenditures for state-of-the-art computerization, trucks, manufacturing processes, and facilities. Their innovation into totally centralized and vertical operations allowed them to expand rapidly without big increases in costs. Giuseppe became known for creative financing and extremely efficient and cost-effective operations. Jeff's most obvious talent was in product leadership, recruiting and training excellent personnel for the sales force, and managing the rapidly expanding businesses of raw materials, styling, manufacturing, distribution, and marketing.

***

The second package arrived at the hotel just after Midnight. It was especially bleak outside. The howling, gusting, wind blew unceasingly. Heavy snow and a sharply lower temperature announced the permanent arrival of Montreal's long winter.

ROYAL REVENGE

Remnants of a half-eaten meal were left on the table. Jeff Royal slumped on the couch, his head in his hands. His face showed signs of fatigue and defeat.

Inspector Roch chain-smoked silently in a chair beside the fire. The ashtray beside him overflowed and smoldered.

Giuseppe and Carmen were on the floor, her head resting in Giuseppe's lap, her eyes closed. Giuseppe idly rolled brandy around in a glass, staring sightlessly ahead.

At that moment, the phone rang and jarred their collective nerves. Inspector Roch held up his hand to Jeff as he ran to the bedroom. He picked up the bedroom extension at the same time that Jeff picked up the receiver in the living room.

"Jeff Royal," he answered wearily.

"*Monsieur* Royal? This is the Concierge speaking. We have a taxi here with a package for delivery. The driver says you were expecting it. Because of the serious situation..."

"This is Inspector Roch," Roch interrupted. "Alert my man in the lobby to hold that driver. The sergeant will be down in a moment to get the package."

Jeff and the inspector put down the receivers at the same time. Jeff slumped back down on the couch, saying nothing. Inspector Roch opened the door to the hall.

"Go to the Concierge with Jean-Jacques," he said to the sergeant. "There is a package brought by a taxi. You bring the package here. Have him question the driver. Hurry!"

The sergeant and the other officer left immediately.

"Were you expecting anything, *Monsieur* Royal?" the Inspector asked Jeff.

Jeff shook his head, mute.

"All we can do is wait and see. The package will be here soon," the Inspector said to no one in particular.

Roch opened the door as the sergeant walked up. Breathless from the hurried errand, the portly sergeant handed the package to Inspector Roch.

"We used the metal detector on it. Nothing." said the sergeant. "And the paper is again too damp for fingerprints."

As before, the package was wrapped in brown paper, damp from fresh snowflakes, and addressed to "M. Royal, Royal Floors". It was much larger than the previous one, and cube-shaped.

"What of the driver? Where did he get this?" Roch asked the sergeant.

"He says a man gave it to him at Dorval Airport. He paid double the full fare downtown. He said *Monsieur* Royal would give him a generous tip when he got to the hotel," the sergeant replied.

"Does he know anything about the man who gave him the package?" Roch asked.

"Only that he looks much like the man who left the first package with the Concierge," replied the sergeant.

"Nothing else?"

"Jean-Jacques is still questioning him."

Roch placed the package on the table. Carmen and Giuseppe came and stood by Jeff.

With a weary nod, Jeff indicated that Inspector Roch should unwrap it. Upon carefully removing the wrapping, Roch found a box from the same department store as before. "*Chapeau pour Monsieur*" was embossed in gold script on the top.

Carefully loosening the string holding the top and then discarding it, Roch removed the lid. The front of the box fell away.

With a fixed expression of unspeakable horror and suffering, the head of Connie Royal gaped back at them with sightless eyes. Her long, dark hair was matted with dried blood. There were deep cuts and bruises on her formerly beautiful skin. It was obvious that her nose had been broken. Her left ear, severed cleanly from her skull, diamond earring intact, lay in a small pool of blood in the bottom of the box. Her sightless eyes were open, glazed over.

Roch cursed in guttural French. The fat sergeant blustered and then gagged.

Carmen stared with a face full of horror, and then whimpered and fainted. Giuseppe laid her gently on the floor and then stood to be beside Jeff. His face darkened with outrage, but he said nothing.

Jeff Royal stood silently swaying, tears streaming down his cheeks.

The enclosed note, carefully removed and then opened by Inspector Roch, was in the same hand as previously. It said,

>"Leave us while you still can.
> *FLQ* "

4

Montreal

The two couples had arrived in Montreal two days before, on a beautiful, crisp day, just before the advent of winter. The changing leaves painted the mountains of Quebec. The spectacular scenery at this time of year was well known and was an annual attraction for tourists.

They looked forward to the fabulous food of old Montreal, and the hospitality of Les Quatre Saissons, one of Jeff's favorite hotels. It seemed that nothing could mar their visit.

Jeff and Giuseppe were very excited about completing the final stage of their latest acquisition. The time together also gave them an opportunity to resolve some of the differences they'd had over the takeover of Dominion.

Jeff, while very enthusiastic about the deal, was the more cautious of the two. He had tried to reduce the ill will resulting from Royal's takeover of Dominion. He realized the failure of the company was not totally due to their mismanagement. It was partially because of the laws and customs and the complicated Francophone/Anglophone society of Canada. Accordingly, he had worked especially hard to protect the dignity of the old management group.

In contrast, Giuseppe had been totally ruthless in his dealings with the former owners and managers. He had used Dominion's financial weakness, their strained relationship with their primary bank, and his new alliance with the US State Department representatives, at every opportunity to improve

ROYAL REVENGE

Royal's position and weaken Dominion's. Their opposing positions had created a great deal of conflict between the two men.

During the explosive growth of their company, Giuseppe had become increasingly greedy and dogmatic in Jeff's opinion. While certainly not altruistic, Jeff realized that people working for them and for the companies they acquired required respect and often compassion. Giuseppe, on the other hand, expected and demanded results above all else and was often ruthless in dealing with honest mistakes and ill-advised approaches. In several of their past acquisitions, Jeff had been required to repair relationships damaged by Giuseppe's autocratic approach. They had also often disagreed about compensation, not only for those former employees of the companies they acquired, but for themselves as bonuses after a successful acquisition.

Over the years, Jeff and Giuseppe had resolved such differences by taking a few well-deserved days together, far away from the business. These "time outs" had allowed them to renew their strong friendship and to enhance their business relationship. The last "Mutt and Jeff" crisis had been two years before. It was precipitated when Giuseppe's careless and brash affair with Carmen had ruined his marriage. He had then blamed his problems with his wife and his marriage on the demands of the business. In reality, Giuseppe's personality had changed, apparently as a result of his personal problems, and not for the better. He was much more demanding of his employees and much less likely to forgive common mistakes. His divorce also placed increased financial pressures on him and increased his demands for more and more compensation as a result. Jeff also noted that Giuseppe had been spending virtually every weekend away, mostly in Miami, often leaving early Friday afternoon. The whole situation had caused problems between Giuseppe, Jeff, and everyone who worked around them.

They had temporarily resolved that situation with a two-day stag trip to Acapulco, sobering up only just in time to make their flight back to Atlanta. Giuseppe had agreed to work on his relationships with the employees and had agreed that his marital problems were making him difficult to work with. He had pledged to improve. Jeff was always amazed with what just a couple of days could do to refresh their minds and renew the strong bond between them.

The couples' arrival at Dorval airport in Montreal was on time and uneventful. Even passing through customs was unusually efficient, thanks partly to Jeff and Giuseppe's Government-issued priority work permits. After getting their luggage and picking up their rental car, the four drove downtown. They, as usual, lost their way in the complex maze of one-way streets, construction, and French-only road signs that mark downtown Montreal. They arrived at the hotel grateful they had survived the drivers of Montreal.

Montreal is the second-largest French-speaking city in the world, after Paris. The island upon which Montreal was first established as a fort was populated by the French as early as 1611. In 1832, Montreal was incorporated as a city. By 1860, it was the largest municipality in British North America and the undisputed economic and cultural center of Canada. In the 1970's, Toronto surpassed Montreal as the largest metropolitan area in Canada. It is no coincidence that Montreal is second only to Paris in romance, cuisine, arrogance, and traffic.

Their arrival was like returning to Paris, with everyone they encountered preferring to speak only French, even though Montreal is the most bi-lingual city in Canada with over 60% of the population speaking both French and English. Those visitors who weren't able to speak French often found a resulting severe drop in service. Fortunately, Giuseppe's Spanish-accented French was generally good enough to get them by.

ROYAL REVENGE

And their corner suite in the hotel, Montreal's finest, was lovely. They had two large bedrooms connected by a large living room. The suite was furnished in a tasteful decor, with expensive accent pieces and pictures to create the feeling of an apartment rather than a hotel. Each room in the suite looked west onto Mount Royale, around which the city is built. The changing colors of the heavily forested mountain were beautiful, a rainbow of warm hues ranging from blood-red maples to bright yellow aspens. The beauty of Montreal was a preview of the even more notable sights they would see on their planned afternoon tour of the Laurentien Mountains further west.

Their hotel had welcomed them with a bottle of expensive champagne and fresh flowers in every room, compliments of the hotel's manager. This courtesy was a result of the many rooms Royal Distributor personnel had occupied in the hotel over the past three months during their management contract with Dominion.

This was the first trip Connie and Jeff had experienced with Giuseppe without his first wife, Maritza. This, of course, created some tension because the four of them had often said that they had given birth to the company together.

Jeff Royal had a special affection for Maritza, and he didn't really care much for Carmen. He found her to be cold and demanding, and he felt she had contributed to much of Giuseppe's negative change in personality. Maritza and Connie were lifelong friends, and both Connie and Jeff had deeply resented the way Giuseppe had treated Maritza as a result of his affair with Carmen. In the months both before and after the divorce, Jeff found relations between Connie and Giuseppe quite strained and he hoped that this trip would help repair that damage.

Connie still had some resentment toward Carmen, due to her part in the break-up Giuseppe's marriage. But she resolved to do everything possible to learn to like her. After all,

Giuseppe's life was his own to live, and he was irrevocably attached to her husband through their business and friendship. She was uncomfortable about traveling with what amounted to someone's mistress, but that was the way it was done now, she guessed. Connie realized that it was important that they all relate well together, since Jeff and Giuseppe were so close personally and professionally. There was nothing she or anyone else could ever do to repair the rift between Maritza and Giuseppe. Besides, Carmen seemed to have an unnaturally strong hold on Giuseppe. Connie resolved to accept that fact and to do the best she could to avoid any conflict. She was more than a little surprised at the way Carmen could manage Giuseppe. It was plain that the "Spanish/Portuguese macho" he had always exhibited was greatly tempered in his new relationship with Carmen.

After settling into their suite, they had the hotel pack a light picnic lunch and bring their car around. Jeff drove northwest out of Montreal on "The 15", as the Inter-Province Highway 15 was called. They laughed as the digital speedometer registered 120 km/h (72 mph) and they were still passed by most cars. After about 70 kilometers, they arrived at the quaint mountain village of Sainte-Agathe-des-Monts.

There they embarked on the two-hour boat tour of the beautiful lake that winds around the foot of the mountains surrounding the Sainte Agathe ski area. Like the entire large group of tourists on the boat, they were enthralled with the last flash of color created by the changing leaves.

Drinking white wine on the boat, laughing and singing with his lovely wife and his friend, Jeff felt a surge of delight and relief. He had been worried about how Connie would relate to Carmen. But the day together had been most pleasant so far. It was apparent Carmen was making a concerted effort to warm up to Connie, and Connie was certainly reciprocating. They had all gotten along very well, which he had hoped would happen.

ROYAL REVENGE

They ended the evening at the *Bistro L'Uni Verre* in Saint-Jérôme, about 60 kilometers northwest of Montreal on the Rivière du Nord, with a relaxed dinner of *Raclette,* the local delicacy of broiled rounds of cheese, accompanied by huge chunks of fresh bread and homemade sausage, washed down with several bottles of the excellent local wine. Driving back afterward to Montreal, they chatted and sang like old friends, the uneasiness with Carmen temporarily forgotten.

Light snow began to fall just as they crossed the long bridge over the mighty St. Lawrence River. They arrived excited and refreshed at the hotel just after midnight.

The hotel's Concierge staff had started a fire in the small fireplace. The foursome looked out over a sparkling city around them as Giuseppe opened the champagne. The Dom Perignon was consumed with toasts of victory, love, and friendship. They all went to bed a little drunk from the wine and the champagne, each of them a little surprised that they had gotten along so well.

Jeff left the curtains open so the lights from the city bathed their bedroom. He contentedly leaned on his elbow in the luxurious bed and watched the falling snow as Connie brushed her hair before she crawled in beside him.

"I had a wonderful afternoon and evening. Thank you, darling," Connie said, as she snuggled up to him.

"I knew you'd like the Laurentien Mountains. One of the managers up here recommended we take the boat trip. No wonder so many people come to see those colors. I think it helped us all to take some time together and play tourist," Jeff said.

"I'm hopeful it will work out, Jeff. Carmen is trying very hard to be accepted by us. Maybe she and Giuseppe will get married. I bet they do, and probably not very far in the future. She sure handles him better than Maritza did. I think she's just part of Giuseppe's life now and we need to adapt."

"She plays him like a violin. It's beautiful to see him so docile," Jeff said, amused. "And yet it's kind of scary."

"She's beautiful, the leaves were beautiful, the dinner was beautiful, the wine was beautiful," Connie giggled.

"You are beautiful, darling," Jeff said as he cupped her breast.

"And you are getting beautiful," she giggled again as she felt his erection. "I'm glad I came."

"I just wish you'd waited for me," he laughed. Her retort became a murmur as he covered her mouth with his.

5

The next morning, they woke to a dreary overcast and heavy, wet snow. Connie and Carmen joined Jeff and Giuseppe in the living room for coffee and croissants. After some discussion, Carmen suggested that the two of them "power-shop" on St. Catherine's Street, Montreal's eclectic shopping district. Connie eagerly agreed, sure they could occupy their entire morning while Jeff and Giuseppe finished their business at Dominion.

Giuseppe was nursing his weeks-old cold that seemed to never improve, and which seemed worse this morning. Jeff was very nervous with anticipation at finally finishing the "bullshit of acquisition". The two of them kissed their companions and left the hotel early.

"Are you the good guy or the bad guy today?" Jeff asked Giuseppe as they walked to their meeting, snow swirling around them.

"As usual, I'm the hard ass," Giuseppe replied.

"Just don't be too hard on these guys. We've already won, and there's no need to beat them to a pulp. We need to remember that they negotiate from a different perspective than we do, with the Government so involved. They have many other priorities to consider than we do. I'm sure this whole thing is very difficult for all of them."

"Okay, Jeff, I'll be gentle," Giuseppe laughed.

The meeting was with the banks, US and Canadian lawyers, several of Dominion's board members, and former executives of Dominion. Also, there to approve the significant changes in work force of Dominion as well as their part of the financing, were three Canadian Government officials. Vice-Consul Lawrence Carter was there as representative of the US Government to facilitate the sale. The financing package was one of Giuseppe's masterpieces and was very complicated, involving participation from the Canadian banks, the Canadian Government, Royal Floors' US Bank, and limited financial guarantees from Royal Floors.

At first, the meeting went along as planned, largely a formality. But it soon became a battle when the owners asked for a major change in the purchase price and terms. Jeff and Giuseppe were shocked. They were used to the American custom of agreeing in advance on everything important, then signing papers only as a formality. Giuseppe was utterly furious and threatened to walk out without further discussion. The meeting erupted into a chaos of French and English. The senior Canadian Government official eventually restored order with some difficulty.

When the room became quiet again, Jeff addressed the owners. "Gentlemen, please. We have already agreed on the price and the terms in prior meetings, weeks ago. Surely, you don't want to go back on your word?"

"But the price is no longer fair," one of the owners said. "The profits of the company have been much more than we could have anticipated."

"That's because we made the difficult changes you weren't willing or able to make," Giuseppe snapped, standing up. "Without those changes Dominion would still lose money! That's why we agreed to a price at the beginning."

"But we could not have known you would be permitted to dismiss all of the administrative people in Montreal. The severance costs we will incur as a result will be very substantial, much more than we planned," the manager said.

"The people in Montreal were the biggest part of the problems," Giuseppe retorted. "We tried very hard to work with them. They refused to work with us. They went on strike almost immediately. Then they sabotaged the facilities. We had to dismiss them. You agreed to give us control. We made the company profitable."

"But now that the company is doing so well, surely you could hire back some of the workers," the owner said.

"The workers were the goddamn problem! We got rid of them once. Why would we want to hire them back, for Christ's sake?" Giuseppe demanded.

"They will work better now that they understand the power you have to remove them. Surely you must realize the extra costs we will incur as a result of these actions."

"You are partially correct. You could not have anticipated the number of people we dismissed. We will agree to pay one-half of the additional severance cost you will incur over what we had predicted. But we will not hire back the workers. That is our final concession," Jeff said firmly.

"Bullshit! We have no obligation..." Giuseppe began.

"We will make this concession in the spirit of fair play," Jeff interrupted. "Mr. Portales is right, we certainly have no obligation to do so. We could not have anticipated them walking away from their jobs, either. I suggest you accept our offer. Now! It is final."

Another unexpected stumbling block was immediate five-year priority work permits for Royal's American managers in Montreal. These would replace the temporary permits the government had issued. Expiration of the permits could have forced the company to replace the Americans Royal Floors had installed at Dominion with Canadians. Jeff was totally adamant on this topic.

The Government finally agreed. The owners reluctantly agreed to the revised purchase price and the other terms when they realized Royal now had the full support of the Government.

Documents signed, permits in hand, the meeting ended with congratulations from the Canadians to the Americans. Only the former management of Dominion seemed to harbor resentment because of the takeover. And strangely enough, they seemed to direct it toward Jeff in particular. Jeff was somewhat annoyed but shrugged it off.

Jeff and Giuseppe walked back to the hotel about eleven o'clock, grateful to have finished the last step in the most complicated deal they had ever done. They were thankful for the typically overheated and very dry climate of the hotel's dark lobby after walking through the cutting wind and driving snow of the first storm of winter.

"Can you believe that last minute crap?" asked Giuseppe. "I was just about ready to tell them to shove the whole thing up their ass."

"It's the same thought process every time we do one of these," Jeff answered, "although we've never had someone renege after the deal was done before. When the people doing the selling smell what we can do to improve the profits, they want everything back that they gave away to get us to buy it in the first place. It's amazing how they think. I guess it's human nature to feel that you could have done something, after you've seen it done. None of these people really understand that most of the big expense cuts we get come from prior huge investments in centralizing our operations and becoming vertically integrated. They would never have gotten the same economies."

"I was surprised they had the balls to ask us to rehire some of the old staff," Giuseppe said. "They were unable to make it work because they couldn't reduce the costs of their operation. They didn't have the guts to get rid of the people when they had control. Now, they want us to make the same mistakes with the same people. It doesn't make any sense at all. It's obvious they're feeling the pressure from the employees we let go."

"Not only the employees; they're getting shit from the Government also! That's why I agreed to the deal on the severance pay. I know you didn't agree on that," Jeff said.

"No, I didn't. We didn't need to give anything away. I think we should have made them stick to the original deal. It kind of pissed me off when you did that. We should have discussed it. Fuck 'em if they have added expenses. Those people would have lost their jobs anyway and the Dominion folks would have had nothing if we hadn't saved the company!"

"But, the one thing we didn't think of was long-term work permits for our American managers. The severance concession helped give us the Government's support. I don't think we would have gotten those permits without doing something for the terminated employees. I think we'll come out way ahead in the long run. We've got our people in place, with no Government hassles, and no bureaucratic bullshit for at least five years."

"Hell, Jeff, we turned it around. We made Dominion profitable where they couldn't. And we did it in three months. They couldn't do it in thirty years!"

"Profit or loss is not the main question to them." Jeff said. "They're all under pressure from forces we never feel in the U.S. They have a totally different set of rules. Their society is almost socialistic. Then they have the dual language and dual culture thing. It's amazing how they operate at all. We're going to have to learn to deal with some of these things in the future."

"As Free Trade becomes truly a reality, these assholes are going to have to adjust, too," Giuseppe said. "More American companies are going to buy businesses up here. This kind of thing is going to happen to companies up here hundreds of times in the next few years."

"That doesn't make it any easier for them to deal with now," Jeff said. "It's no fun to admit that foreigners can be successful where you couldn't. Especially when the Government doesn't allow you the flexibility to change the work force or the work rules. And then, oftentimes, the new company replaces the workers with foreigners. It's got to be maddening! Besides, they're just jealous because we're so damn good-looking."

Laughing merrily, they met Carmen at the elevator. She had come back to the hotel alone, complaining of the cold and slush.

On the way up in the elevator she said, "Connie decided to keep on shopping. She wanted to look for something to get for her mother. She promised to be back before twelve-thirty for lunch."

"You thought I gave a lot away at the meeting today," Jeff said to Giuseppe. "Another hour of Connie's shopping will make that seem tiny!"

They were laughing together as they walked down the hall to their rooms. Giuseppe opened the door as Carmen, eyes twinkling, said, "I have just what you need for that cold, Giuseppe!"

"Call us when Connie comes back," Giuseppe said to Jeff, pushing Carmen in ahead of him. "I have to take care of myself," he laughed, closing their door.

Jeff, mildly envious of Giuseppe, utilized the time prior to Connie's return to answer the long string of phone and e-mail messages taken by the hotel while he was out. There were too many to finish. Fortunately, most were not urgent, so he completed the most important ones and then began reading the morning papers.

When Connie didn't return by lunch, Jeff became concerned and quite annoyed. He was sitting in the living room, considering whether to go to the shopping district to look for her, when the doorbell interrupted him. He opened it to find the hotel concierge.

"*Monsieur* Royal? This message was to be delivered to you immediately. The gentleman who left it said it was most urgent, so I brought it to you myself. He said there was no need to wait for an answer. He wouldn't leave his name, although I asked him. He said you would know what to do."

Jeff expressed his thanks and gave the man a generous tip. Closing the door, he sat down and looked at the envelope.

On the front, in flowing Gallic script, was written:

"M. Royal, Royal Floors."

With curiosity, he ripped open the envelope. It was written with more of the same flowing script on a flat card. His curiosity turned to horror when he read...

> "Your wife is ours, leave Quebec.
> *FLQ*"

Too stunned to react intelligently, Jeff pounded on the adjoining bedroom door and yelled for Giuseppe. He came from his room, red-faced, nose running, bare from the waist up, dragging on his pants. Jeff had obviously interrupted the pre-lunch "cold treatment" administered by Carmen. Still stunned by the contents of the envelope, Jeff handed him the note without a word.

"Oh shit!" Giuseppe said after he read it. Without another comment, he phoned his contact at the American Consulate, Lawrence Carter. Carter had been a great help to Giuseppe when they began the negotiations with the management of Dominion. In fact, Giuseppe and Carter had become somewhat friendly as Giuseppe navigated the financial intricacies of making a deal with an old-line Canadian company, big Canadian banks, and the Canadian Government. A career diplomat, Carter had been stationed in France, Peru, Columbia,

Venezuela, and even Ecuador, and so spoke perfect Spanish and French. He and Giuseppe often conversed in Spanish and had been to dinner together a few times on Giuseppe's many trips to Montreal. Jeff didn't particularly like him, thinking him somewhat pompous, but Giuseppe felt he had been extremely helpful in putting their Canadian deal together.

Carter, after expressing his shock at the turn of events, promised to contact the proper authorities at once, and to meet them at the hotel as soon as possible. He contacted the Montreal Police, and in just under one hour, Senior Inspector Roch presented himself, accompanied by Vice Consul Carter, at Jeff's suite.

Carter was a large florid-faced man with a diplomat's demeanor. Dressed as always in an expensive suit with a perfect tie and gold cufflinks, he brought the weight of the American government with him. It was obvious that Inspector Roch was very aware of his influence. After the formal introductions were completed, Inspector Roch took charge.

The subsequent "interview" became an interrogation of Jeff, Carmen, and Giuseppe.

"Where did you see her last?" Roch demanded of Carmen.

"At *Chapeau du Cerisse* on St. Catherine Street".

"Exactly when did you leave her?"

"As I told you before. Moments before I caught a cab for the hotel."

"Why did you leave?"

"I told you already. I had finished shopping. I was cold!" she sniffed, obviously irritated.

"And you, *Monsieur* Royal. Can you imagine why your wife would be abducted? Or who would do this thing? Have you been threatened before?"

Jeff answered almost absentmindedly in a voice totally devoid of emotion. "The only people who knew she was here were some of those we met with this morning and people from the hotel and ..."

Carter interrupted, "Inspector, isn't there some other approach we should be taking here? After all, the note is signed by the FLQ..."

"What <u>are</u> you doing to find her? And what the hell does FLQ mean?" Giuseppe asked.

"FLQ is the abbreviation for the *Front de Liberation du Quebec*, a Separatist terrorist group. They were actively involved in criminal terrorist activities until the bombing of the Montreal Stock Exchange in 1969 and the kidnapping of two government officials in 1970. Those responsible for the crime escaped to Cuba or were imprisoned. By the early 1980's most of them have been paroled or are still in Cuba. The FLQ has not been involved, to our knowledge, in anything other than legal activities for almost twenty years now. Most of their activities concern labor disputes. I am frankly surprised to see someone using their name, although we have been watching several of the known members closely with all the troubles lately," he explained.

"As to what we are doing now, I have two investigators interviewing everyone here at the hotel who may have had contact with the man who brought this message. Others in the Department are rounding up three activists in the FLQ, although it has been a long time since these violent ones were active. Four of my men are at this moment interviewing every recently released employee at Dominion Distributors as quickly as we can establish contact with them. We are not sitting on our hands," he said, looking at each person individually.

Ignoring Jeff's obvious desire to ask more, Roch turned to Giuseppe. "*Monsieur* Portales. Can you think of any reason for the disappearance of Madame Royal?"

"We have had a great deal of trouble with the people we released from jobs at Dominion, as we have explained over and over to you for the last two hours. We had more problems about that at our meeting today," Giuseppe said in a low even voice, his black eyes flashing. "Why don't you leave us alone and look for the people responsible?"

"It is our experience that there will be more actions to follow from people who do such things as this," said the Inspector. "Obviously, there will be specific demands made, possibly for ransom. They know you are at this hotel. So, we will wait to have them contact you here. We have made arrangements to trace any telephone calls and have alerted the management of the hotel to assist us. We are also concerned about your security which is why we have arranged to have additional men posted on this floor and elsewhere in the hotel," he continued.

"We will also want you to communicate as soon as possible with the local management at Dominion Distributors. We will need the same cooperation there," he added.

Giuseppe moved toward the phone.

"So now, all we can do is wait for something to happen? You can't be serious about that," said Jeff incredulously.

"Other than the measures we've already taken, that is correct," said Roch.

"Bullshit!" exclaimed Giuseppe, slamming down the phone before he completed dialing. "That's ridiculous. I think we should hire our own investigators. We can't just sit here and wait for the people who took Connie to react."

"That would be ill-advised," said Lawrence Carter. "Inspector Roch here has the best record of any investigator in Montreal. We've worked with him before and I have the utmost confidence in him. I know it is most difficult, but you must cooperate, at least for the time being. Besides, Giuseppe, you must remember this. You are in a foreign country, with different requirements," he emphasized. "This is not the United States."

ROYAL REVENGE

"No it's not," said Jeff bitterly. "It's obviously a country that somebody wants us to get the hell out of!"

***

The two men looked at each other with barely disguised dislike and body language that revealed that relationship to anyone looking – but no one was. One the trainer, one the dog. The short one, with the sinister face and the lopsided sneer, took a long drag off his unfiltered cigarette and exhaled vigorously into the face of the other. The dark warehouse was cold and bleak, and the wind outside was howling and driving snow and sleet under the old overhead doors. The filthy windows rattled with the wind and the driving snow and sleet.

"I have done what you wanted. Now it is time for you to honor your commitments. I must be able to resume my former employment," he said in heavily-accented English.

"In good time. As soon as possible," the big man replied condescendingly in French. "There is much to do. We must be patient. This is only the first part of the plan. Are you not comfortable in the apartment we have provided you?"

"I am too exposed. Eventually one or the other will find me. I even fear the police!" he said in disbelief.

"We will do whatever is required to make you comfortable. Women?"

A shake of the head. "I need more comfort than a woman can give. See if some of the samples from the South have made it here yet. I want to go where only the powder can take me. Then perhaps a woman – or more than one," he said with a sinister laugh.

"We will honor our side of the arrangement," said the other. "Continue with the plan. You will receive a delivery within hours after you have finished here. I'll have a woman suitable for your tastes to deliver it to the apartment. Do with her what you wish," he said as he stood to go. "Remember, however, you must follow the plan. Do not leave this building!"

The dark one put out his cigarette on the dirty floor. Only the fact that the dark one was eight inches shorter than he prevented the other man from an inward shudder of fear. How could something so evil have grown in such a diminutive body?

6

Atlanta, September.

Buckhead United Methodist Church was unique in that it had been built only seven years before and <u>looked</u> like a church. The white stone structure, crowned by a traditional white steeple, was visible from great distances for those seeking a traditional place to worship.

The church sat at the top of a hill at the end of a long, winding drive, which led back from the noise of Paces Ferry Road. The building was much longer than it was wide, with side walls full of beautiful, tall, stained glass windows with old-fashioned religious scenes. Huge doors in the front opened into a large assembly area where worshipers were greeted before and after services.

From the assembly area, one entered a vaulted sanctuary that inspired silence and reverence. Behind the pulpit was a very large, simple, wooden cross. The huge pipe organ to the side gleamed with brass. In front were dark wooden pews, which somehow had been finished to look old and well used. They encouraged the worshipers to slide closer together. Encased by the beautiful trees common to this wooded section of Atlanta, the building could have easily been located in a small village in Vermont, dating from the late 1800's.

The orthodox look of the building was one of the things that had induced Connie to convince Jeff to go visit the church for the first time with her four years before.

"Maybe the traditional style of the building means they have a traditional style in the church. I certainly hope so, because that's what I'm looking for." Connie had said that first Sunday as they were getting dressed.

"I just hope no one tries to save me on the first day," Jeff chuckled, as he brushed his lips down the nape of her neck.

"I'm sure they won't," answered Connie, pushing him away tenderly. "Anyone who knows you well would realize that saving you will take more time than they are probably willing to allow, if it's possible at all. I know how you feel about organized religion, Jeff. Just go with an open mind. Please. Think of this as a place to be for us to be social and to make new friends. And remember, we do know several of the people who started this congregation, so you need to be on your best behavior."

On this beautiful fall day four years later, Buckhead Methodist was filled to capacity. Connie Royal had been a very popular member of the congregation and most of her fellow members were to be found at her memorial service. The Royal's many other friends, business and personal, swelled the gathering for the service into the assembly area in the front of the church, where temporary seating had been arranged to accommodate the crowd.

The Atlanta police were there in force to control the traffic from the worshipers and well-wishers, and to search for suspicious persons attending the services. They were also necessary to control and restrict the crowd of cameramen, reporters, and morbid curiosity seekers who congregated at the entrance of the church's drive.

There had been many sensational and detailed stories in the Atlanta papers since the day after Connie's murder. Local, national, and international television coverage had been constant and thorough. The resulting invasion of reporters was incredible. The morbid aspects of the packages and the international flavor of the unsolved crime attracted them. This, combined with the prominence of Royal Floors in Atlanta business circles, resulted in a broad spectrum of news coverage.

Not only had the normal daily newspapers been involved, but also every paper from the Wall Street Journal to The Enquirer had assigned reporters to cover the story. Television coverage had been even more complete. There were daily requests for interviews from anyone connected with the business or the family. Giuseppe had finally been forced to restrict, and protect, employees at all Royal offices from contact with the press, requiring all contact regarding the tragedy to be handled by his office.

The publicity had reduced Jeff Royal to a prisoner in his own home since his return to Atlanta. Pinkerton Security guards stayed at the front gates full-time. He had not yet dealt with his personal loss and shock. He was furious with the notoriety and unceasing invasions of privacy that resulted from the surge of reporters. He had not handled it at all well, and the memorial service was his first appearance in public since returning to Atlanta from Montreal.

Fortunately, Giuseppe's friendship, and his strong measures to protect Jeff and Royal Floors from the publicity, and to allow Jeff to isolate himself, gave Jeff some peace. Giuseppe had done everything in his power to reduce Jeff's stress and responsibilities. Giuseppe had assumed all of the daily duties in the business that normally belonged to Jeff, so as to allow Jeff time to himself without interruption. Jeff was comfortable with Giuseppe's ability to run the business in his absence and he had not gone to the office since returning from Montreal.

While Jeff had remained sedated in the hotel suite for an entire day, it had been Giuseppe who had arranged for Connie's identification and subsequent cremation in Montreal. He had also made all of the travel arrangements for their return to Atlanta.

The morning after the receipt of the second package, Inspector Roch called the suite. Jeff was still unconscious as a result of the powerful dose of Valium administered by the hotel physician the night before. Giuseppe answered the phone.

"*Monsieur* Portales? Inspector Roch. We have recovered what appear to be the remains of *Madame* Royal. I would like to avoid disturbing *Monsieur* Royal at this time. Would it be possible for me to have you collected in the next few minutes, so you might attempt the necessary identification?"

"Of course, Inspector, I will do anything I can to help," Giuseppe answered. "But how will I identify ..."

"There are still the personal items of clothing and the jewelry she was wearing. You can identify those things. In addition, *Monsieur* Royal had mentioned a distinctive scar on *Madame* Royal's leg, which she acquired in an automobile accident. It occurred to me, that since you had known her for a very long time, you could possibly recognize this mark," he said.

"Of course, I had forgotten that until now. Since I was the driver of the car when she was injured, I'm sure I can identify that. It's on her left leg just below the knee. Will this enable you to avoid disturbing Mr. Royal further? He is still asleep from the sedative and the doctor said that he needed to rest," Giuseppe said.

"Yes. If you will sign a statement to the effect that you are sure that this body is that of *Madame* Royal, I will release the remains to the mortician you have hired," Roch answered. "The sergeant will collect you in the lobby in fifteen minutes."

Giuseppe had gone with the sergeant to Montreal's morgue. In the presence of Inspector Roch and Vice Consul Carter, he went through the grisly ordeal of identifying what was left of Connie Royal. The sight made him physically ill. Inspector Roch, having had this reaction from family members before, did everything possible to alleviate Giuseppe's discomfort. Giuseppe came back to the hotel immediately after making the final arrangements with the funeral home for her transfer and cremation, and eventual transfer of her ashes to the airport.

By early evening, he had made all their travel arrangements. With Carmen's help, he packed Connie's and Jeff's clothing, and arranged for their secretary, Olivia Henson, to meet them in Atlanta on their arrival late that evening.

Giuseppe also arranged for the key people at Dominion to handle the few remaining details of the acquisition's closing, the rental car return, hotel bills and the like. He instructed the Dominion advertising agency to field any inquiries from the press. It would be up to the agency to control the information going out in Canada regarding Jeff and Royal Floors.

They checked out of the hotel as evening fell. The three traveled in silence to Dorval in the hotel's opulent limousine. Heavy snow continued to fall, and the roads were getting worse. The wind blew unceasingly.

Lawrence Carter met them as the limousine pulled up to a private entrance of the terminal. Avoiding the reporters at the public entrance, Carter had arranged for the U.S. Customs Inspector to be on hand to expedite the departure of the Americans. Giuseppe had chartered a Learjet to take them to Atlanta, so that they could avoid the expected reporters at Hartsfield International and land in privacy at Fulton County Airport, also known as Charlie Brown Airport, a small private airport on the north side of the city that Royal Floors had used before.

"Mr. Royal, you of course know that you have our deepest sympathy in your loss. The U.S. Government and our Canadian office will do everything possible to help you at this end while the investigation goes forward," he said to Jeff.

Jeff looked at him as if in a trance.

J. Trey Weeks

"We appreciate your help, Lawrence. It is most important that I be kept informed about any progress the police make in their investigation during the next few days while Jeff is recuperating from the shock," Giuseppe intervened.

"Of course. I'll call you every day, if required. The only reason I won't call is if I have no news. I am sure Inspector Roch will also communicate with you regularly," Carter said. They shook hands and then they headed toward the plane.

The Lear 500 was fast and comfortable. They arrived in Atlanta before midnight in just under three hours. Jeff, still dazed from shock and the drugs given him, had refused to eat the meal the pilots had put on board. He had avoided all attempts at conversation and, simply stared out the window most of the flight, sometimes sobbing quietly. Their secretary, Olivia Henson, and two company drivers met them with two cars to transport them home.

Olivia had brought Dr. Ezell, Jeff and Connie's personal physician, with her. Dr. Ezell agreed to accompany them to Jeff's house and sedate him further. He rode in the second car with Jeff, which followed the car with Olivia, Carmen, and Giuseppe.

"There were TV vans and cameras at the front gate. Rena called me earlier. I took the liberty of posting one of the company's security men at the drive for tonight and tomorrow." Olivia said to Giuseppe. "You can reach him from the car phone. He is staying by his van so we can reach him and he expects us to call when we are a couple of blocks from to the house. He will clear away the reporters. His name is John Rodgers."

While en route to Jeff's house, Giuseppe called the guard who answered on the first ring. "This is Giuseppe Portales. We'll be there in about a minute, John. We want to go directly in the gate and up to the house without any delay. Will there be any problems with reporters?"

ROYAL REVENGE

"There's a bunch of 'em here, Mr. Portales, but I'll move 'em away from the gate," Rodgers replied. "Just drive straight in and don't stop for nothing."

The two cars were bathed in lights from the cameras around the entrance gate as they sped past the gathered mob of reporters and television vans and up the drive to Jeff's home. Rodgers closed the gate after them.

Jeff had always been averse to flaunting their newly acquired wealth after the company became successful. He drove a domestic mid-size car and required all of upper management of Royal Distributing to do the same. He and Giuseppe had furnished all the company's offices, theirs included, in an almost Spartan fashion. Albert Henry had impressed upon him that controlling expenses in a business was a matter of setting the right example at the top.

But as to the house, he had allowed Connie an unlimited budget. "What else am I going to spend it on?" he asked Giuseppe one day. "We might as well enjoy it while we can. Connie is in hog heaven about this house."

They had lived in the house only one year. Jeff and Connie had purchased the two-acre slightly hilly site with the dilapidated old house and servant's quarters that rested on it five years before. They had planned their "dream house" for three years before beginning construction. The only word to adequately describe the result was "spectacular".

The entire property was bordered with a stone and ironwork fence that was, in itself, a masterpiece. The grounds in front, split by a winding drive, were left in their heavily wooded natural state. Halfway to the back of the deep lot, shielded by huge old oak trees, was the house they had built with adjoining servant's quarters. It was made of dark red antique brick, salvaged mostly from the old house and outbuildings they had torn down. Windowless from the front, the structure appeared to be one story. Upon closer inspection, one found that the walls in front surrounded various courtyards. These gave total privacy to those inside the house and were planted in a variety of rich gardens.

In back, the grounds were exquisite, manicured, and opulent. The entire rear walls of the house on both the first and second stories were glass. From inside one looked out on a magnificent swimming pool, regulation tennis court, and beautiful huge terraced gardens of roses and azaleas. Running through the grounds from a wooden deck near the tennis court was a small burbling stream that appeared natural but was man-made. It ended in a natural rock waterfall that emptied into the pool.

One could enter the massive swimming pool from inside the exercise room by diving into a huge heated spa and swimming underwater in a canal to the outside. There was a large pagoda-like structure on the other side of the pool, which housed an immense grill, bar, bathroom, shower, sauna, and complete kitchen. A large greenhouse was attached to the pool house. Inside the fence in back and surrounding the perimeter was a jogging path. In the far corner was a picnic table and swing set, for "visiting children", Connie had said.

Inside, the furnishings could only be described as elegant. And yet, the total effect was very comfortable and warm. Connie Royal had spent virtually all her time for three years designing, decorating, and then furnishing this house. Every detail of the house and grounds showed her excellent taste and perfect planning.

Before she and Jeff had married, Connie knew she couldn't have children. After resigning herself to Jeff's unceasing refusal to even consider adoption, she plunged into every project she took on with the same dedication most women devoted to their children.

In addition to her large circle of friends, she had become involved in numerous projects for charity and the church. She was also very active in an ongoing campaign to increase adult literacy. Connie started as a volunteer and progressed to being one of the most convincing and prominent members of the adult literacy movement in Georgia. In addition, she was always at hand for functions required by her position as the wife of the President of Royal Distributors.

But her house and its surroundings were her pride and joy. There were three large and comfortable guest bedrooms upstairs, each with a private bath, surrounding a large sitting room. The servant's quarters were equally as nice.

The balance of the downstairs living area had every luxury available. Off to the side was the master suite, with a huge bath, sitting area, and two walk-in closets. The public areas included a formal dining room suitable for a seated dinner for twenty. The huge den, formal living room, game room, the large kitchen and breakfast area were tied together, and could easily accommodate more than one hundred people for informal parties. There were two private studies, four bathrooms, a formal and informal bar, and the exercise area. They all were decorated and furnished to perfection.

Everything about the house was devoted to comfort for her and Jeff and their guests. Connie had planned for ease of entertaining large groups, which they often did, and for visiting overnight guests, which were frequent.

Rena Miller, Jeff and Connie's live-in housekeeper for three years, was standing in the open front door as they drove up. She was one of those black women who looked anywhere between forty and fifty. In truth, she was well over sixty. Rena treated Jeff and Connie like her own children, and the kitchen was considered her supreme domain. Giuseppe had phoned to tell her of Connie's death before they left Montreal. Rena had taken the news hard. She was still clearly distraught, and very concerned about Jeff. Giuseppe, Carmen, Olivia, and Dr. Ezell entered behind Jeff.

"Oh God, Mr. Royal. I'm so sorry, I'm so sorry," she said with tears streaming down her ample black face, hugging him and patting his shoulders. "Come inside and get to bed. Have you eaten? Do you want anything to eat?"

Jeff, arms at his side, moved his head slightly from side to side in answer. Still in a trance-like state, he allowed Rena to lead him to the back of the house to bed. The doctor followed. After attending to him and then leaving him in Rena's tender care, Dr. Ezell joined the others in the living room.

"He needs immediate psychiatric attention, once he comes out from under the Valium and the initial shock. Although he's still in shock, I'm very concerned about his total lack of response to any stimulus. We can't keep him sedated forever. Eventually he'll have to face this thing and go on living his life," he said to Giuseppe.

"Compounding his problem is that he's lost his family before, and he felt responsible. He told me several times yesterday that he wished he hadn't taken Connie to Canada. Connie helped him overcome his guilt thing, but she was all he had left in the way of family. The way he's reacting to this is really kind of predictable. I don't know how he'll cope with being alone again," Giuseppe said. "Losing her was one of his greatest fears. When she got sick a few years ago, he was a basket case until the tests came back negative. He'll be incapacitated at best, if this thing doesn't kill him. At the very least, it will take him a very long time to recover and return to his normal life."

"I am aware of his background," said Doctor Ezell. "I've been thinking about possible treatment plans since Olivia called me. When I come by tomorrow morning, I'm going to bring John Fitzhugh. He's a psychiatrist and has been a close friend of the Royals for several years. I'm sure he's the right person to deal with Jeff now."

"I know Doctor Fitzhugh. He's an excellent choice. Jeff likes him a lot. I think that's an excellent idea. I'll come here before going to the office," volunteered Giuseppe, "if you think I can help, that is. And Carmen will do anything..."

"That's very kind of you. But I think he needs privacy and professional care right now," the doctor interrupted. "Rena can take care of Connie's things. Jeff will be glad to have you attending to the business, so he won't have any of that to worry about. I'll call you tomorrow after we leave and tell you how things went. I'm pretty sure this will be a long-term treatment program. It will take weeks, probably months. Will you see that Rena has everything she needs to run the house?"

"Of course. Olivia will help take care of that. She handles many of his personal affairs. She can call Rena tomorrow to make sure she has everything she needs," Giuseppe said.

Olivia nodded. "I already take care of most of his finances and can sign on his accounts. I'll take care of Rena and help her with the other household things, too," she said.

"You might as well go on home now," the doctor said to Giuseppe and Carmen. "I'm sure this whole ordeal has been rough on both of you, also. I'll call you in the morning, Giuseppe. Do you need something to help you sleep? And have you got something for that cold?"

"After the last two days, I think we all just need to sleep in our own beds," said Carmen. "I think Giuseppe just needs some rest, also. He'll eventually wear the cold out. I'll make sure he takes his vitamins. What about the reporters outside? Will they follow us home?"

"I already took care of that," Olivia said to her. "You have a guard at your apartment, too. His name is um ... Jerry Rodgers. He's John's brother. We can go through the same drill on the way to your place, although there weren't any reporters there when I checked before."

Turning to Giuseppe, she said, "I've increased security at the offices, too. I thought we should be prepared for anything. There were a lot of them there this morning. I'll make more permanent arrangements with Pinkerton tomorrow."

"As usual, you thought of everything," said Giuseppe.

With a catch in her voice, near to tears, Olivia said, "I just wish I could have done something..."

"You've done everything you can. You can't prevent crazy people from doing crazy things. There's not much any of us can do now, except to take as much pressure off Jeff as possible," Giuseppe said, putting his arm around her.

They left after arranging for the driver to take Doctor Ezell home.

7

Atlanta, April

Atlanta was in for a bright, hot day. The sun was just coming up as Jeff Royal climbed out of the spa. Water streamed off his body in rivulets. He had completed sixty laps in the pool, the second part of his morning routine. The first part, begun at four a.m., was a five-mile run through the neighborhood with a five-pound dumbbell in each hand.

Jeff peeled off his swimsuit and began to towel himself off. The suit was one of those abbreviated ultra-thin bikinis like professional swimmers wear. Colleen Schaeffer, Jeff's physical trainer, had insisted he buy that type.

"I'll look like a damn porpoise in one of those things," he said.

"That's part of the plan. You'll look absolutely awful. That ought to help you be more determined to work at it. When you look good in one of these, you'll be in shape," she said.

After drying himself, he put on a new bathing suit and went to the Soloflex machine. In the wall mirror, he looked at his reflection. The image looking back was totally different from that of seven months before.

His stark white hair was cut very short. His blue eyes sparkled, highlighting his clean-shaven face. While tanned, somewhat handsome and healthy looking, his thin face was severely lined. Jeff, only thirty-six, now had the look of someone in his late forties. The light hair on his chest was also white. But his body was very young looking. His stomach was flat and hard. His waist was slim. His arms and shoulders were lean and muscular. His chest showed the effects of regular weight training. His long legs were powerful and very firm. There was not an ounce of fat on his frame.

After months of regimen, Jeff looked good in the skimpy bathing suit. He began his hour-long workout vigorously, while Colleen counted repetitions.

It had been seven months since Connie's memorial service. For the first two months, Jeff had spent most of his days in bed. His hair had become long and filthy and had turned totally white. His body became pale and flabby, with rolls around his middle and "man-boobs". He rarely got dressed (since his clothes didn't fit) and wore a bathrobe and boxer shorts most of the time. His scraggly beard was virtually all gray and untrimmed. His formerly sharp blue eyes were dulled and bloodshot. His scowling face was puffy, with deep black circles under his eyes. Once Jeff had been fanatic about personal hygiene. Now he bathed only sporadically. He had gained almost twenty-five pounds because of his inactivity, overeating, and his vast intake of alcohol.

He avoided everyone, even refusing to talk on the phone. His only contacts with other people were meals in the kitchen with Rena and daily two-hour sessions in his study with Doctor Fitzhugh. Jeff had consented to the sessions with Fitzhugh only after strong urging from his personal physician, Dr. Ezell. He had even avoided any but the briefest phone conversations with Giuseppe.

He had remained in his room except for meals and Doctor Fitzhugh's visits. He refused to allow Rena to clean the room. The bedroom had become filthy, the floor covered with empty bottles and the residue of food wrappers of every description.

When Rena had finally refused to buy him more liquor, Jeff had found a store that delivered. He instructed the guards at the gate to bring it up to the house. On the weekends, when

Doctor Fitzhugh didn't come, Jeff would stay in bed and drink himself into a stupor. He had toyed dangerously with suicide during the first few weeks after Connie's death.

Doctor Fitzhugh was very good and very determined. But, he had made little progress after many hours of therapy over the last two months. Finally, after eight weeks of trying, Fitzhugh had finally broken through.

He feared that Jeff would try suicide, or worse, succeed at suicide. On that day, he confronted the problem directly. "You know that the children of parents who commit suicide are more in danger of suicide than the rest of us, don't you?" asked the doctor.

"You've told me that before."

"I know you've thought about it. Suicide."

"Yes."

"What did you think of your father when they told you he killed himself?"

"I felt grief ..."

"No. I don't want to know *your* feelings. What did you think of *him*?"

Jeff squirmed in his chair. "It ... It pissed me off that he would leave me alone. I thought it was a chicken-shit thing to do. I guess I lost respect for him," he finally answered.

"Do you want someone to think of you that way?" asked the doctor.

"There *is* no one. I don't have any family now. You know that."

"But you have your friends; your business associates; your company and your employees; Connie's parents. Think about Rena. You're all she has left. You're like a son to her. And what about Connie's killers? Don't you want to know if they're ever caught and punished?"

"You're right about Rena. But most of our former friends are tired of trying to be friends after this deal. I certainly haven't helped that. Connie's parents have their own problems and two other children. I guess I'll have to go back to work, sometime. I've heard nothing from the Montreal police. Giuseppe said that Lawrence Carter has called several times, but they still don't have many leads. I sure can't do anything about that."

"You could get out of bed and stop killing yourself with too much booze. You could clean yourself up. You could lose all the fat you've put on around your gut. What about the book you always wanted to write? If you don't want to go back to the office, you could try working on that again. Why don't you dust off that project? You need to go on with your life, Jeff."

"I know I need to do something. But I don't have much of a life left. I just can't get used to the fact that Connie's dead. And now I'm alone again."

"You must accept that. Connie would want you to accept it and go on."

"Go on to what?"

"To whatever you want to do. You're young, rich and intelligent. You built a big business that is very successful. Most people would envy that. You're healthy, at least you could be if you'd stop drinking and eating so much. Surely you can find something to do that you enjoy. Why don't you take it one step at a time? Get yourself back in shape first, and then go on to doing other things. You don't have to have contact with people now. Giuseppe is handling the business. But you do need to quit the pattern of self-pity and self-destruction you've gotten into. You're feeling sorry for yourself and it's getting you nowhere. Actually, you're somewhat pathetic."

Jeff looked up in shock. Fitzhugh nodded. "Pathetic is a strong term, Jeff, but you're there."

The next morning Jeff appeared in the kitchen with a garbage bag full of the detritus from the bedroom. Rena was pleasantly shocked to see him dressed and clean-shaven. He was even whistling.

ROYAL REVENGE

"Good morning, Mr. Royal. Would you like me to fix you some breakfast this morning?"

"Just juice and coffee, Rena, thanks. I need to go on a diet and lose this," he smiled as he patted his paunch. "And would you plan on making a light lunch for two? I'm going to ask Mr. Portales to meet me here about noon. Oh, and when you get a chance, would you clean the bedroom? I've cleaned out the trash," he said as he held up the garbage bag. "I think it's time to get back to normal."

Singing merrily to herself, happy to the point of bursting, Rena prepared coffee and juice while Jeff phoned Giuseppe to ask him to lunch.

Giuseppe was surprised at the invitation but readily agreed to lunch. Jeff met him at the door.

"You look like shit. How'd you get so fucking fat?"

"You look good, too. I'm glad you're here to cheer me up," Jeff laughed, patting Giuseppe on the shoulder as he ushered him in.

They sat outside in the bright November sun and allowed Rena to clear away the dishes. They had eaten on the patio. It was unseasonably warm, and the sun felt good, especially to Jeff. It was the first time he had been outside the house in weeks. Giuseppe was the only person, other than Doctors Ezell and Fitzhugh, Rena, and the guards, that Jeff had seen since Connie's memorial service.

Giuseppe still had a cold. He sniffed and blew his nose frequently.

"Are you ever going to get well?" Jeff asked. "You always seem to have a cold."

"I think it's allergies. Carmen thinks it's Cuban cigars."

They were laughing as Rena brought fresh glasses of iced tea and cleared the dishes as Giuseppe lit one of his cigars. Jeff, obviously very uncomfortable, with fat pushing out over the top of the tie-waist chinos he wore, slumped and squirmed in his chair. His clothes were stretched to the limit and his shirt buttons threatened to pop off.

"So that's the financial picture," Giuseppe was saying. "Profits are up. Collections are up. Cash flow is terrific. The biggest problem is where to put it all. We have only a few branches, mostly in the Northwest, that are not performing well. I'm sure those will come around soon. George is out in Seattle now, hammering on the sales force. I'm sure he'll get them turned around.

"You'll be happy to know that the Canadian division is doing very well. Sales are way ahead of forecast, and expenses are lower than we thought they would be. We're having no problem handling the added workload here, both in manufacturing and operations. I'm sure we'll be able to pay off the owners and the Canadian banks next year, which will give us a huge fucking discount. Increased sales have allowed us to reduce the management charges to the branches. Dominion may be one of our best deals yet. Overall, business has never been better," he concluded.

"You've done a great job. With everything else, I couldn't have asked for things to be in better hands," Jeff said. "I hope you know how much I appreciate it."

Giuseppe shrugged.

"I've decided to take some more time off from the business," Jeff continued. "First, I have to get myself in shape, so I can wear my clothes. Can you believe these are the only pants I can get on?" he laughed with Giuseppe. "And my boxer shorts are more like yoga pants!" he laughed. Then, I plan to try writing again. That means you'll have to take my place, and still continue to do your own job a while longer. Does that present any problems?"

"I can handle it for now. The people we have in place now are good at what they do. If we made another acquisition, I couldn't."

ROYAL REVENGE

"I don't see how another acquisition could help us. There's no place else for us to go, except Mexico, and I don't see that as much of an opportunity. Besides, I don't really know how much appetite I have for expanding the business in the future," said Jeff.

"I don't either," said Giuseppe. "I think we have enough for a while. We can get good growth for several more years. But a lot of people have been asking about you. What should I tell our own people? What do I tell the vendors and the banks? Some of them have been very concerned. Especially the fucking bankers. They always seem to think the sky is falling or has already fallen. I need to tell all of them something. When do you plan to come back to work? Actually, do you really intend to come back to work may be a better question."

"From what you've told me, the company has never done better. That fact should make our suppliers and the banks happy. Just tell the employees I'm taking some time off. And make sure we have plenty of cash if you're worried about the banks. If it's longer than six months before I'm ready, we'll promote you to President and George to Executive Vice President."

"I won't tell George," Giuseppe said. "He'd think about nothing else. Right now, he needs to keep things going with the sales force."

"You're right about George. How about money? Do you want to pay yourself more now?"

"I already am. You got a raise, too. Olivia has been handling your checking and savings accounts, so you don't know yet. Under the terms of our contracts, the two of us get 50% of the profits as bonuses, assuming the cash flow is there. We've never taken it before, but the profits are so big right now, and the cash flow so good, I figured we might as well take something out. We sure don't need it for the operation.

"Besides, since you have been gone from the business, our biggest bank has shown a lot of concern. There is always a chance they will reduce our revolving credit lines and tie up more of our cash. I figured we'd be better off with the money in our own accounts. I went over it with Dick and he has figured out how to shelter most of it from taxes."

"How much extra are we getting?"

"Last month you got $65,000 extra, and I got $35,000. I think we can take out about that much each month for the next six months, before we adversely affect cash flow. I also think we should take it out, since we don't need it in the company. If things change, we'll adjust accordingly," Giuseppe said.

"Good Lord! Business must be good. Keep on doing whatever you're doing. Just don't work so much you forget to enjoy life."

"You know how much I like to work. Carmen has been super. She even helps me in the office a lot now." Giuseppe said, puffing on the cigar. "We're talking about getting married. We've also decided to build a new house. I bought a big lot on Paces Ferry last week."

"That's wonderful. Building a house will drive you crazy, but the result is worth it. I'd like to see the plans sometime. Back to business, if you think I need to meet with some of the key people to settle them down, I will. But I'd prefer not to come to the office for a while."

"Everyone understands that. I see no problem at all. I'm just glad you've decided to do something with yourself."

"I think the worst is over. Tell me what you've heard from the police."

"I talk to Lawrence Carter frequently, at least once a week. I also usually see him for dinner when I travel up there to review our progress with Dominion. Inspector Roch has called a couple of times. They say they have one or two suspects and they're getting close to capturing them, but they haven't found them yet. To tell you the truth, I really don't think they know much more than they did before. The press coverage has really died down since the police have nothing more to report."

"No further problems at Dominion? That's good, but it's hard to figure," Jeff said. "Why the sudden change? We're still running Dominion."

"Inspector Roch thinks they're laying low for a while. The cops really put the heat on after what happened to Connie. Troubles have slowed at the other companies in Montreal, too. Also, their elections are next week. Maybe they're waiting for those to be over. Who knows in that crazy place," said Giuseppe.

"Maybe it will stay peaceful now," Jeff said. "I hope so."

"I do too. Well, I'd better get back to work. Thanks for lunch. How often do you want to meet and go over things?"

"Why don't we meet here for lunch once a week," Jeff said. "That will help me keep informed."

"I have no objection to Rena's cooking once a week. I'll call you in between if anything comes up that you need to know. I'm really glad you're back among the living, Jeff. You know I'll do whatever is necessary to help you and to guarantee our success."

"It's friends like you…," Jeff choked and then brought himself under control. "I'd like you to tell Inspector Roch and Lawrence Carter to call me here from now on. I think I can handle more direct involvement. You'll have enough to do without that." Jeff said.

"I don't mind talking to them, but if you want to handle it, fine. I'll have Olivia call them today. I can do the rest regarding the company. Don't worry about the business." They shook hands warmly and embraced.

"Take care of yourself. Go on a fucking diet," Giuseppe said with a twinkle in his eye as he left.

Jeff watched as Giuseppe drove away. He was very content with Giuseppe running the company. He knew it would do well financially and that he wouldn't have to worry. But Jeff was a little irritated at the big cash bonuses Giuseppe had decided to take out. He had resisted doing it in the past. But those were their agreements, and, the cash was certainly there. "Why not?" he thought.

***

The third shift was running full blast. 35 trailers were lined up against the loading dock with forklift drivers loading huge rolls of carpet into them as fast as they could be checked off. As soon as forty-odd rolls were loaded, the trailer was closed, sealed, pulled away, and another took its place. Royal Floors shipped almost 200 trailer loads to 58 destinations every weeknight except Saturday. The forklift trucks moved rapidly through the warehouse, rolls of carpet sticking 12 feet out in front of them, waiting to be shoved into the waiting trailers. Considering the amount of movement, it was fairly quiet in this part of the operation. 800 yards away, carpet was being tufted, backed, finished, inspected, and wrapped at the rate of 2,000 running feet a minute. The chemical smells, noise, heat, and human activity seemed to be organized chaos there.

Jeremiah Farley turned his forklift into the aisle at the far end of the 500,000-square-foot warehouse and turned so his load was perpendicular to the aisle. His friend, Davey Hale, cut the straps holding the 120-foot long roll of carpet tightly together. Rapidly unrolling about forty feet, Davey cut a 20 by 8-foot square out of the middle, leaving twenty feet at the end of the roll and 2 feet on each side. When rolled up, this left an empty compartment inside the roll about six inches high and going completely around the center core. Davey, with Jeremiah's help, rolled up the carpet until the compartment was fully defined. The two men then hurriedly stuffed heavily wrapped plastic bags into the hidden compartment. After rolling up the rest of the carpeting and putting new straps around it, the only evidence of their work was the 20 by 8-foot piece lying on the floor. They rapidly rolled that up and bound it together. Davey jumped on his truck and lifted the piece 30 feet in the air, depositing it on the top shelf of this most remote part of the warehouse.

"I'll take this up and re-wrap it," Jeremiah said. "It'll be in Oklahoma City by morning. Oklahoma must be a good market! We shipped one to Tulsa yesterday."

"We need to clean up those extra pieces this weekend," Davey said. "There must be thirty of them up there."

"Not a problem," said Jeremiah. We're both on overtime Saturday. You know none of the suits will be around on the weekend. I've scheduled a disposal shipment to the off-goods guy. Not only does he come and get it, he pays cash for it!" he laughed.

***

After Giuseppe left, Jeff went into his study. It was time for him to decide what to do with himself. As he often did when faced with a situation, he mentally outlined the problems and the solutions in almost flow-chart fashion:

- *"I'm fat and out of shape. Quit drinking! Diet (severe, nutritionist?). Exercise (personal trainer?). Daily regimen. Call Doctor for physical.*
- *Brain dead. Begin new book outline, start writing. Read two books weekly (1 fiction, 1 non-fiction). Reduce sessions with Fitzhugh. Quit drinking. Study foreign language (correspondence? Berlitz?). Weekly sessions with Giuseppe.*
- *No hobbies, no fun. Greenhouse/gardening? Buy a new car (what kind?). Travel, cruise (people contact!). New clothes (wait for diet).*

- *Get back in society. Companionship? (not now!).*
- *Financial - no problems.*
- *Investigation - put heat on Roch (go to Montreal?). Meet with Olivia, go over accounts. Handle Connie's clothes and other things (her sister? Maritza?)."*

The next day Jeff began a completely new existence. He interviewed several people who advertised their services as personal trainers in the newspaper. After several interviews, he found that most of them simply held your hand and helped keep you on whatever program you started. He hired Colleen Schaeffer because of her degree in nutrition, and her insistence on total control of his diet, as well as the varied physical exercise regimen that she required. She also taught Spanish at Berlitz. She was a very strong individual, and Jeff knew he wanted to be led around for awhile.

"Essentially, this will be a full-time job. Can you take it full-time?" he asked.

"I now do personal physical training and teach weekends at Berlitz. I make about $33,000 per year between the two jobs. I can't make less than that. What are you going to do after I put you in shape? I'll need to make a living after I finish working with you," she said.

"Let's agree on $3,000 the first month. I have over 300 people at my company here who could use your services. After one month, if you're as good as you say, I'll give you a three-year contract for $40,000 per year, plus benefits, to be our health consultant. After you finish with me, you'll work there. I guarantee that will keep you busy for years. Okay?"

"Only if you agree to do everything I put into your plan. Diet, nutrition, exercise, everything in the package is important. And, you want an immersion course in Spanish. I'm going to be a very tough taskmaster. Agreed?"

"Done," Jeff said as they shook hands.

ROYAL REVENGE

Colleen Schaeffer came to the house every day, five days a week, at four a.m. At first, they walked through the neighborhood. Then Jeff swam while Colleen watched and counted laps. Then she would take him through light exercises on the Soloflex. Each day she required more. Faster walking, then jogging, then running. More and more laps in the pool. More repetitions with more weight. After two months, the three-part exercise regimen took almost four hours.

Also, each day, Colleen gave Jeff a two-hour lesson in Spanish. She was very articulate and patient. Jeff found he liked her a great deal. And, because of all the exercise she got, she was quite attractive. With all the time they spent together, there could have been some physical attraction. But, Colleen had addressed that issue the day she returned to start Jeff's training.

"Here's a list of foods you can't eat. Also, nothing can be fried. Give this to Rena. She can give you reasonable amounts of anything else. Here's a list of vitamins and supplements I want you to take each day. I'll order them for you if you wish," she said. "You'll need some new equipment, exercise clothes, and so forth. Here's that list. I can get that for you too."

"Thanks. You order all of it. But wouldn't it have been easier to list what I can eat?" Jeff laughed as he perused the very long list of foods that were forbidden. "What's next?" he asked after they had stopped laughing.

"Take off your clothes down to your underwear. I need to see how much work we've got to do," she said.

"You're kidding!"

"Don't be so nervous. I'm not interested in men," she said. "You can take off everything and it won't appeal to me. We're going to spend a great deal of time together from now on. I'm being hired to get your body into top shape. There's no reason to hide it from me."

J. Trey Weeks

The exercise became his substitute for therapy. His visits with Doctor Fitzhugh were reduced to weekly. After another month, they ceased altogether.

He observed a very rigid diet, much to the consternation of Rena. "No red meat? No bread? What in the world will you eat?" she asked.

"Vegetables, all kinds of fish, lots of fruit. I can eat anything that's not on this list. But, nothing else," Jeff said.

"I'm too old to eat this stuff, Mr. Royal. You're going to starve me, too."

"You can keep other food here for yourself. Just don't tempt me with your Southern cooking. And absolutely no booze, not even wine."

"You know how I feel about liquor. I won't tempt you. But I think you're crazy. I <u>know</u> that woman is. But that's better than what you've been doing," she said. "Anything's better than that!"

"This is something I want to do," he said as he hugged her. "Thanks for being so patient with me for the last few months." Rena's eyes filled with tears as Jeff hugged her.

Jeff's days became filled with self-imposed routine. He continued his isolation. Colleen always left just before lunch, the Spanish lesson over. Once a week, Jeff would have lunch with Giuseppe at his house. Lately they had had their meetings in halting Spanish. On the other days, he ate in the kitchen with Rena.

After lunch, he worked in the gardens or the greenhouse. He found comfort in the smell of earth and flowers, and in running his hands through the dirt. He had developed an interest in roses and had planted several new varieties.

The balance of the afternoon was spent writing his book. He now truly enjoyed writing and attacked the project with vigor. He had progressed from his old outline to the basics of a rough draft. Jeff had completely lost himself in his novel, and eagerly devoted several hours each day to it.

Each evening he read, alternating between fiction and non-fiction. The only TV he watched was the 6 o'clock news. By nine p.m. he was in bed.

Once a week he would call Lawrence Carter and Inspector Roch. The investigation into Connie's murder had not progressed at all.

On this bright April morning, Colleen counted the last of the repetitions. Jeff had finished his hour on the Soloflex and weights. He was red and sweaty from the exertion. He went to shower and dress while Colleen prepared for their Spanish Session.

The phone rang as Jeff went out to the patio to meet Colleen. Rena answered it in the kitchen.

"Mr. Royal. That Inspector Roch is on the phone for you," Rena called out to him.

"Wait a minute, Colleen. I'd better take this call," he said as he went for the phone.

"Good morning, Inspector. This is Jeff Royal."

"*Bon jour, Monsieur* Royal. Excuse the interruption. I felt that I should call you immediately. We have arrested the man who we think was responsible for the death of your wife."

Jeff's heart pounded. His mouth was very dry. "Who is he? Have you questioned him? Why did he do it?" he stammered.

"A moment, please. The man is in hospital. He was shot during the arrest. He is not expected to live. We have not been able to question him as of this moment," the Inspector said.

"I'll be there as soon as I can," Jeff said. "I'll leave at once."

"But *Monsieur* Royal ..."

"I'll be there this afternoon," Jeff said as he slammed down the phone.

8

Atlanta, Montreal, Miami

Jeff was ready to smash his fist into the recorded voice in the train between terminals at Hartsfield International Airport. The delays buying his ticket, checking documents, and going through security had made his connection close enough. But, now, some damned idiot had his baggage cart caught in the doors.

"Pow! Pow! Someone is interfering with the doors," the electronic voice was saying, over and over, with little inflection.

He moved to the doors, pushing the other passengers aside. The little cart was stuck between the car and the platform. With one smooth motion, he pushed the doors aside and grabbed the sweating salesman's bag and cart and pulled them inside the car. One of the straps on the bag broke with the effort.

"Goddammit, you broke my strap," the salesman said as he looked up into Jeff's face. Looking back at him was a face set with barely controlled rage and ice-blue eyes that seemed to bore a hole in his brain. The salesman wisely said nothing else. The rest of the people in the car looked ahead blandly or silently at their feet, as the train made its quick journey to the first concourse.

Jeff ran up the escalator, taking the steps two at a time. The escalators at Hartsfield are among the longest in the world, and some of the busiest. Most of the passengers moved aside voluntarily to let him pass. Several were irritated when he pushed by but said nothing after he gave them a withering look.

ROYAL REVENGE

"A" Concourse is about a block long. Gate 29 is at the end of the concourse. At two o'clock on a normal weekday afternoon this part of the airport contains over four thousand people. Jeff felt that every one of them was conspiring to keep him away from the gate.

He pushed his boarding pass at the gate agent standing at the head of the Jetway. Her smile was as phony as her hair color. She fumbled with the paper and finally dropped it and the others she was holding. After a few long moments of fumbling and sorting, she handed the stub to Jeff and let him pass. "3-D, Sir. On your left," she croaked.

Jeff was lucky to get a seat on one of the few one-stop Delta flights to Montreal, through Boston. The seat beside him was the only empty one in the front cabin. He sat back, waiting for the door to close, hoping no one would sit beside him. They finally closed the door moments after the last passenger bustled aboard. It was the sweating salesman from the terminal train. He crammed his luggage and cart in the overhead bin and sat down beside Jeff without a look or a word. Jeff was alone with his thoughts for the entire first leg of the flight to Boston.

He called Inspector Roch from the noisy, congested, dirty concourse in Boston's Logan Airport. "I'll arrive about 6:30 at Dorval. Where can I meet you?" he said.

"The sergeant will pick you up outside of Customs. He will bring you to my office. But ..."

"Thank you. I'll see you in two hours," Jeff interrupted as he hung up.

Jeff ran most of the long way from the plane to the Customs area at Dorval. The line at Customs was as long as he had ever seen. It took almost twenty minutes for him to reach the agent. He wisely used the time to calm himself and put on the proper mask of humility.

He pushed forward his declaration card and passport.

"The purpose of your visit, *Monsieur*?"

"Business."
"How long will you stay?"
"Three days."
"Nothing to declare?"
"No."
"Ah. You have a permit. *Merci, Monsieur.*"

Fortunately, he had carried his luggage and avoided the long wait the other passengers had to endure. He met the sergeant at the exit from Customs. After the necessary greetings, they drove downtown in silence.

Inspector Roch was a Senior Inspector. Jeff couldn't imagine how bad the office of a lower level Inspector must be. The Inspector's scarred and battered wooden desk had to be sixty years old. The window was bare, covered with drops of moisture. One could hear the frigid North wind blowing against it and feel a cold draft all through the office. The area was too small for the desk, wastebasket, coat rack, and three chairs it contained. The Inspector's huge ashtray smoldered from a mound of days-old cigarette butts. It was surrounded on the desktop by piles of paper and two telephones. Lawrence Carter was the third man in the office. He had been there when Jeff arrived. Inspector Roch had informed them both of his current knowledge of the case, which had seemed very little.

"... and so, you see, there is nothing you can do. The killer is dead, and we know nothing else. I am sorry you came all this way, *Monsieur* Royal," the Inspector was saying.

"I promise I won't bother you further after tonight. But I want to know everything there is to know about this man. Why do you think he did it? What proof do you have that he is the killer? What motive is there? Did anyone else help him? Just tell me what you know about it and I'll leave."

Lawrence Carter caught the Inspector's eye and nodded. Roch threw up his hands in resignation. He got up from his desk and closed the door. The stale air in the tiny office was quickly thick with the smoke of Roch's cigarette. The wind continued to howl outside.

"I will tell you everything we know. He told us nothing before he died. Much of what we know is from our sources – various informers who travel in the same circles he traveled in.

"The man we believe killed Madame Royal was named Jean-Claude Gaspar. This is his picture. *Monsieur* Gaspar was a Cuban citizen. He was born in Havana. His father is Cuban and died many years ago. His mother is French-Canadian and was originally from Montreal and moved back from Havana ten years ago. She lives here now. Her house is where we eventually found him. He was what you call in your country a 'hit man', one who kills for money. Please understand that he was not a highly-paid assassin for hire. He was, quite simply, a low-level butcher of people. We think this was his first visit to Canada in many years."

"So, he was in the country illegally?" asked Jeff.

"Yes, *Monsieur*. Of course, we have no restrictions in Canada for Cubans to enter. But he did use a forged passport. He entered the country about five months before your wife's death.

"We are quite sure he killed two other people besides Madame Royal in the time he was here. Their bodies were also maimed and disfigured. In one case, the victim's hand was sent as a warning. When we caught Monsieur Gaspar, he was involved in the process of planning another murder. But we believe they were all unrelated to Madame Royal. Rather, they were all for the money paid him."

"How do you know he did it?" asked Jeff.

"His picture was identified by the people at the hotel as the man who left the note and the first package. The taxi driver who delivered the second package also identified his picture as possibly being that of the man who gave him the package. Part of a fingerprint was on the inside of the envelope containing the note. It was enough to identify as probably his, although it was not enough to bring up his name in our initial search for suspects. We feel that print is so coincidental that it is conclusive. Our informants also indicated he was responsible.

"Both of those he killed, and the one he was about to kill, were involved in the sale of drugs. They were apparently caught holding back large amounts of cash from their superiors."

"Drugs?" questioned Jeff, perplexed.

"*Oui, Monsieur.* Drugs. Mostly heroin and cocaine. *Monsieur* Gaspar worked for several years for the Fabriza family of Miami. We believe that the Fabriza family controls much of the drug supply into Canada, especially Quebec. That is apparently the only reason Gaspar was in Montreal. Interested people in your country lost track of him about a year ago. We were surprised to find him here. In the past he worked only in the United States."

"But why would he do this to Connie? What do these people and their drugs have to do with Connie? I don't understand the relationship," Jeff asked, pleading for understanding.

"That is the question we cannot answer. We are absolutely certain he had no connection to the FLQ. We know *Monsieur* Gaspar did no independent work. Based on our understanding the Fabriza family would forbid that. The only conclusion we can come to is that he still worked for the Fabriza family and he must have done this at their request. Although we don't have any proof of this, we think that for some reason the Fabriza family wanted you and your associates out of Quebec, and they were willing to kill to accomplish this."

"But we're still here. Why wasn't there more trouble?" Jeff asked.

"Again, we cannot answer that. The problems at your company were caused by some of the more militant of the workers that you released. The troubles stopped when we

ROYAL REVENGE

pushed very hard on them after *Madame* Royal's murder. We are as certain as we can be that those problems and *Monsieur* Gaspar are not related. We are also sure that the *FLQ* had nothing to do with your company's troubles."

"But you're saying that Connie's murder has nothing to do with Dominion at all. Then, why did he kill her? What possible reason could he have had for this?" Jeff asked of both of them.

"Only *Monsieur* Gaspar and the people who paid him could know that. And he is dead, unfortunately."

"But, the people who paid him know something. He's not the only one who knows the reasons. Someone in the Fabriza family must know. They could tell us the answer. I want to know why they did this. We must ask someone in the Fabriza family," Jeff said.

"*Monsieur* Royal, there is nothing to link *Monsieur* Gaspar to the Fabriza family except his past association. Besides, you can hardly expect them to claim responsibility for this."

"No, but I intend to find out if they were responsible," Jeff said in a low, even voice.

"Mr. Royal, this is something that the proper authorities must handle. I will report Inspector Roch's findings to my superiors. Only the FBI is qualified to follow up the possible connection to the Fabriza family. They will investigate thoroughly. You must allow them to do so. You cannot take this matter into your own hands," said Lawrence Carter.

"I appreciate that, Mr. Carter," Jeff said thoughtfully. "And, I agree. You're right, of course. The FBI should handle it. I guess I should contact them also. Please keep me informed if you find out anything else. And, by the way, I do want to thank you for your help with this and with Dominion. I know I haven't properly thanked you before.

"And, you, Inspector. I also want you to know how much I appreciate everything you've done. May I have this?"

hesitatingly he indicated the picture of Gaspar. "I want to remember this man's face, forever," Jeff said.

"But, of course, *Monsieur*. I have other copies. We are closing our investigation at this point. I am sorry we cannot do more," he said as he closed the file, handing the picture to Jeff.

"Would you like to go to your hotel now? Either of us can take you."

Jeff looked at his watch. It was almost ten o'clock.

"There's an early morning flight back to Atlanta. I think I'll go the airport and stay at the Hilton there. I'll take a taxi. There's no reason to trouble either of you any further."

"I live near the airport. I'll take you. It's really not out of my way. It's no trouble at all," Lawrence Carter said.

After saying good-bye, Carter and Jeff stepped out into the cold and slush. They walked the long block to Carter's car. Since it was so warm in Atlanta, Jeff had neglected to bring a coat. It was very cold. The wind seemed to go right through him. He had forgotten how different the weather was up here.

"I don't see how you stand this weather. Is it ever warm and dry here?" he asked Carter, shivering, his teeth chattering.

"Of course, in the summer and early fall. It's beautiful then. Otherwise, the weather here is generally awful."

"I couldn't live here with this weather, and with all the problems the city has," Jeff said.

"But it's a very interesting place to live. The European aspect of this city, its dual cultures, and its unique problems, make this one of the most desired posts in the diplomatic corps. Progress with Free Trade will make it all the more important. I've been posted in Columbia, Peru, Venezuela, Ecuador, and France. I've been here in Montreal for five years, and I find it to be the most interesting post yet. I hope to stay until Free Trade is fully implemented. That will possibly take ten more years. Then I'll go somewhere else," Carter said.

ROYAL REVENGE

They chatted amiably in the car on the way to the airport. Jeff told Carter how well the company was doing in Canada. He touched briefly on how he had coped with Connie's death, and again, expressed his appreciation for Carter's help. Carter dropped him off at the Airport Hilton.

"Good night. Thanks again for everything you've done for me." Jeff said, retrieving his luggage from the back seat. "I'll keep in touch."

"Good night, Mr. Royal. Have a pleasant flight. I will get my report off within two days. Hopefully, the authorities can do more in the States. They will give this case high priority. I'm quite sure they will be contacting you soon. You must have confidence that they will do everything possible to help," Carter said.

"Of course. I'll wait to hear from them. I'll call you when I do. Good-bye, and thanks again for everything," Jeff said as he closed the door.

Carter drove slowly out of the Hilton parking lot. He was not at all sure that Jeff Royal was going to wait for anyone. His face was worried as he mentally jotted a reminder to call his friend at the Dalton office of the FBI in the morning. After that he would talk again with Giuseppe.

After checking in and leaving an early wakeup call, Jeff went to his room and hung up his bag. He propped the picture of Gaspar up on the desk. He sat down and stared at it. It was a typical police department front view and profile with a number below. Under the number was printed "Miami Police Department, 4/20/86".

Gaspar's wicked face looked back at him. His facial expression was one of total boredom. The black eyes were deep pools, devoid of emotion, bordered by heavy eyebrows on the top and dark circles on the bottom. His mouth turned down in a natural sneer. His drooping moustache accentuated the sneer. His dark skin was heavily scarred and pockmarked. The long nose twisted slightly to the left, obviously previously broken. There was an earring in his left ear. The lobe on the right ear was missing. His long hair was thick, black, and straight.

Jeff resisted the temptation to tear the picture to bits. Tears streamed down his face as he thought of this man with his wife. His hands crawling over her skin. His fists beating her without mercy. Jeff tasted the terror Connie must have felt. Bile rose in the back of his throat. His body shivered as he felt the horrible pain she had endured. He pictured her finger in the box, lying on the blue velvet. Her head, the eyes dead, the skin bruised and cut, nose broken, face fixed with such awful terror, filled his mind. He sobbed as he remembered the severed ear lying in the pool of blood in the box. Suddenly he gagged. He ran to the bathroom, vomiting violently, his body heaving.

Eventually, he got to his feet and washed his face with cold water. He brushed his teeth. He sat on the side of the bed a long time, staring at nothing, thinking nothing, hearing only the whistle of the cold Canadian wind outside.

Jeff stripped to his underwear, got on the floor, and began to exercise as fast as he could. He grunted with exertion as he pushed himself to the point of pain. An hour later, he was exhausted. He lay on the floor, his face in the dirty carpet, heart pounding, his breathing very rapid. Sweat poured off his body. He lay quietly, breathing deeply, with great concentration, until he was utterly calm. He shivered as his body cooled down. He showered, as hot as he could stand it, then finished with cold water. As he pulled on clean shorts, his face was set in grim resolve. His mind cleared, and he began to plan his next steps. Jeff sat on the bed in his shorts, took a yellow pad from his suitcase, and began an outline:

1. Trouble at Dominion
   - Started before we came up here. Trouble at other companies here at the time. Got worse when we took

over. Continued until we purchased. Stopped shortly after Connie killed. Stopped at other companies also (coincidence?).
2. No trouble after Connie killed
   - Police say Connie unrelated to problems with workers. No connection between Gaspar and FLQ. No connection between FLQ and troubles at company. Police sure Gaspar killed Connie.
3. Gaspar
   - Drug family killer. Killed two others here (drug related). Connected to Miami family (Fabriza). Gaspar here to do jobs for family. No connection between Gaspar and Dominion. No connection between Connie and family. What connection between Gaspar and Connie? Only reason was to threaten me. Why? Some connection between family and me. What?
4. Fabriza Family - Miami
   - Source of drugs for Quebec. Had Gaspar kidnap and then kill Connie. Only apparent reason was to threaten me or company. Company is unrelated. Family wants me out of Canada. Why?
5. Options
   - Contact FBI, put on pressure.
   - Do nothing, wait for FBI.
   - Go to Miami

Jeff looked at the outline, and then studied his three options. The decision was plain to him. He continued the outline:

6. Miami
   - Contacts - Mayor Castillo, Julio Pozo.
   - Money - call Olivia and get wire transfer. Check to see if condo occupied. Clothes, car, etc. - buy everything

He finally found Delta's number in the thick phone book. He got through quickly.

"Yes sir. We have a flight to Miami at 7:55 in the morning. It's non-stop. Shall I book you on that?" the reservations clerk asked.

"Yes. First class. And would you please cancel my flight tomorrow to Atlanta? It's flight 1780 through Boston."

"I've cancelled the Atlanta flight. I have you booked first class on flight number 215, leaving at 7:55 a.m. and arriving Miami at 11:15, Mr. Royal. You are in seat 1-A. When will you return?" she asked.

"I don't know," Jeff said. "I'll figure that out later."

"Do you need a car, hotel reservations, anything else?"

"No, thank you," he said as he hung up and turned off the light.

He tossed and turned all night. Hazy images of Gaspar's face merged with sharp images of Connie and flitted across his brain. He killed Gaspar a hundred times in a hundred different ways in his mind. The wind gusted against the window. It sounded like a terrified woman's scream.

The sheets were twisted and soaked with sweat. He finally dozed off again as dawn was breaking. The phone rang shortly after with the hotel's mechanical wakeup call.

***

The big jet shuddered a bit as it ascended and then finally broke through the dark clouds covering Quebec. Above the clouds the sun was bright, the sky blue and clear. Below, it was cold and snowing. Jeff reclined in his seat and slept soundly, despite the constant chattering announcements from the pilot and the flight attendants over the PA system.

Three hours later, Jeff looked out the window as the plane descended through a cloudless sky and circled over the sparkling

ROYAL REVENGE

blue ocean for the final approach to Miami's busy airport. It was a beautiful, sunny, perfect spring day in South Florida. The white beaches of Miami's Gold Coast were filled with people basting their bodies in the hot sun. The blue sky was virtually without clouds. The city shimmered in the heat.

The plane's tires thumped as they hit the runway. Jeff was the first passenger off. Having cleared customs in Montreal and carrying his luggage, he had no further delay. He went at once to the Crown Room where he grabbed a phone and called his secretary, Olivia Henson.

"Olivia, this is Jeff Royal. I'm down in Miami but I really don't want anyone to know I'm here. I need for you to do several things for me. Okay?"

"Of course, Jeff. It's nice to hear your voice. What do you need?"

"First, is the Miami Beach condo available? I need a place to stay. I'd rather not go to a hotel."

"Let me check for you. It will just take a moment. ... Yes, it is. Giuseppe has someone coming in to use it in three weeks. But, it's empty now. It should be clean. They clean it every other week."

"Good. Put me down for the next three weeks. I want you to call Rena and tell her where I am. Be sure she doesn't tell anyone else. Ask her to cancel Colleen Schaeffer for the next week. I'll call her soon and tell her when I'm coming home. I also want you to transfer some money. Send it to the SunTrust Bank, Miami Beach branch. Make it for $150,000. Call someone there and tell them I'll be by to open a checking account there this afternoon."

"All right. Anything else you need? What about your lunch with Giuseppe this week?"

"Oh, I forgot. Cancel that, too. He can reach me at the condo if he needs me. That should do it, thanks."

"Jeff, are you in trouble or anything? Is something wrong? Can I help you?" she said, her voice full of concern.

"No, Olivia. I just decided to take some time off down here and I'm going to buy that car I've been promising myself. I'm fine, really."

"All right. I'll take care of everything. I'll transfer the money from the company account in Miami. It's too late for a wire transfer from here. But I'm sure they won't give me any trouble. Please call me if you need anything else. Good-bye. And Jeff, take care of yourself. "

"I will, Olivia. Thanks again," Jeff said as he hung up.

The Royals and the Portales' had kept a condominium in the Art Deco district of Miami Beach for several years. They had often used it when visiting Miami. The district had undergone substantial renewal in the past few years. They now loaned it to friends and customers and used it themselves only occasionally, although Giuseppe had started using it very frequently before his divorce. Jeff and Connie hadn't been there in about a year.

He gave the cabby the condo's address. Jeff was a little surprised to find that he had to talk slowly since his Berlitz Spanish was difficult for the Cuban cabby to understand. While Jeff went inside to turn on the air conditioner and drop off his luggage, he had the cab wait outside.

Next, Jeff took the cab to the bank, where he opened a checking account with the $150,000 Olivia had arranged to transfer. He got $5,000 in cash, some preliminary checks, and left with the bank's manager walking him to the door.

"I'm buying a car today. I'm sure they'll call to see if the check is good. Should I have them ask for you, Mr. Cantu?" Jeff asked.

"Yes, Mr. Royal. Here is one of my cards. If you need anything, have them contact me directly. I'll make sure there is no delay. I will be happy to help. We appreciate your business."

ROYAL REVENGE

Returning Cantu's "thank you's" as he rushed out the door, Jeff ordered the cabby to the nearest Mercedes dealership.

"This will be the last place, *Señor*? You're buying a car here?"

"Only if the price is right. Wait until I tell you to leave. I don't want to be completely at their mercy," Jeff laughed.

An hour later he dismissed the cab and drove out in a new, bright metallic red Mercedes 500 SL convertible. He drove about eight blocks further to an exclusive menswear store he had patronized many times in the past. The tiny wizened proprietor, Hyman Feld, bowed slightly as he entered.

"Mr. Royal. How very nice to see you. It's been a long time since you've come to our store. We've missed you. You've changed sizes, I see. I can tell just by looking, you know. I'd say a thirty-two waist. Correct? What do you need today?"

"I need just about everything, Hyman. And I need it all by tomorrow. Can you do that?"

"Stock cloth, yes. Special order, no. Of course, there will be some extra charges. How many suits? And what else will there be?"

"Two suits, two sport coats, four slacks to match, three casual outfits, shirts, shorts, jeans, shoes, polo shirts, socks, underwear, ties. Any problem?"

"For that we'll close the store if there's a problem!" Hyman said in his heaviest Yiddish accent. "Let me get some of these lazy sons of mine around here to help."

Two hours later Jeff had ordered and been fitted for a complete new wardrobe. He took a change of clothes for the next day. Hyman Feld, for a small delivery charge, of course, agreed to finish all the alterations and have everything else delivered to Jeff's condo early the next day.

His next stop was the Miami Beach Health Grocery. Jeff ordered a week's worth of food, vitamins, bottled water, and toilet articles from the helpful clerk. She scheduled delivery for the next morning.

Next door was the Miami Beach Sport Store. Their only Soloflex machine, a set of dumbbells, running shoes, swimsuits, and jogging clothes would be delivered before noon the next day. The manager agreed to set up the Soloflex when they delivered everything else. Jeff took a swim suit, the dumbbells, and a jogging outfit with him.

Electronics Superstore was across the street. Jeff bought a laptop computer, software packages, large monitor, stand, and printer. He also got a small headset radio for jogging, an answering machine, and a small cassette recorder. The store didn't deliver, but the salesman agreed to deliver everything himself the next morning.

One block further south, he found a florist and a bookstore side by side. He bought four books, writing supplies, and a reading lamp. He took them with him. He asked the florist to deliver four miniature potted roses to the condo.

Jeff drove further south and across the bridge west into Miami. He passed from the glitz and glamour of Miami Beach to the dingy ghetto of Liberty City. From open lobbies and beautiful Art Deco storefronts, he traveled to barred windows and boarded-up or burned-out buildings.

He stopped at a pawnshop and put up the top, locking the car before he went inside. The place was dark and dingy, and the air smelled of stale sweat, machine oil, and cigarette smoke.

"What do you need today? Let me guess. You're not selling. You must be buying," said the pale, obese man behind the counter. His lisp was plainly from his two missing front teeth. The tattered and filthy undershirt he wore showed scores of tattoos, on virtually every inch of exposed white skin. His head was completely bald, his body hairless. He was sweating heavily. Even from the other side of the counter, he exuded the combined smells of stale sweat, smoke, garlic and onions. His

ROYAL REVENGE

cheek bulged with a huge wad of tobacco. He spat noisily into a cup before Jeff could answer.

"A pistol. An automatic. For protection," Jeff said.

9

Miami Beach

At four a.m., the next morning, Jeff got back into his routine. He tuned his headset radio to a local Spanish station and ran three and a half miles up Ocean Drive with a dumbbell in each hand. The jogging path ran parallel to the white beach that soon would be filled with the oiled bodies of tourists baking in the hot sun. At this time of the day there was little traffic, and no pedestrians. It was still dark and hot with no breeze and a little muggy. Jeff was sweating profusely.

He jogged to the end of Ocean Drive, and turned north on Collins Avenue, and began running. After he reached Bal Harbour, he turned back south and jogged easily toward his condo. Dawn was breaking as he got back. The morning run was important to Jeff. It helped clear his head as well as revive him physically.

When he got back to his apartment, Jeff swam laps in the undersized pool. Other residents of the complex were plainly not early risers. The only other human he saw the entire morning was an old man delivering the Miami Herald to each unit. Jeff ordered a month's subscription and took the morning paper from him.

Finished with his swim, he spent an hour on push-ups and sit-ups. After a hot shower, he shaved and dressed in jeans and golf shirt. Jeff looked forward to getting his project under way.

At exactly eight o'clock, Hyman Feld appeared at the door with two of his sons. At Hyman's insistence, Jeff tried on all of the clothes he had purchased. And he felt that everything fit perfectly. Hyman, of course, had a different opinion. He fussed with tucks and turns and then had his sons remove all the labels and stray threads and hang the suits and slacks neatly in Jeff's closet. They also arranged the other garments neatly in the bureau drawers.

The Sports Shop delivered the Soloflex Machine while Jeff was trying on clothes. They set up the equipment in the spare bedroom, which had been converted to a study. Hyman's sons put away the additional articles of clothing Jeff had purchased from the Sports Shop.

The salesman from Electronic Superstore arrived at the same time as the deliveryman from the grocery. He set up the computer stand and connected the printer to the laptop. He also hooked up the answering machine to the phone. The roses arrived shortly thereafter. At one point there were eight people in the small apartment. Jeff bounced from one to the other giving instructions, sometimes in a suit, sometimes in his underwear. Hyman patiently trotted behind as he patted, poked, and pinned.

"You have improved the economy of Miami Beach in a single day! You bought something from everyone! I guess this means you'll be staying a while?" Hyman Feld said, inquisitively.

"At least until I finish what I came for," said Jeff. "Thanks for everything. I appreciate the service," he said sincerely as he ushered Hyman and his sons, the last to leave, to the door.

Hyman paused in the doorway. "I sat *Shiva* for her, Mrs. Royal. I offer my deepest sympathy to you. If you need anything, just call," Hyman said as he grasped Jeff's hand firmly and looked directly into his eyes. "Anything."

"Thank you, Hyman. I appreciate your kindness. You can help right now by not telling anyone I'm here. I don't want to be bothered. I'll certainly call if I need anything. Good-bye."

J. Trey Weeks

The condo was part of an old forty-unit hotel-apartment complex built in the early 1920's. For many years, rich northerners had rented units like this one as summer retreats in glamorous Miami Beach. In the late fifties, the demographics changed significantly downward. Retirees on limited incomes, poorer minorities, and then the second Cuban invasion had changed the glitter of Miami Beach to a ghetto of blight and poverty and disrepair.

In recent years, the Art Deco architecture had appealed to new investor groups who purchased the units at distressed prices and renovated them. One key to the recent rise in value was the City's fanatic attention to detail in keeping the 1920's look and feel of the area through total control of the renovation process. Of course, the significant tax benefits from the Federal Government helped also.

The apartment had a large living room with glass doors at one end that opened onto a small balcony. From there one looked across Ocean Drive into Lummus Park and out onto Biscayne Bay. Adjacent to the living room was a small kitchen and dining area.

Jeff's unit had three bedrooms, one of which he and Giuseppe had converted into a study. It was in this now very crowded room that he had set up his exercise equipment and his computer.

Connie had been busy working on their house while Jeff and Giuseppe were purchasing the condo. Maritza Portales had hired a local designer friend to decorate and furnish it. The designer had assured them they would like the décor, and that it would exemplify "the South Florida lifestyle". After over four years, Jeff still wasn't sure he liked it. In fact, he was pretty sure he had never liked it.

There was lots of lime green and lemon yellow, an overstuffed couch, and bamboo-trimmed chairs. Most of the furniture was too large for the small rooms. Jeff resolved to

ROYAL REVENGE

have it redone sometime in the future. But the condo was quiet, private, comfortable and convenient. And at the moment, it was much nicer than a hotel.

Jeff walked around the apartment, looking at the things he'd purchased, organizing the few items that had been left out.

After a few minutes, he went to the bedroom, reached under the bed, and retrieved the pistol he had bought the night before. Sitting on the edge of the bed, he took it out of the leather holster. He placed the two boxes of Hornet hollow-tipped bullets beside the gun. Jeff then ejected the clip and familiarized himself with the weapon. He inserted nine bullets. The clip dropped back into the handle smoothly and closed with a snap.

It was a 9 mm. Mauser, obviously well used. The stubby black barrel and thick wooden grip gave it a sinister, wicked appearance. Jeff had owned guns all his life and had once been a frequent hunter. But, he had never before owned a gun like this one, designed specifically for use on humans.

Jeff settled into his condominium, finally alone, thinking about his course of action over the next few days. He had thought of only two contacts for help in Miami. He was sure he wanted to avoid involving the local people from Royal Floors since he had had virtually no contact with any of his employees for almost seven months. Besides, they probably couldn't have helped much.

The two people who he felt could, and would help, were Miami's former mayor, Jesse Castillo, and Julio Pozo, a writer for the <u>Miami Star.</u>

Julio Pozo was the only person at the <u>Star</u> who still maintained contact with Jeff. They had started reporting for the paper at about the same time and had become quite close. Julio fit perfectly into the style of the <u>Star</u>. He had a natural love for writing and tended to throw himself into a story, often elaborating it into complete fiction with his vivid and unlimited imagination. Where Jeff objected to the style of the paper, Julio reveled in it.

"This is entertainment to tens of thousands of people. They can't be rich and famous like the ones we write about, but they enjoy reading about rich and famous people. We're entertainers. Everyone knows that most of the shit we write is exaggerated and generally overdone. It's entertainment, nothing else," Julio had urged.

"But when it ruins the life of someone we write about, when the things we write aren't even true, how can you call it entertainment?" Jeff asked.

"The people we write about are above all that. This crap gives them free publicity and enhances their careers. They love it!" Julio responded.

But even Julio had objected to the treatment of the Mayor. He had been very sympathetic when Jeff got fired because of alerting the Mayor's staff to the slanderous story in the Star. Julio had made sure the key people on the Mayor's staff knew Jeff and were aware of his sacrifice on the Mayor's behalf. He was also responsible for Jeff's current long-standing acquaintance with the Mayor, having introduced them shortly after Jeff lost his job.

Jeff called Julio's office and was immediately put through. Julio seemed glad to hear from Jeff and agreed to meet him at the condominium early that evening. From there they would go out to eat.

"You can buy me drinks, dinner, and more drinks, and then you can tell me what's so important and mysterious," Julio had said. Julio didn't ask why Jeff wanted to see him, but he did seem a little reserved. Jeff didn't tell him his reasons, preferring to explain his project in person.

Over the years Julio had become something of a celebrity in Miami, and he was very well connected with both the Cuban and Anglo population. He was on everyone's key guest list. He still had a fondness for Jeff, and they had seen each other occasionally over the years. It was a compliment to Jeff that Julio took an evening to spend with him. The social schedule Julio kept was full to almost inflexible, with events almost seven days a week. According to Julio, his social schedule had ruined two marriages. In fact, Julio simply wasn't marriage material.

The second call was to former Mayor Jesse Castillo's office. Castillo had become a very successful investor and businessman after dropping out of politics since the Star scandal. Of course, Mr. Castillo was in a meeting, but his secretary assured Jeff he would call as soon as he could get free.

Jeff put the evil-looking pistol under the bed and fixed himself a light lunch while he waited for the call from Jesse Castillo. As he began to read the morning newspaper, he suddenly realized that Julio knew why he was in Miami, and probably knew why Jeff wanted to see him. On the third page was the story. He read it with great effort.

CANADIAN KILLER CAPTURED
Miami Man Killed During Montreal Arrest

"Montreal, Que. (AP) The Montreal Police announced yesterday that they had captured a suspect in the killing of Mrs. Connie Royal of Atlanta, Georgia. Mrs. Royal was abducted, tortured, and brutally murdered last September while on a business trip to Montreal with her husband, Jeffrey Royal, President of Royal Floors. The motive for the murder has not been determined.

"Royal Floors is headquartered in Atlanta and operates branches throughout the United States and Canada. The company maintains offices in Miami and throughout Florida. Both Mr. and Mrs. Royal graduated from the University of Miami

"The suspect died in a Montreal hospital of multiple gunshot wounds suffered during his capture at the suburban Montreal home of his mother. One Montreal policeman was seriously wounded by gunfire in the incident and is currently recovering in the hospital. The suspect has been identified as Jean-Claude Gaspar, 31, of Miami. Gaspar is alleged to be a longtime employee of the Miami Underworld family allegedly headed by Carmino Fabriza of Boca Raton. Miami police report that Gaspar has been arrested thirteen times in the last five years for suspicion in various crimes of assault and murder. He was never indicted nor convicted in any of the resulting investigations.

"There was a current warrant for his arrest for suspicion of murder in the killing and disfigurement of Jose Gilberto Lopez, an illegal Cuban immigrant, in April of 1989. Gaspar disappeared immediately after the warrant was issued. He had apparently entered Canada illegally.

"Royal Floors' Executive Vice President, Giuseppe Portales, declined comment on the capture. Jeffrey Royal has been unavailable for interview since the murder of his wife last September.

"The Montreal Police report that they suspect Gaspar of several other murders in the area over the last eight months. Their investigation into the crimes is continuing."

Jeff almost gagged. He wadded up the first section of the paper and threw it across the room. The thought of Connie's suffering being exposed to the public again was almost more than he could take. He felt unbridled hate for Gaspar rising in his chest. It took several minutes to get himself back under control.

He was sitting on the balcony, staring at the hordes of tourists on the beach, his mind nowhere, when the phone rang.

"Jeff, this is Giuseppe. What the hell are you doing in Miami? Olivia told me you went there yesterday. Rena said you were in Canada. Have you read the papers? They caught and killed the guy who murdered Connie. Did Inspector Roch tell you that? Is that why you're in Miami? What the hell is going on?"

"Well, it's good to talk to you too, Giuseppe. I'm here to get away, to run on the beach and to relax. Yes, I read the paper. I went to Canada yesterday. I knew most of that stuff from what Inspector Roch told me in Montreal. That has very little to do with me being in Miami, although I do plan to find out a little more about this Gaspar."

"You're crazy to get involved in that Gaspar thing. Lawrence Carter told me he's apparently in the mob down there. The publicity is going to pick up again. We've had twenty reporters call already this morning. Let the police handle it, for Christ's sake. Surely you're not going to try do something about him yourself?"

"I'm only going to try to find out some things about him and answer some of my questions. I'm no vigilante. Don't worry. And I'll stay away from reporters. Virtually no one knows I'm here. Any other questions?" Jeff asked, piqued.

"Yeah. Why do you need $150,000 in cash? Olivia told me you had her transfer funds from the company."

"I asked her to transfer my own money. She decided to transfer money advanced from the company to save me time. I assume she's paid it back by now out of my account. What I needed it for is none of your fucking business," Jeff said evenly.

"Oh Jesus, Jeff. I'm sorry," Giuseppe said with sincerity. "I know it's none of my business. I was just worried about you. Forget I asked. I apologize."

"Accepted," Jeff said with resignation. "Don't worry about me, Giuseppe. I'll be fine. I just needed to get away. And wait until you see the new car I bought. It's a red 500 SL convertible. It's unbelievable. People stare at me when I drive down the street," Jeff laughed.

"Congratulations. I'll bet it's beautiful. You deserve it. Just don't drive it to work. You'll cause dissension in the ranks. Maybe I'll come down this weekend and see it. How long are you going to stay there?" Giuseppe asked.

"I only have three weeks in the condo, and then it's reserved. But, I'm sure I'll be home before then. How's business? Are sales still good?" he asked, purposefully changing the subject.

"It's terrific. Even better than last fall. We're up over 24 percent excluding Canada. Include Canada, and we're up almost 30 percent. I don't know where it's all coming from."

"Great. Keep it up. If you want to come down ..." Jeff said.

"Maybe I will. I'll call you Friday. Be careful."

Knowing Giuseppe would never tear himself away from the business and Carmen long enough to come down and bother him gave Jeff some comfort. He knew Giuseppe would be a real pain in the ass if he came to Miami. He also resented Giuseppe's curiosity about what he was doing there.

Jesse Castillo called shortly after Jeff hung up from his conversation with Giuseppe. "Jeff, it's very good to hear from you" he said in his deep Spanish-accented voice. "I read the papers this morning. I'm sorry you must go through all this publicity again. I of all people know how painful the constant publicity can be. I'm afraid the press will be hard to discourage. They never seem to leave one alone. When can I see you?"

"Thank you, sir. Fortunately, I don't have to deal with the press like you do. I would like to see you as soon as possible. My schedule is very flexible. Can you work me in tomorrow?" Jeff asked.

"That will be difficult, unless it is very early. Can you meet me in my office before eight o'clock? I know it's early..."

"I get up very early. It's kind of you to work me in. Shall I be there at seven?"

ROYAL REVENGE

"Fine. My secretary Maria will give you directions to the office. I'll look forward to seeing you in the morning then."

After getting directions to the former Mayor's office, Jeff hung up. The Mayor was plainly not surprised to hear from him, and probably knew he wanted information. He thought about how to approach Castillo.

Jeff knew that Julio and Castillo both would give him any information they could. He also knew that they would try to discourage him from acting on his own.

After finishing the lunch he'd prepared, Jeff tried to work on his book. Two hours later he'd made no progress whatsoever.

He pulled out the outline he had made in Canada. What did he really want to accomplish? What could someone like him do that the police couldn't do? He reviewed it again and again. He kept drawing blanks.

Just before seven o'clock, Julio came to the door. After he entered, he held Jeff at arm's length and looked at him as if seeing him for the first time.

"You look terrific. Slim, trim, physically fit. Jesus, I need the same diet you're on. What have you been doing? Did you buy a new body?"

"Just about," Jeff laughed. "I decided I needed to get myself in shape. I'm now one of those health nuts we used to hate. I even exercise every day."

"You're gorgeous! I can't wait for some of the rich bitches I know to see you. They'll be all over me just to get at you."

They were both laughing as Jeff fixed Julio a drink.

"Vodka, rocks, no fruit. Right?" Jeff asked.

"Obviously a great mind to go with the body. What are you having?"

"I've pretty much quit drinking. I'll have fruit juice. But please, enjoy your drink," Jeff said, somewhat self-consciously. "I promise I won't preach to you on the never- ending evils of

Demon Rum," he said, laughing, remembering how many times he and Julio had painted the town red when they were together at the <u>Star</u>.

"Don't worry about me. Your new-found sobriety doesn't bother me. That just leaves me more to drink," Julio laughed with him. "Besides, Carrie Nation wouldn't have a chance with me."

A sudden poignant silence and Julio's serious look indicated that he was ready for Jeff to tell him what he wanted.

"You've read the paper. You know they caught Connie's killer?" Jeff asked.

"Yes. And, I guess I know that's why you're here. But what do you really expect to do? What do you want from me?"

"What I want to do is to find the connection between me and the killer. I guess that means finding the connection between me and the Fabriza family since this human scum, Gaspar, worked for them. I can't understand why they would have any interest in me. And, therefore, I can't understand why they would kill Connie to get at me. Until I answer those questions, I can't really get myself back on track. I know it won't bring Connie back and I'm not out for revenge. I just have to know the answer. That's what I expect to find. That's why I'm here."

"And what do you want from me? Have you considered that the guy Gaspar could be acting on his own? Or that someone in Canada hired him? It certainly could have been someone at the company you took over up there."

"The inspector who handled the case in Montreal said that Gaspar wouldn't work for anyone else. The Fabriza family would forbid that. It certainly couldn't be a random killing. He knew too much about me. He also sent those three notes. The inspector also said that the other troubles at the company were unrelated. He's good at what he does. I trust his judgement."

ROYAL REVENGE

"Okay. Let's assume that Gaspar did this for Fabriza, although there is certainly nothing to connect them to you or Connie. What do you want from me?"

"You know everyone in Miami who's anyone. Who can I talk to who knows people in the Fabriza family? I need someone who will talk without endangering himself or me. Maybe I can find the connection that way. I want to try to find out who ordered Gaspar around. Maybe then I'll find out why they aimed at me through Connie."

"I know some people who are close to these people but there's no way in hell they'll talk to you about those things or anything else. If you start asking those kinds of questions about that bunch, you're liable to wind up fucking dead in Biscayne Bay or in the Everglades. They're very powerful here, Jeff, and they don't mind using their power. And they are very well connected. Maybe I'd better tell you a little about this group, so you'll know what you're up against.

"Carmino Fabriza came to Miami in 1959, just before Castro was coming to power in Cuba. Although he was supposedly well connected with the mob in Cuba, no one had anything on him, and he entered with his entire extended family, totally legally. He's now a naturalized citizen. He built an organization here that initially was involved only with the Cuban population and only Cuban expats worked for him. They were involved in prostitution, protection, gambling, that sort of thing. He was a master at organizing it and has never even been arrested.

"His brother, Alphonso, who wasn't quite as squeaky clean, went to Columbia at about the time Carmino came here. When drugs became the big moneymaking thing to do, Carmino and Alphonso were ready. Carmino set up a complete distribution system. Alphonso set up manufacturing. Alphonso supplies the drugs, Carmino provides the market. He now controls most of the import of drugs from Columbia to Florida, and apparently to Canada.

"Carmino is over sixty now, but he's never been more powerful. He's also totally ruthless. The only chink in the armor is that he has no clear successor. His only son is named Raphael. Raphael is thirty, very handsome, of course very rich, and really lives the good life. He's not nearly as dedicated as his old man and has never worked actively in the business.

Currently, Carmino is trying to mold Raphael into a successor. He's not having much luck, though. Raphael wants to stay a playboy and hasn't earned the respect of the rest of the family. Of course, there are lots of others in the organization to take the old man's place when he dies. But he doesn't seem to plan on dying anytime soon. I'm telling you, you don't want to get involved with these people. You're in way over your head."

"But I am involved, Julio. I don't know why, but they must have some reason for doing this. I've got to find out what it is."

"I know you don't want to hear this, but I really think you ought to forget doing anything on your own. I also think you should realize that nobody else is going to penetrate the Fabriza family either. There's not much further to take it. The investigation will stop with Gaspar. You read the paper. The cops never even put Gaspar in jail. And he supposedly worked for Fabriza for years. Fabriza hasn't even been indicted before. How the hell do you think you can do anything when the cops haven't been able to get anything on him in thirty years?"

"Dammit, I have to do something! I can't just forget it! At least help me try to do something."

"You're crazy. I'd be crazy for having anything to do with this. I really don't think there's anything you can do, Jeff. I really don't," Julio said as he looked down at the floor.

"Julio, please! Help me with this. You'd want to know if this happened to you. You knew Connie. She didn't deserve anything like what happened. I need to know why he did it. Please," he pleaded as he grasped Julio's hands.

Julio looked up into his friend's eyes. His resolve and some of his fear melted when he saw Jeff virtually begging. "Okay. We're both crazy as shit. I'll do what I can. I really don't think I can do much. We'll start with a lady named Catarina Contreras. She's Raphael Fabriza's longtime girlfriend. Maybe she can point us in a direction that's not dangerous.

"Cat Contreras is the only woman who's ever been really close to Raphael. He gave her an apartment in the Gables, where she lives with her brother, Claudio. Claudio works for Raphael as a driver, bodyguard, valet, whatever.

"She's a classy woman and stays very remote from the rest of the Fabriza family, so she keeps out of trouble. I've known her for several years, and we've been very good friends. I've done her a few small favors, and, she's done a few for me. Maybe she can tell us something. I will tell you that she's the most beautiful woman in Miami. She's also smart. Old man Fabriza thinks a lot of her. He wants Raphael to settle down with her. I'll have to interpret, 'cause she doesn't speak very good English."

"*Gracias, mi amigo, gracias. Pero, ahora hablo muy bien el Español.* I've been taking lessons," Jeff replied in rapid Spanish.

"Very impressive. A little too much Berlitz Castilian, but very good! You'll do well where we're going. Just pretend that you don't understand what we're saying until we see what happens and who we want to talk to, okay? You can't pass for Cuban, so there's no reason for everyone to know you speak the language. *Comprender*?"

"You're the *jefe*. Where are we going?"

"Some place where Anglos fear to tread. Put on some Miami Vice clothes and let's get going. Do you have a car? We'll need something flashy. My second ex-wife owns my flashy car, now."

"How about a red Mercedes convertible? I just got it yesterday."

"Perfect. I knew you'd be prepared. Get dressed. I'll fortify myself with one more drink while I wait. I'll probably need it," he laughed, weakly.

Jeff came out in a cream-colored sport coat with light blue slacks and a pink open collar shirt.

"This is as close as I will ever get to Miami Vice," he laughed.

"You're gorgeous! I'll be covered up with pussy just by staying close to you! I'll tell you everything you need to know in the car," Julio said.

With the top down the two men headed across the Venetian Causeway toward Little Havana, the *Calle Ocho* district centered on Southwest Eighth Street. The sun was just setting, and the warm air was very comfortable. Julio loved it.

"What I could do with this car and your money in this city. After a month, my pecker would fall off! At that point, I wouldn't care," he exclaimed, laughing. "Now to be serious. We're going to a very private club, *Casa de Liberacion*. Only members and their guests are permitted, and, there are no Anglo members.

"It's owned by a Venezuelan named Hector Rodriguez. But it's well understood that old man Fabriza ponied up the money to start it. It's also well known that Hector paid him off in a year, with interest. This has gotta be the most successful club in Cuban Miami. I guarantee you'll never see anything like it in Atlanta or anywhere else in the States."

Julio was right. The front of the club, in a four story rather unremarkable building in the middle of Southwest Miami, was plain whitewashed stucco. There was no identification on the building except a small brass plaque beside the door that said, "Private Club". A hint that inside would be found an expensive and exclusive club was the presence of six uniformed attendants presiding over a sea of expensive automobiles of every make and model. The front door, a huge fixture of polished brass, was protected by an awning held up by gleaming brass posts. The door had to be eight feet tall, and the doorman who guarded it looked as if he would have to stoop to enter. He was very muscular with a shaved head, and a perpetual scowl on his face.

Julio handed his club card to the doorman after Jeff turned the car over to an attendant. They waited only seconds while the doorman entered the card into a slot on the wall beside the door and a green light came on over the slot. The doorman, without speaking, then opened the door with a loud "click" by pressing on the green light.

"I guess I'm still *persona grata*," Julio said as they walked past the doorman into the club. "If the light turns red, the door won't open. It doesn't matter anyway, because, by then that big bastard has your ass back in your car. I saw him do it once and he's very efficient."

They passed into a very large entry area with comfortable lounge chairs set around the walls and leading to a beautiful bar. Waiters in elegant tuxedos circulated among the few guests who waited there. Jeff felt a bit out of place, since everyone he'd seen so far appeared to be Hispanic.

A smiling Maître d' stood at a podium, guarding another door that led into the club. Julio showed his card again. It was again pushed into a slot and a green light went on by the door. They were immediately admitted into the most incredible nightclub Jeff had ever seen. The noise and the smell of smoke, expensive perfume, sweat, and liquor hit Jeff like a blast from a furnace.

It was almost as if the club's interior had been dropped in from outer space. The entire dance floor was Plexiglas, with an intricate pattern of neon lights under the surface, which throbbed and undulated to the rhythm of the music. The dance floor was bordered by thick white carpet. Six steps led up to two levels of totally enclosed Plexiglas booths around the entire perimeter, serviced by beautiful young waiters and waitresses dressed only in tiny bikinis of various bright colors. In the booths were tables set with linen and crystal, candles in the middle of each. They were all full of people, eating and drinking.

The music from the combo on the raised stage at the far end was so loud it vibrated Jeff's inner organs. Laser lights darted around the room. The floor was packed with gyrating couples.

Hanging from the ceiling near the center of the dance floor were five Plexiglas cages. Inside were totally nude dancers, each with a perfect body. In one, there were a man and a woman. Another had two men, another two women, another two men and a woman, and the last held two women and a man. They were all engaged in various erotic routines, enacted in ritualistic dance to the rhythm of the pounding music and the pulsating lights.

Just to their right was a Plexiglas elevator. Julio grabbed Jeff's arm and pulled him toward it. Guarding the door was another huge man, this one dressed only in a neon purple bikini. His arms were like tree trunks and he looked strong enough to break a normal man in half. This guard took Julio's card, again without a word, and inserted it into a slot in the elevator. When the light turned green, he pushed it and the doors opened. He ushered them into the elevator and the doors closed. The resulting silence was almost shocking.

"This is card controlled, too. You can see there's no way to get up here unless they really want you to," Julio said.

Jeff laughed nervously, amazed.

The car stopped, and the doors opened. The second floor of the club was an elegant casino, with roulette, craps, blackjack and baccarat tables. Soft classical music flowed from hidden speakers. All the tables were Plexiglas, the tops covered in gold felt. There was the low hum of lively conversation virtually all in Spanish, but little of the noise one usually found in a casino in Las Vegas. This atmosphere was much more European.

One whole side of the large room was arranged with tables for dining and drinking, and the other side consisted of the longest bar Jeff had ever seen. The dealers and waiters were again young, good-looking men and women dressed only in black silk bikinis with white collars and black bow ties. The pit bosses were all dressed in perfectly tailored tuxedos. Virtually all the tables were full of obviously wealthy Hispanics. The area around the bar was packed with people.

"This is one casino where you don't have to worry about them having cards up their sleeves," whispered Julio, giggling slightly. "Let's get a drink and then we'll wait for Cat. We're a little early. She's usually not here 'til after eight."

They found a spot at the crowded bar. Jeff ordered while Julio held court with the many guests he knew in the casino. Jeff joined them, bringing the drinks, and was introduced, always in Spanish with subsequent English translations, to Julio's friends. The Spanish was so rapid that Jeff was often unable to understand it. He was amazed at how many beautiful women there were around them, but Julio had always attracted women.

After Julio's second drink, they were briefly alone. Julio smiled at him.

"Now you see why everyone comes here. The most beautiful women in Cuban Miami are here every night. It's incredible. I don't know how Hector got them to start coming here, but it's made him a fortune. Of course, the gambling doesn't hurt either."

"How does he get away with it?" Jeff asked. "The gambling, I mean."

"Calle Ocho is a different world. It's like Chinatown in San Francisco. We cause the city no trouble, pay significant taxes, and so they leave us alone. They have lots of other things to worry about without concerning themselves with what happens down here. Besides, you saw how restricted this place is. It's hard to become a member of the lower level. You must have six recommendations from current members to get in there. Less than one-fourth of the members are ever allowed to get up here to the Casino. The people who can get in aren't going to talk about what they do here."

Jeff was about to ask another question when the elevator doors opened, and from it emerged the most beautiful woman he had ever seen. He was speechless. Julio saw Jeff's jaw drop and looked to see what had interrupted their conversation.

"That's Cat!" he whispered. "I told you she was the best-looking woman in Miami, probably in the world."

She was more than beautiful. She was ravishing. Her light olive skin was flawless. Her long, wavy hair gleamed with gold and auburn highlights. She was tall, wearing high spike heels, and her body, encased in a shimmering green sequined dress, was perfect. But her eyes were the most stunning feature. She had huge eyes of the most amazing bright green Jeff had ever seen, with long lashes on a perfectly sculptured face. Jeff hadn't really looked at a woman in over seven months. He was instantly attracted to this one, however.

"Jesus."

"I told you," Julio gloated as he waved to attract her attention.

She soon saw Julio, and her face broke into a dazzling smile. She turned gracefully and came toward them. Jeff's heart was beating rapidly. He realized that he was sweating like a schoolboy on his first real date.

Her low, throaty voice was like a cat's purr when she greeted Julio with a kiss on the cheek. Instead of the clipped

ROYAL REVENGE

Cuban Spanish Jeff was just beginning to understand well, she spoke slowly with a much softer accent. Each word seemed to flow into the next in an almost musical fashion.

Jeff unconsciously wiped his palms on his pants. Julio turned to Jeff and introduced him to Cat in Spanish.

She extended her hand, and said in heavily accented English, "I am happy to know of you, Mr. Royal. Julio is my very good friend."

Her English may have been heavily accented, but it sounded like Shakespeare to Jeff. Her hand was warm and very soft, but her grip was quite firm.

"The pleasure is certainly mine. But please call me Jeff," he said in English.

Cat turned to Julio who translated rapidly. She turned back to Jeff and fixed him with another dazzling smile. "Jeff." She made the name sound like music. "Okay. I am called Cat."

Julio went to find a table, leaving them alone. Jeff shuffled his feet. He was almost giddy from the aroma of Cat's perfume.

"A drink for you?" he asked, using his hands to pretend he was drinking.

"No, *gracias*. Later, I think."

He stood there staring, frustrated at being unable to converse with her as a result of Julio's instruction. She held his eyes a very long time, and then looked demurely at the floor. Julio rushed up. "Follow me. We have a table," he said to Jeff as he took Cat's arm and ushered her toward a table across the room.

Somewhat lightheaded, Jeff followed. He couldn't take his eyes off the beautiful woman walking in front of him. Julio and Cat stopped several times to greet friends. Finally, after what seemed an eternity, they were seated at a small table at the edge of the casino.

"I think it's time we spoke Spanish," Julio said in Spanish to Jeff.

Lifting one eyebrow in mild surprise, Cat again smiled, melting Jeff's insides, and said, "I am so glad you can speak my language. It is much easier for me to get to know you. Speaking English is very difficult for me."

"Getting to know you will make all the lessons worthwhile," he said in Spanish as he smiled and looked into her eyes.

She threw her head back in a musical laugh. "He is a charmer, Julio."

"Yes. And a good friend. One who needs your help," Julio answered. He ordered drinks from a passing half-naked waiter.

Julio told Cat of Jeff's tragedy. He outlined what Jeff hoped to accomplish in Miami. Other than an arching of one of her eyebrows occasionally, she listened intently but without reaction. When Julio was finished, she sipped her drink thoughtfully.

Finally, she looked at Jeff and said, "I am sorry for what has happened to you. I don't know if I can help, but I will be willing to try. You must understand the danger. The Fabriza family will not like it when they find you are asking questions. You must be very careful."

She reached into the small silk bag she carried and took out a pen and a small piece of paper. "Here is my address and phone number. My apartment is in Coral Gables. I will meet you there tomorrow morning at ten o'clock. Okay?"

"I'll be there. Thank you very much," he said.

Without warning, she stood to leave, extending her hand to Jeff, embracing Julio.

"Entonces. Nos vemos manana. Tomorrow then," looking at Jeff with that incredible smile. *"Buenas noches."*

She left the club without another word. Jeff's eyes didn't leave her until she had disappeared into the elevator.

"You're lucky. She must really like you. I've never even been invited to her place. She will do whatever she can. Now let's drink. I believe you have been hypnotized," Julio laughed. "Scotch?"

"No, thanks. ... Yeah. Just one. To settle my nerves."

"It might help get rid of that hard-on, too!" Julio laughed gleefully.

Jeff continued to stare at the elevator, his mind a thousand miles away.

After a light dinner of *tapas*, they left at 11:00 p.m., incredibly early by the standards of the *Casa de Liberacion*. The gambling was becoming more intense and the crowds and the noise had increased by the time they made their way down the elevator. Jeff's one drink, or the lingering image of Catarina Contreras, or both, had made him a bit dizzy. He and Julio stepped out of the silent elevator into the same blast of smells and noise he had experienced earlier.

The dancers in the cages had changed, but the performances hadn't. Julio and Jeff stood near the door, looking at the performers and the crowd.

"Does this place ever close?" Jeff asked.

"Absolutely. At two a.m., sharp. But between now and then, there's a hell of a lot of action we'll be missing. I really hate to deprive these needy and available women of our expert services."

"I'm sorry to be so dull. If you want, I'll take a cab and leave the car for you to use. You can bring it back later."

"No. Maybe tonight I'll even get some sleep for a change. Let's go back to your place."

Most of their ride back was ruled by silence. Julio tried to make conversation, but Jeff's mind was obviously somewhere else. He finally gave up and slept most of the way back.

Jeff parked and put up the top. They got out of the car and embraced.

"Call me after your meeting with Cat. Also let me know what the Mayor says," Julio said, eyes twinkling.

"How ..."

"Deduction, my boy, deduction. He's the only other guy in Miami who comes close to being as well connected as I am. He had to be the next person you saw. Just remember, be very careful. And don't mention your meeting with Cat Contreras to anyone! It could be dangerous for her."

"I won't, Julio. I promise. Thanks, and good night," Jeff called over his shoulder as he walked up the stairs, humming to himself.

10

It was a little harder than usual for Jeff to get up at four a.m. After leaving Julio at almost midnight, he couldn't sleep. Visions of Catarina Contreras kept moving through his mind interrupted only by thoughts of his meeting with Mayor Castillo in the morning.

After a very fast run down Collins and cursory laps in the pool, he dressed in one of the new suits from Hyman Feld. He was adjusting his tie when he realized that it was the first tie he'd worn in over six months. "My life is really changing," he thought to himself as he looked in the mirror. At 6:15 a.m. he was headed across the causeway toward downtown Miami.

The former Mayor kept a small suite of offices on the fifteenth floor of a gleaming new downtown bank building. Because of the early hour, Jeff was forced to have the security guard in the lobby call the Mayor's office to get access to the floor. After a rapid ascent, he found the offices. Castillo, the only person in the office at that early hour, greeted him with a cup of steaming coffee.

The Mayor's large office was conservatively furnished with dark wood and leather. The entire outside wall, floor to ceiling, was glass and looked out on the city and Biscayne Bay. One wall was completely covered with plaques and pictures from Castillo's twelve-year reign as Mayor. The opposite was devoted to pictures of his large family. They sat on either end of the leather couch, facing each other. The Mayor lit an expensive and illegal Cuban cigar and exhaled with pleasure.

"One of the benefits of getting out of politics is that I can smoke these now instead of those terrible imitations made in Tampa," he said. "Based on what you've done to get yourself in such good physical shape, I don't suppose you want one?"

"Thank you, but no. Getting in shape was tough, staying in shape is almost harder. I've had to give up many of life's simple pleasures, like eating and drinking."

Castillo laughed, but soon his face became very serious. "You know how sorry I am about what happened to Connie. Everyone who knew you both felt the tragedy of her loss. I suppose you're here to find out more about why it happened. I'm not sure you are informed enough to know the difficulties you will face. I'm also equally sure I won't be able to dissuade you. So, I guess that means I'll do whatever I can to help. Why don't you tell me what you wish from me?"

"You always were quick to get to the point. I will be, too. You've read the newspaper story. The man, Gaspar, ... the man who killed Connie, had no motive unless he was paid to kill her. From what the Canadian police tell me, his employer was apparently the Fabriza family. I simply want to know why they wanted to threaten me so badly that they would do this to someone totally innocent like Connie."

Jeff's voice cracked as he concluded, and it took him a few moments to regain control. The Mayor compassionately stared at the floor.

"What will you do when you find out? How will you get revenge?"

"I'm not looking for revenge. Oh, I'd want them punished. But I'm not naive. I know they're powerful and dangerous. They also seem to be immune to the law. I'd turn any information I get over to the FBI. What I really want to know is why? There's no connection to me that I can find. I just can't understand why it happened and I don't know how I can live with that for the rest of my life. You know about me and about my business activities. Can you think of any reason they'd want to do this to me?"

"Not unless you're involved in some activity that threatens them. Are you sure this man Gaspar still worked for them?"

"The police in Montreal think so. Apparently, the other murders he was involved in were related to the Fabriza's drug business up there. I'm working under the assumption that he was still on their payroll. There's really no other conclusion."

"Unless he worked for someone else. But let's assume that he still worked for Fabriza. What possible relationship do you, your business, or anyone in your business have to the Fabriza family?"

"There's none. None! That's why I'm so mystified. None of this makes sense. There's no connection."

"There must be. You just don't know what it is. Have you heard of Pablo Espinoza?"

"No. Who is he?"

"He's head of the number two family in the Miami underworld. He used to be second in command of the Fabriza family but realized several years ago that Camino Fabriza's son Raphael is the only candidate Carmino will endorse for the next number one. Now he's a competitor. Someday the two families will kill each other off, but right now they seem to have an uneasy truce. The financial brain of the Espinoza group is a young guy by the name of Herman Guerra. He's absolutely brilliant. I hate to admit it, but he worked for me years ago. In fact, I'm sure you have met him before. He was on my staff when the *Star* story broke. He might know something. I'll give you his number. If you want, I'll try to set up a meeting with him for you. He probably won't talk to you, but it's the best idea I have. However, my friend, I strongly suggest that you drop the whole thing. You're not capable of working in these circles. You must know that. Why don't you give it up?"

"I can't. And, you must know that."

"I can accept it, but you're still on very dangerous ground. I hope you have sense enough to quit if one of these people makes a move. Do you?"

"I think so. But they won't know anything until I start asking questions."

"That's where you're wrong. They probably know you're here already. Who else knows you're here, besides me and my secretary?"

"Giuseppe, Julio Pozo, my secretary."

"No one else?"

"Well, the guy at a men's shop I go to, the bank ..."

"Which bank?"

"SunTrust, Miami Beach branch. Why?"

"Jeff, wake up. These people sell drugs. And they don't take credit cards. They have huge deposits in virtually every bank in Miami. Chances are that someone at the bank knows someone in the mob. Just be damn careful. Call me if you get in trouble, and I'll try to help. I again recommend that you go back home and forget this project."

"Thanks for your concern. I appreciate the help. I'll try to stay out of trouble," Jeff assured him.

"I think you probably are already in trouble. But there's nothing to be done about that. Call me if you need me," he said as he rose, indicating the meeting was over. He went to his desk and wrote a phone number and the name "Herman Guerra" on the back of one of his business cards. Handing it to Jeff, he said, "Again, be very careful, and call me for help if you need it."

"I will. Thanks again. I appreciate your time," Jeff said as they shook hands.

It was only eight o'clock, so Jeff headed back to the condo to change before he met Cat Contreras. He had forgotten how impossible the traffic was in Miami. After he finally reached Miami Beach, he barely had time to change to white slacks and a dark blue golf shirt and still get across the causeway and then make it to her apartment in Coral Gables by ten o'clock.

As he was running out the door, the phone rang. He answered it.

"Jeff? Giuseppe. I won't be able to come down there on Friday. I just can't seem to get away. How are you doing? Have you found out anything?"

"Not really. Julio Pozo and I met last night. He introduced me to a woman who may know something. I'm going to see her now. In fact, I was on my way out the door."

"How is she connected to this thing?"

"She's the girlfriend of the son of the head of the Fabriza family. She's gorgeous besides. I need to run. Can I call you later?"

"That's okay. I just wanted to tell you I couldn't come down this weekend. Call me if you need anything or if I can help you. You know I'll do whatever I can. And be careful. Those people are fucking crazy!"

"I will. Good-bye."

Jeff parked in the "guest" space in the back of the building, leaving the top down. Cat Contreras lived in a lavish apartment on the third and top floor of an old building built in the Spanish design common to this exclusive section of greater Miami. The renovation of the building had obviously been expensively and painstakingly done to recapture the original look. Cat's apartment was one of two on the third floor. It was serviced by a small antique elevator. After reaching the third floor he rang her doorbell and waited with anticipation as he heard the clicking of her shoes as she approached.

She came to the door in a red silk blouse worn over white pants with white open sandals. The red fabric accentuated her olive skin and the reddish highlights in her hair. Her eyes seemed impossibly green. Jeff felt his heart pounding rapidly. She invited him in with one of her dazzling smiles and a firm handshake. He settled on the couch after accepting her offer of coffee, which she served on a silver tray in expensive china cups.

The apartment was warmly and expensively furnished. The very large living room had a limestone tile floor with tastefully arranged, expensive oriental rugs. Most of the wall facing the quiet tropical street had been modified to accept floor to ceiling glass windows. The whole effect was quite beautiful and very peaceful.

"Thank you for permitting me to visit you," Jeff said in Spanish.

"As I told you, I am not sure if I can be of help to you. Julio Pozo has been a very good friend. He would not ask if he didn't feel I would want to try to help you. Now, would you please tell me again of how you know Julio so well?"

Jeff gave her a short history of himself, beginning with his brief tenure at the Star. He found her easy to talk to and found that he revealed more of himself than he had intended. He concluded with telling her again, but in more detail, why he was in Miami.

"Julio has told you of how I know the Fabriza family?" she asked, when Jeff was finished.

Jeff nodded.

"I rarely ask about their affairs because I don't want to know. My brother works for Raphael Fabriza. This morning I asked my brother about the man Gaspar. He says he knows nothing of him, that he doesn't work for Fabriza. I am sure he knows of him, because he was very curious as to why I would ask. I told him it was because of the story in the paper.

"There is really nothing more I can do now. If I ask any more questions, it will cause suspicion. I would suggest that if you want to continue, you go back to Julio and ask him for someone else to contact who may know more. I'm very sorry I can't help you."

ROYAL REVENGE

Jeff's face fell. He was very disappointed. He had hoped for much more than this. As he stood up, he said, "I understand, of course. I hope that your inquiries won't cause problems for you. Thank you for trying. I appreciate it very much."

He moved toward the door to leave. She also stood and moved very close to him. She took his hand. Her aroma was intoxicating.

"I am very sorry for you. I think you should go back home to Atlanta and forget this thing. It would be very dangerous for you to continue. I know how they think."

Jeff opened his mouth to respond when the large living room window shattered inward. Stunned, he turned toward the window. Cat pushed him to the floor just as he heard the rapid sound of a machine gun. Bullets struck the couch near the top of the back, shredding the expensive cloth, and tearing away bits of the frame. The china cups on the table exploded from the rapid impact of more shots. Marble chips flew in every direction as the coffee table disintegrated.

Jeff pulled her arm and pointed toward the heavy table in the dining room. They crawled toward the room, flinching as the destruction of her apartment continued. Lamps, pictures, chairs, and the walls were hit repeatedly by volleys of bullets from the street. Jeff and Cat were covered in plaster dust and bits of glass and sheetrock.

"What the hell ..."

"Oh God! They must know you are here. They must know I talked to you. We must get out of the apartment! They will surely kill us if we stay," she said, tears beginning to brim from her eyes, fear evident on her face. She was shivering violently. Jeff's mouth was so dry he could barely talk. His heart felt like it was coming out of his chest.

"How do we get out?"

"Through the kitchen. Down the stairs. This way."

J. Trey Weeks

They crawled through the dining room into the kitchen. The noise from the machine guns and the destruction of the apartment's furnishings continued unabated. Jeff looked over his shoulder as he crawled around the corner into the kitchen. The living room of the beautiful apartment had been virtually destroyed. The floor was covered with debris. Plaster dust created a fog that was not thick enough to hide the unbelievable devastation.

They reached the door leading from the kitchen into the hallway. Jeff stood up just as the noise stopped. He opened the door and looked down the narrow hallway. It was only about ten feet to the door of the stairs. The hall was completely empty. Cat stood up, still shaking, almost uncontrollably. He grabbed her arm and pulled her toward the stairs. The bell from the arriving elevator sounded just as they passed through the door and started down. They had gone down five steps when the wooden door at the top of the stairs splintered with bullets exploding through it. The bullets ricocheted off the concrete walls of the stairwell. They ran down the stairs and reached the second-floor landing when the door above them burst open. They had barely turned the corner, half stumbling, half running down toward the first floor when Jeff heard someone shout, "*En las escalaras. Por aqui! Sigueme! Prisa!* (On the stairs. Through here! Follow me! Hurry!)"

Bullets thudded into the floor just a few feet behind Jeff as they clambered down the last few stairs to the first-floor landing and burst through the door to the outside. Sirens wailed distantly as they ran away from the street. There was a dark blue car in the middle of the street with the driver half in and half out. In his hands was a small machine gun. He turned toward Jeff and Cat and raised the gun.

Two men burst through the door behind them. A ripple of bullets from the man in the street pounded into the grass just behind them. Jeff pushed Cat violently to the right toward a cluster of palm trees in the adjoining lawn. Bullets from the men behind him exploded the bark on the palm trees with a smacking sound. He pulled Cat toward the trees and down on the grass as the sound of sirens became very loud.

Jeff looked down the street and saw a police car, siren screaming, lights flashing, turn into the street about two blocks away. The two men behind him ran toward the car, now more worried about their own survival than their prey. The man in the car fired another burst toward Jeff and Cat as his two accomplices reached the car. The bark from the trees peppered them as they lay in the minimal shelter of the spindly palms.

The gunmen's car skidded from curb to curb as they fled, motor roaring, tires screeching. One of the men in the back fired a short burst at the approaching police car, shattering its windshield. It skidded sideways and jumped the curb on the other side of the street, crashing with the sound of buckling steel and breaking glass into another cluster of palm trees.

Jeff heard more sirens approaching. He pulled Cat up and dragged her toward the parking lot behind the building. He reached the Mercedes, fumbling awkwardly for his keys, dropping them to the pavement in his haste, finally getting the car started. Cat, unquestioning, got in the passenger's seat.

"Go this way. You can get to the street behind." she pointed.

The tires thumped with a sickening sound as Jeff flew over the speed bumps in the alley. He skidded around the corner and headed away from the sound of the screaming sirens as fast as the car would accelerate. They wound their way back to Eighth Street before Jeff slowed down and then pulled into the parking lot of a grocery store. He parked in an empty space and turned off the motor.

His hands were shaking violently. He felt mildly nauseous. He turned to Cat. Her formerly olive skin was the color of curdled milk. Tears streamed down her cheeks. She was shivering. Jeff put his arms around her, wrestling with the console between them. She leaned into his embrace. He held her until her shuddering body calmed.

"Do you have any place to go?" he asked, tilting her face up gently.

"I don't know where to go. I don't know what to do. I am afraid. I am very afraid," she said in a throaty whisper.

"Will you come with me? I have a place that is safe. No one knows I'm there but Julio. Do you want to go there?"

"But I have nothing. No clothes, nothing," she said as she gestured at her torn and soiled pants. "What will I do?"

She sobbed as an unbroken stream of tears fell down her face. She buried her head against his shoulder. Jeff hugged her closer.

"I have a friend who can help. I'll call him. We can take care of everything you need while we think of what to do."

Jeff put the top up and turned on the air conditioner. He pulled out into the street and drove back to Miami Beach. When he got to the street with his condo, he pulled into a similar unit about a block away.

"Stay in the car. Keep the motor running and the doors locked. If anything happens, or if I'm not back in ten minutes, take the car and go to Julio. You know where to find him. Okay?"

Cat nodded meekly.

Jeff took the key to the condo off his key chain. Cat lifted herself over the console and into the driver's seat.

He jogged easily toward the condo, slowing to a walk as he approached. He warily looked at every car in the street. There was no one in sight, even at the pool. He walked up to the unit and inspected the door, then let himself in. The only sound was the hum of the air conditioner. He walked from room to room. As far as he could tell, nothing seemed to be disturbed. As he was leaving to go back to the car, the phone rang. Jeff let it ring until the answering machine clicked on with his answering message. He listened as it finished, and the recording began.

"Jeff? This is Giuseppe. Give me a call tomorrow. I want to go over the terms of our bank loan. They're getting impossible to deal with lately. I think we should pay it off now. I'll explain more when you call."

He closed the door as Giuseppe hung up.

Jeff was sweating again by the time he got back to the car. Cat was sitting behind the wheel with the motor running, her face still white. She was staring vacantly ahead. They changed seats and he drove to the condo and parked. Once inside, he locked the door, and headed for the bar.

"Would you like a drink? I think I'll have one."

"Yes. Please. Do you have rum?"

Jeff fixed them both a drink and then called Hyman Feld.

"Hyman? This is Jeff Royal. I do need something. I have a friend who just came into town and her luggage with all her clothes and personal things has been lost. Can you get a wardrobe for her like you did for me? We can't leave the condo. I'm expecting an important call."

"Of course, Mr. Royal. My brother owns a very nice woman's shop. His name is Arthur. Give me your number and he will call you immediately to get the appropriate information about sizes and so forth. He can supply anything your friend needs. I'm happy to help."

One hour later Arthur Feld arrived with his wife and daughter, each with an armful of clothing. He chatted with Jeff in the living room, studiously ignoring Jeff's torn and grass-stained slacks, while Cat tried on clothes in the bedroom. The Felds even brought a selection of makeup and toilet articles. After they were finished, Arthur told him that Hyman would bill him together with the things Jeff had purchased.

Jeff thanked them profusely and ushered them out. He locked the door and looked at Cat. She was now quite composed, and sat, barefooted, wearing a green silk blouse with matching pants. Her hair glowed red with the sunlight from the window. Her breasts rose and fell with her breathing, making the blouse taut, as she sat quietly, looking back at him, meeting his gaze directly. She put her drink down on the table and rose with a movement that revealed the sculptured perfection of the body beneath the silk. Her beautiful eyes, now calm and clear, glowed like jade.

"What do we do now?" she said.

"First, my third drink in five months. Then you tell me everything you know about Fabriza. Then, we decide what to do. In the meantime, you can stay here. I'll sleep in the other bedroom."

She came up to him and put her arms around his neck. Her body melted against his. He felt her firm breasts against his chest, her soft breath on his neck. She pushed her body against him and raised her face to his. She brushed his lips with hers, then together they kissed, first tenderly, then passionately, then hungrily. Her hips moved against him, and she felt his hardness. Her hand moved to his cheek, and she stroked him tenderly. He placed his hand on her breast, feeling the erect nipple through the silk of her blouse. Her kiss became more urgent, her tongue searching. She tilted away from him and turned her mouth to his ear.

"I think I'll sleep with you," she said huskily as he picked her up and carried her to the bed.

11

They lay in each other's arms for most of the afternoon, mixing passionate sessions of lovemaking with intermittent sleep. The ringing of the phone awakened them. The answering machine began recording as Jeff reached the phone, pulling on his pants.

"Jeff, this is Julio. You must call me at once. Something terrible ..."

Jeff picked up the receiver and interrupted. "This is Jeff, Julio, what's wrong?"

"I think you know already. Cat's place was shot to pieces this morning. The police are looking for her. They're also looking for some white-haired old fart who can run like the wind who was seen leaving with her. I imagine you know who that was. Is she safe?"

"Yeah. She's here with me. I think we're okay here."

"Okay! You're out of your fucking mind! Half of Miami is looking for the two of you. A policeman was injured when his windshield was shot out and he wrecked his car. The Miami Police tend to get real pissed off about things like that. If the guys who shot her place to ribbons don't get you, the police will. They want to question her, and I'm sure they'd like to know a little bit about you. At the very least, you're guilty of leaving the scene of a crime. Who knew you were there besides me?"

"No one knew, Julio. Cat said she'd talked to her brother about Gaspar and he seemed upset that she was asking questions, but she certainly didn't think ..."

J. Trey Weeks

"That's the problem. You're not thinking, either of you. Lots of people saw the three of us together last night at *Casa de Liberacion*. Those guys with the machine guns saw you today. You've struck a big fucking nerve somewhere. They will figure out who you are and where you are before the police do. The motherfuckers are probably going to start looking for me, too. I <u>knew</u> you were going to fuck up my life when you started asking questions. I assume you don't know who the guys doing the shooting were. Does she?"

"No. She was as scared as I was. I assume they were from the Fabrizas."

"Who knows where you are now?"

"Not many people. You and a few others. Giuseppe, Mayor Castillo, some others."

"That's several too many. Here's an address in Coral Gables. Write it down. It's one of my rental units that I never rent. I'll meet you there in an hour. Bring stuff to wear and anything else you think you need. I'll go out and get some food. In a couple of days maybe we can figure out what to do, besides shit in our pants. Don't tell anyone where you're going. No one, absolutely no one! Okay?"

Readily agreeing, Jeff scribbled down the address as Cat emerged from the bedroom, towel around her, fresh from the shower. She looked incredibly beautiful.

"We're going to a place Julio has. He doesn't think we're safe here," Jeff said, wanting nothing more than to take her in his arms and hold her close again.

Her face turned ashen. She moved toward the bedroom as she said, "I'll get my things together. Julio is usually right." Within minutes she emerged in a simple dress, carrying a plastic garbage bag full of her new clothes and her personal things. "I'm ready to go. Please let me help you with your things," she said calmly.

ROYAL REVENGE

Jeff hurriedly threw the things he needed in another garbage bag. They locked the door and rushed to the car. He jammed everything he could in the tiny trunk of the Mercedes and stuffed the rest in the limited space behind the seats. He opened the door for Cat and then put the pistol in the glove compartment. Cat's eyes widened, but she said nothing. Jeff put the car in gear, screeched out of the parking lot, and headed for the causeway.

Julio's rental unit was an old apartment in a section of Coral Gables that had escaped any attempt at renewal. It was very old-fashioned, but clean, with a well-stocked bar and kitchen and two bedrooms. Julio, with a drink in his hand, answered the door when they knocked.

"This is where I play around when I'm married," Julio explained as he showed Jeff and Cat around and helped them bring up their things. "No one knows about it. The only guests I've had here are usually too drunk or stoned or horny to know where they are or who they're with. I've told the paper I'm taking a few days off, so no one will miss me. Now, why don't you tell me what happened, and maybe we can figure out what to do next."

Jeff and Cat sat close together on the couch, as Jeff recounted the morning's events. Julio remained silent, but his practiced reporter's eye noted the tiny signals of body language and eye contact that passed between the pair he was facing. When Jeff had finished, Julio said in English, "I think you've fallen in deep, deep, love and deep, deep, shit at the same time, Jeff, my boy. I don't think you know how deep this hole can get."

Jeff smiled as Cat looked questioningly at him, not understanding most of what Julio had said. Jeff looked at her and took her hand, explaining in Spanish, "Julio said he's very happy to see that we care about each other so much."

"I also said you're in deep, deep, *Mierda*," Julio said to Cat in Spanish as he looked at his watch. "Let's watch the news and see what they think they know up to now."

The six o'clock news was beginning just as Julio got the picture tuned on the ancient television set. The announcer, with his perfect features, hair so well arranged that it looked like spun glass, was just beginning the broadcast.

"In Miami, police are looking for a woman who was apparently abducted at gunpoint today after her Coral Gables apartment was virtually destroyed by several unidentified men with machine guns."

"Jesus! I'm surprised you got out of there," exclaimed Julio as the pictures of the remains of Cat's apartment flashed on the screen.

"One policeman was injured when his car was hit by gunfire as he arrived at the scene. He was treated for minor injuries and released. The woman abducted was identified as Catarina Contreras, rumored to be close to Raphael Fabriza, son of the alleged head of the noted Miami underworld family. Police are searching for three Hispanic men last seen leaving the area in a blue, late-model Cadillac, with a Florida license. The men are heavily armed and should be considered very dangerous.

"Police are also searching for an unidentified Anglo male about six feet tall with white hair and about forty-five to fifty years old. He was last seen dragging Miss Contreras from the area."

"I told you they were looking for an old white-haired fart," Julio laughed.

"Miss Contreras is thirty-two years old, five feet seven inches tall and weighs one hundred and ten pounds. She is assumed to be held against her will and the police are asking that anyone with information regarding her whereabouts or the identification of her assailants ..."

ROYAL REVENGE

Cat gasped as the screen filled with her picture.

The announcer continued, "The attack may have been drug- related, sources said, although police have not confirmed that speculation. Informed sources maintain that the Fabriza family controls much of the drug traffic into South Florida and throughout the United States and Canada. We will have more on the story on our eleven o'clock edition. Turning to national news ..."

"Well, Ollie, it's a fine fucking pickle you've gotten us into this time," Julio said in his best Laurel and Hardy imitation as he turned off the set. And then in Spanish, "Cat. Tell me everything your brother said when you asked about this guy, Gaspar. Then I want you to tell Jeff about your boyfriend, Raphael, so he'll know just how screwed up this whole situation is. Tell him everything. Don't leave anything about Raphael out," Julio emphasized the last sentence with a serious look.

Cat moved almost imperceptibly closer to Jeff and began to talk, hesitantly at first, as she described her brief discussion with Claudio Contreras that morning. Then, calmly, and without emotion, she told Jeff of her three-year relationship with Raphael Fabriza and the Fabriza family.

Raphael Fabriza had first met Cat about a year after she came to Miami from Caracas with her brother, Claudio. Cat and Claudio had come to live with wealthy friends of their parents. They were lucky, escaping a life of poverty and a bleak future for the wonder of the United States. The friends, Hector Rodriguez and his wife, Maria, who had come to Miami years before, had no children. They had wanted Cat and her brother to come to Miami for many years. Finally, Cat and Claudio had decided to leave Caracas.

Hector operated a marginally successful night club in the Calle Ocho district, as well as a prospering import business, and Cat and Claudio were offered clerical jobs in his import business. They decided to stay in the United States, and through the influence of their hosts, had obtained permanent visas.

Claudio was three years younger than Cat and as handsome as she was beautiful. He had quickly become very frustrated with his small salary at Hector's import-export firm. When Hector launched his newest nightclub, *Casa de Liberacion*, Claudio helped with the opening. He immediately asked to work there.

Over the objections of his wife, who wouldn't understand such things, Hector allowed Claudio to work as a waiter in the club. Claudio's good looks and his excellent performance as a waiter soon allowed him to progress to a dealer and, then, a pit boss in the casino. It was in the casino that he had gotten to know Raphael Fabriza.

It would have been impossible for Claudio to avoid envy of Raphael Fabriza. He was young, very handsome, and always surrounded by beautiful and wealthy men and women. He gambled tens of thousands of dollars in a single night and shrugged off huge losses with the style and nonchalance of one who has unlimited access to unlimited money. Raphael liked young Claudio and often invited him to private parties after the casino closed. Hector Rodriguez was powerless to stop the growing friendship, as Raphael was the son of the man who originally financed and then helped Hector's most lucrative operation to begin and, then, to flourish.

Soon Claudio announced that he was leaving the casino to work for the Fabriza family as Raphael's driver. Hector tried without enthusiasm, and Maria tried in earnest, to discourage him, to no avail. Maria came to Cat in desperation.

"They are *Suciedad* - filth. They are scum - *putas*. He will become like them, like my husband has become, with no morals, no feelings for anything but their slimy money. I have seen what they do to people to change them. Hector was a good man. He thought he could be involved with them without getting dirty.

He was wrong. He is now as dirty as they are. He cannot get away from them, ever. The same thing will happen to Claudio. You must talk to Claudio. It would be better for him to go back to Caracas than to go to be with these people."

Cat was surprised to hear Maria talk so boldly against her husband. "But Claudio will just be a driver for the man Raphael. He says Raphael Fabriza is not part of the things the family does."

"Then where does he get his money? He must be one of them to have all the money he has. You must talk to Claudio. He must not do this. He will become one of them. You are the only one who can stop him. Your poor mother would grieve if she knew what Hector has done by allowing this to happen," she sobbed.

Cat talked to Claudio with no effect. He was plainly enthralled with Raphael and his glamorous lifestyle. He saw nothing wrong with being part of it.

"How can you judge him? He's not like you think, not like Maria has told you. You've never even seen Raphael. Come with me to meet him. Have dinner with us. Talk to him. If you think he is so bad I will return to the casino as Hector's employee. But, I will be surprised if you don't like Raphael as much as I do. He is the most wonderful man I've ever met. He has come to like me and is giving me a chance to be something," Claudio said, with the reverence of someone talking about his hero.

Cat agreed to meet Claudio the next evening for dinner where he would introduce her to Raphael. She dressed carefully, wanting to make a good impression for Claudio. They were to meet in a very famous restaurant in North Miami, one noted for being booked ahead for weeks. Cat was just a little early, having allowed extra time for the usual problems with Miami traffic. Cat's classic beauty always made men treat her with courtesy when they saw her. But, when she told the Maître d' the name of the party she was meeting, she got her first glimpse of the reason for Claudio's seduction by Raphael and by the Fabriza money. The Maître d' abandoned his station like it was aflame, to the irritation of a waiting area full of typically impatient moneyed Miami guests who were ready to be escorted to their tables.

"Of course, *Señorita* Contreras, come this way with me, please. *Señor* Fabriza has reserved his usual private room. There will be three of you, am I correct? He has arranged for champagne for you if you arrived before him. May I pour you a glass?"

Cat accepted as she was being seated at a small table set for three in a luxurious private room staffed by tuxedoed waiters. After helping her with her chair, the Maître d' snapped his fingers. Instantly one of the two waiters came forward with a bottle of Dom Perignon and presented it. The Maître d' examined the bottle and rejected it with a look of disdain.

"This bottle is not the correct one. The 1936 is what was requested. Please get it immediately," he said to the waiter as he indicated total frustration with the poor quality of his help by rolling his eyes.

Moments later, as the champagne, the 1936 this time, was being poured, the waiters snapped to attention as Claudio and one of the most handsome men Cat had ever seen came into the room.

Raphael Fabriza was perfectly groomed in a suit of gray silk that looked freshly pressed. He was very tall for a Cuban, well over six feet. His long torso was powerful, and his waist very slim. His expensive suit was tailored to accentuate those features. His gleaming white shirt and expensive and perfectly knotted blue silk tie looked as if they came from a clothing ad. His face could have been too pretty, but his square chin and a small scar above his cheekbone made him handsome. His head was crowned by razor-cut thick black hair. He was darkly tanned, and his face showed just a shadow of his smooth-shaven dark beard. His nose was straight and complimented his high forehead. His eyes, a very light golden brown uncommon to Cuban Hispanics, danced with delight as they rested on Cat. He smiled at her with perfect white teeth.

He kissed her hand as Claudio introduced them. The waiters hovered throughout their dinner, awaiting Raphael's every command, which he gave frequently without seeming imperious. Their conversation throughout dinner was generally light, but sometimes intense. He seemed very interested in Cat and her brother, and easily talked about any subject that she could bring up. Cat found the man to be incredibly charming, and despite herself, became very attracted to him.

The next few months were a whirlwind. Raphael invited Cat to join him and Claudio at luxurious dinners, lunches, and lavish parties, mixed in with days spent on his sailboat in Biscayne Bay, or a simple picnic to Lummus park. He never made the slightest advance, even in the infrequent moments when he and Cat were alone, always giving her a perfunctory kiss of greeting on the cheek, but only after knowing her for several weeks.

Cat, who had never known young men who were wealthy, had certainly never met any man _this_ wealthy. She had also never before found any Hispanic man who was more compassionate or gentle or less aggressive toward women. Before long, she was as much a captive of Raphael Fabriza as her brother. She was even sure she was falling in love with him. She began hoping for Raphael to become more demonstrative and affectionate with her, as their relationship, had, up to now, been quite platonic.

One day a very excited Claudio called her at Hector's office. "I'll pick you up for lunch. Tell Hector you need the rest of the day off. You won't believe what I have to show you."

Her objections to taking the day off were overcome by Claudio's unchecked enthusiasm. After she talked with Hector, Claudio picked her up in Raphael's limousine and drove her to an apartment house in Coral Gables.

Truly excited, he took her arm and escorted her to a third-floor apartment in an obviously expensive renovated building. "Well, what do you think of this? Isn't it beautiful?" he asked her as he showed her through each room of the exquisite unit.

Cat was overwhelmed. "Yes, it's very, very beautiful, Claudio. But why are you showing this place to me? Who lives here?"

"We do. You and me. Raphael is giving this place to us. We can have an apartment of our own now. Your room is here, and mine is here," he said as he took her through the sumptuous bedrooms.

"You're crazy, Claudio. Why? Why is he doing this? We can't possibly accept this kind of thing from Raphael. My relationship with him isn't that close. We have become good friends, but that's all. I could not accept this kind of thing from him. We can't possibly live here, Claudio," she protested.

Claudio brought her into the living room and sat with her on the couch. He took both of her hands in his. His dark eyes softened as he looked at her. "You must understand something for me, Cat. My relationship with Raphael is very close. I want to be with him, and he wants to be with me. Now we can be together whenever we want, without anyone knowing. Do this for me, Cat. We are in love. He is the most wonderful man I've ever been with."

Cat's eyes got very wide with the shock of what Claudio was telling her. "You and Raphael. You are in love with each other? But ..."

"I didn't realize what was wrong before. But with Raphael, I found that nothing was wrong with me. It was that I had always thought my feelings about other men were bad. Raphael showed me that my feelings for him were okay. Of course, no one can know. His father would be very upset if he suspected. Someday the world will be more understanding. Someday, Raphael will be in control of his father's business. Then, our relationship can be in the open. For now, we must be lovers in secret. You can help us by living here with me. Please do this, Cat. Do it for me," he pleaded.

As a result, Cat and Claudio moved into the apartment where she and Jeff had nearly lost their lives that morning. Cat pretended to be Raphael's mistress, and was seen in public with him almost every day. He often spent the night at their apartment. Raphael paid all of her expenses, and she quit her job at Hector's firm. Raphael and Claudio continued their affair. As far as anyone else was concerned, Raphael spent virtually all his free time with Cat. Claudio was just her brother and Raphael's driver, to whom Raphael was very kind, and who almost always accompanied them.

Jeff looked at Cat with a look of complete shock. "Do you mean that the only reason you've maintained this lifestyle and masqueraded as Raphael Fabriza's mistress is so your brother and Fabriza could hide the fact that they're lovers? That's incredible!"

"It's not so incredible when you know the whole story about Cat and Claudio in Caracas," said Julio. "It's not your place to judge. Some other time she can tell you, if she chooses to, her reasons for this sacrifice. Now you know a secret that only four other people know.

"I think it's time to use that knowledge to get ourselves out of this mess and to get the information you want. The first thing is for us to meet with Raphael and Claudio and see who tried to kill you both, and why. The best one to answer that question is Raphael, so I suggest we set up a meeting with him. But now,

I'm hungry. Why don't we fix dinner and then we'll plan our attack for tomorrow."?

"I will fix dinner. I would like to cook for you. It takes my mind off my troubles. Do you like *Paella*?" Cat asked.

"I'd kill for *Paella*," Julio said as Jeff enthusiastically nodded his agreement. "There's a Spanish market at the end of the block. Let's put together a list and I'll get everything you need that we don't have here."

"While you're at the store, I'm going to take a shower. After what we've been through, I could use one," Jeff said.

While Julio was at the store, Cat began busying herself in the kitchen. After his shower, Jeff came into the kitchen with his hair still damp, a towel wrapped about his waist. He came up behind her and kissed her on the neck, putting his arms around her and cupping her breasts tenderly. He nuzzled her hair and smelled her freshness. She sighed contentedly and turned to him and melted into his embrace. They kissed tenderly and held each other.

Cat softly stroked Jeff's biceps and then moved her hands down his back and pulled the towel away. She ran her hands softly over his buttocks. Her hands fluttered up to his waist, and then circled his chest, moving down to his stomach and then the front of his legs. She kissed his chest, circling her tongue around his nipples. She knelt before him and ran her tongue down his flat belly while she held him softly in her hands. She kissed his shaft and then took him in her mouth. Jeff's knees weakened. He felt himself on the verge of collapse.

Cat kissed him once more before she stood up, smiling mischievously, wrapping the towel back around his waist with some difficulty. "The rest we will save for later, for dessert," she murmured as she took him back into her arms, her tongue searching his mouth, her entire body pushing against him. They stood together, tightly embraced, saying nothing, enjoying the heat and closeness of each other.

ROYAL REVENGE

Eventually, Jeff pulled away and looked into her liquid jade eyes. "I'm sorry I've involved you in my problems and created such danger for you. But I'm not sorry that I found you and we are together. I don't understand why you've lived this lie with Raphael and Claudio so long. But, I don't care. I want you to be with me. I love you."

Cat's eyes misted as she answered. "I've wanted to hear you say that since I saw you last night. I've lived for Claudio, or for my parents, or for someone else, all my life. I love you, and I will help you finish what you've started. Then I want to live for you, and for myself. Someday I will explain what I've done, and why, and you will maybe understand. I will even improve my English for you!" she said as tears began to fall from her beautiful green eyes. The towel had loosened so she wrapped it back around him and then took him back into her arms.

They were still standing together in an embrace as Julio returned with two sacks of groceries. He looked at them with mocked disdain. "It's bad enough that you make me buy the groceries. Then you exhibit yourselves in my kitchen. Then you, Jeff, molest the cook, doing God knows what, but I'm sure they were obscene things, when I'm plainly starving to death. You could at least let the cook finish what she's started. No, forget I said that. Let her finish cooking!" he laughed, and they were all laughing as Jeff went to the bedroom to dress.

Cat proved to be an excellent cook. The three of them finished a huge meal of *Paella* washed down with two bottles of Spanish wine.

They cleaned up the dishes and then sat in the living room. "Tomorrow we need to meet with Raphael. I suggest you call Claudio and we'll ask him to set it up. He's also probably very worried about where you are. Why don't you call him now?" Julio asked Cat.

"I will call the car. Do you want me to have him call us here?" she asked. "I would also like to have him tell Hector and Maria that I am okay."

"Yeah. Just don't tell him where we are. We'll figure out another place to meet him tomorrow. At this point, I don't think we should let anyone know where we are," Julio said.

"I need to call Giuseppe, too," Jeff said to Julio. "I never answered his call from this morning. I'll leave this number if it's okay with you."

"That's fine, but I still think we need to be sure no one knows where we are. We don't need any unexpected visitors. Okay?"

Cat found Claudio in the car and gave him the phone number of Julio's apartment. He was terribly worried about her and most relieved to find out that she was alive and well. He agreed to meet them alone in Lummus Park the next morning. Claudio assured her he would call the Rodriguez' to tell them Cat was safe.

Jeff's call to Giuseppe was less pleasant. "I find out more about your progress from watching the six o'clock news here in Atlanta than you tell me. Tonight, they're talking about a mob war about to erupt in Miami. Was that girl that was kidnapped the one you went to see? Why in the fuck don't you let me know what's going on? I've been worried sick, and I need a little help with the business, too. I've called the condo ten times. Don't you ever check your fucking messages? Where the hell are you? What's going on? Tell me what you're doing," Giuseppe demanded.

"In the first place, I'm safe, but barely. Someone really doesn't want me down here asking questions. In the second place, I think you need to settle down. I don't need any crap from you. I'm getting enough down here. What I'm doing is really not of your concern. And as far as where I am, here's the number. I won't be going back to the condo until some of this stuff blows over. Now let's talk about business. Why do you want to pay off the bank? It's not due and there's no need to pay them early."

"The bank is getting real chicken-shit all of a sudden. They're giving me a lot of shit about the quarterly numbers. Now they want a lot of information they've never asked for before. They're even making noises about requiring a full-blown audit, which they've never required before. I think it's because of their expansion into Texas. They bought a big group of failed banks there from the FDIC. Now the FDIC is looking at everything they do everywhere else. I don't think we need them anymore. Besides, we have so much excess cash that we can pay them off and save the interest we've been paying them as well as the expense of the audit."

"You're talking about just under five million dollars to pay them off! Where did we come up with that much cash?" Jeff asked, incredulous.

"Well, business is still terrific. Collections are coming in faster than usual. And the Canadians have to give us a big discount if we pay them early. We can pay off the bank and the Canadians and still have a reasonable cushion. If you'll agree, I can complete the transactions next week. I will need you to sign some stuff, but I can FedEx it to our office in Miami. You'll need to sign it before five tomorrow, so they can express it back to me."

"Okay, but I hope you're not playing it too close. If business slows down ..."

"Jeff, I'm the money guy, remember? If we need it, we have a five-million-dollar line of credit at Atlanta First we've never used. Trust me."

"Okay. I'll go to the office here tomorrow afternoon and sign the stuff you need. Just have them leave it with the receptionist."

"Good. Now, what in hell are you doing? Why can't you go back to the condo? What happened today? I think you're in over your head. Where are you staying? Can I help you with something? I'll come down there if I need to."

"I'm with Julio Pozo. He's helping me out. There's really nothing you can do, but if the reaction I've gotten so far is any indication, I'm getting really close to finding out who's behind this whole deal. If I can't find out something concrete in the next few days, I'm going to the FBI with what little I have, and then I'm giving up and coming home to Atlanta. You're right, I'm in over my head and I'm starting to get worried about it."

"I still think you're crazy. Come on home, now. I'll go with you to the cops if you want. You're going to end up dead if you keep on fucking around with those people down there."

"I'll be careful. I'll call you tomorrow. Don't worry," Jeff said. Giuseppe hung up reluctantly after reminding Jeff to go to the Miami office before five o'clock the following day.

Jeff joined Cat and Julio in the living room as Julio turned on the eleven o'clock news. The newscaster's hair hadn't moved one iota since six.

"Miami police recovered the car allegedly used this morning in the attack on an apartment in Coral Gables during which a Miami woman was apparently abducted and a Miami policeman slightly injured. The car was reported stolen in Miami early yesterday. The missing woman is identified as Catarina Contreras. A police spokesman said that there are currently no further leads in the case. In other news, the Miami City Council ..."

Julio turned off the set. "Let's get some sleep. We meet Claudio at nine tomorrow and we have a lot to do. You two take the first bedroom and I'll retire with my dreams of days gone by in the other. Good night," he said as he bent to kiss Cat on the cheek and patted Jeff on the shoulder.

ROYAL REVENGE

Jeff watched Julio as he discretely closed the door to the second bedroom. He stood, and Cat stood up and kissed him. Their kisses became passionate, fierce. Jeff picked her up and carried her to the bedroom. He lay her on the bed and gazed at the vision before him. She pulled him down beside her and kissed him again. His breathing became very rapid as she unzipped his pants, and put her hand inside his underwear, caressing him.

He unbuttoned her dress and fell on her breast, his tongue circling the dark nipple. Cat arched her back, pushing his head against her. With a shake of her shoulders, the dress fell to her waist. Releasing him, she began fumbling with his shirt buttons, while slipping one hand inside his shirt, rubbing his chest. Jeff stood up, and hurriedly took off his clothes. Cat stripped off her dress and panties, and propped herself on her elbow, gazing at him standing before her, naked. Her eyes glowed like green coals as she looked at his body, and she moved toward him, sitting on the bed facing him, running her hands over his back, his buttocks, his legs. Her hands caressed his skin from his knees up the inside his thighs, to his belly, and then down. She stroked his length, and then took him in her mouth, pulling him into her with hands clasped firmly against his buttocks. His knees went slack, and he collapsed on the bed.

Pushing her down, he kissed her breasts, tasting her skin with pleasure as he moved down her body. Very quickly Cat shuddered in orgasm, stifling a scream as his mouth covered her and his tongue searched inside her. Jeff moved on top of his lover and entered her, slowly at first, and then with ever- increasing rapid thrusts. His body tensed and every muscle quivered and he came as Cat dug her nails into his back with a small cry of ecstasy.

They fell asleep entwined in each other's arms.

12

Jeff woke at three-thirty, momentarily forgetting where he was. He carefully moved his arm from under Cat's head and she murmured softly before falling back into deep sleep. He kissed her hair gently and then rose.

Dressed in running shorts and shoes, Jeff let himself quietly out of the apartment, leaving the key in the potted plant beside the door. With a five-pound dumbbell in each hand, he began jogging down the street. The air was heavy with humidity, and after about a mile Jeff was soaked with sweat. He continued jogging for almost an hour, and then spurted into a run as he headed back the last few blocks to Julio's apartment.

As he rounded the corner about a hundred yards from the apartment unit, he saw a car moving slowly, lights switched off, and then stopping in front of the unit with a flash of red from the brakes. Jeff veered into the shrubs, breathing heavily from his exertion and his growing panic, and crept slowly up to the apartment building, hiding himself in the foliage. A cold shudder of fear stabbed his gut as he crept ever closer.

The interior light went on briefly as he saw a man get out of the car, closing the door carefully to avoid making any noise. The man walked softly and purposefully toward the entrance to the courtyard. In the dim light Jeff could see that he carried a pistol. He pulled a piece of paper from his pocket and read it in the light at the courtyard entrance, then reached up and unscrewed the bulb, leaving the apartment entrance in darkness. As he reached up, Jeff got a good look at his face. He was one of the men who had chased them down the stairs at Cat's apartment!

His heart hammering in his chest, Jeff was careful to conceal himself from the second man waiting in the car, who was now revealed only by the glowing ember on the end of the cigarette he was smoking. Jeff silently dropped one of the dumbbells he was carrying into the bushes. He followed the man with the pistol into the courtyard and then up the stairs to the door of Julio's apartment.

The man checked the number on the door and then moved back slightly before removing a ring of keys from his pocket. Fumbling in silence, he tried several different times before picking the lock. He quietly opened the door. Jeff crept up silently behind him as he entered the apartment.

Jeff was temporarily blinded when the living room lights went on suddenly. In the following split second, he registered the sight of Julio, standing in his underwear with his hand on the light switch, in front of the man with the pistol. Jeff hit the man over the head with the five-pound dumbbell he still carried. He used all the force he could muster.

The man's head split open with a "chocking" sound like that of a baseball being hit into the stands. As he fell forward, the gun made a spitting noise, the bullet splatting the wall between Julio's legs, an inch or so below his body.

"Kill the lights!" Jeff hissed as he kicked the man's body over, grabbing the gun from his clutching fingers. Julio switched off the lights as Jeff ran to the window in time to see the car door open again. The second man got out, closing the door softly, and looked up toward the window where the light from the apartment had shone onto the street seconds before. He threw his cigarette into the street and came forward to the courtyard entrance in a crouching run, with a pistol in his hand.

"There's another one coming up the stairs. Get down and don't make a sound," Jeff whispered as he crawled toward the still open door. He heard the second man's steps scratching softly on the concrete stairs as he came up to the apartment. His head, shoulders, and the arm with the gun in it appeared in the light of the door as Cat suddenly came out of the second bedroom wearing Jeff's white shirt. "Jeff, what's wrong. Where ..?"

Julio jumped up and pushed her back roughly through the bedroom door as the man's body came rushing through the front door. His gun popped and spit a burst of flame. Jeff pulled the trigger of the gun he was holding reflexively. His gun popped three times and the man dropped like a stone.

"I think I'm hit, Jeff," Julio moaned. Cat turned on the light to the bedroom as Jeff dragged the dead man's inert body all the way into the apartment and closed the door. He rushed to Cat and Julio.

Julio lay on his belly on the floor, a red streak growing into a large stripe across the back of his boxer shorts. Jeff pulled Julio's shorts down and found an oozing pool of blood in a narrow groove across Julio's buttocks. "I don't think it's any more than a deep scratch, Julio. Stay there and we'll wash off the blood." Cat ran to the bathroom and returned with a wet washcloth and tenderly washed the blood away. The bullet had made a three-inch-long furrow across Julio's butt.

"A couple of big Band-Aids and some clean shorts and you'll be good as new," Jeff laughed nervously, his voice quaking.

"I'm sure glad he didn't shoot on the other side. I thought I was headed for the priesthood with the first guy. It hurts like hell and I'm scared to death. Are you okay, Cat?" Julio said as Jeff moved closer to her, putting his arm around her.

She nodded mutely, shivering, and grabbed Jeff's hand fiercely. She then asked, "What do we do now? Where can we go now?"

ROYAL REVENGE

"Finish helping Julio and then put on your clothes. I'm going to go move their car to the back. Then, I'll put these guys in it and take it somewhere and leave it. After that I guess we go back to the condo in Miami Beach. Do you have any better ideas?" he asked Julio.

"Not unless you want to leave the fucking country as fast as our legs can carry us, but I'm sure that's too intelligent a solution for us to contemplate. Help me up and then we'll clean up the mess. Are they both dead?"

"Yes, and I'm sure this one is one of the guys who came to Cat's apartment," Jeff said as he felt for a non-existent pulse on the first man. He went to the kitchen and pulled on the rubber gloves used hours ago to do the dinner dishes. He then rummaged through the pockets of the second man until he found the keys to their car.

"Get dressed, pack up everything again, and don't touch anything on them. We have to hurry before it gets light," he said as he went out the door.

After moving the gunmen's car to the back, Jeff carried the bodies down the steps and dumped them in the trunk. The sickly stench of human excrement and blood, combined with the sight of the first man's smashed head, made him sick before he finished. He used one of Julio's towels to wipe himself off and then drove the car to another apartment house about a mile away. He parked the car in a vacant space and locked it.

Careful to avoid being seen, Jeff then wiped himself off again, and ran rapidly back to Julio's apartment, dumping the gloves and the towel in a Dumpster a block away. On the way upstairs, he picked up the dumbbell he had dropped in the bushes earlier.

Cat and Julio had the Mercedes and Julio's car packed with everything they were taking. Jeff showered and dressed while Cat and Julio finished cleaning up the gory mess in the apartment as best they could.

Dawn was breaking over the bay as they arrived at Jeff's condo. They parked both cars in the back and unloaded them. After lugging everything up the stairs, Cat made coffee while Julio and Jeff sat talking softly on the balcony.

"We need to go to the police, Jeff. We can't keep this up much longer. We were lucky this morning, but somehow they knew where we were. How much longer will it take them to find us here? Someone is bound to know those guys didn't get us this morning. They aren't going to give up. Let's quit before we all get killed."

"I want to meet with Raphael Fabriza first. Then we'll go to the police. Let's just get through the rest of the day."

"I hope we can survive the rest of the fucking day! Frankly, I'm scared shitless, and you should be too. Cat is terrified! And my ass hurts."

"After what they've tried so far, they're not going to give up, no matter what we do. How could they have found us last night? I thought no one knew where your place was. And how could they have known we were there anyway?"

"Only two people knew even the phone number. It's unlisted so they couldn't have linked it to me unless they own someone at Ma Bell. Claudio Contreras and Giuseppe Portales are the only ones who knew for sure.

"Maybe Raphael, assuming Claudio gave the number to him, but hopefully he isn't that stupid. Besides, I really don't think Raphael is behind this. He's as fond of Cat as I am. He also needs her as a cover for his thing with Claudio. There's a rotten apple somewhere else. Obviously, we can eliminate Giuseppe. And, this morning we can find out just who Claudio gave the number to. Then maybe we'll know something. Can you see the place in the park where Claudio is to meet us from here?"

ROYAL REVENGE

"Yeah. It's right over there," Jeff said, pointing to the east and south. We'll be able to see his car when he comes up. Why?"

"When he comes up, let's call his car and have him walk up the park. Then, we can see what happens from there," Julio said, as he squirmed uncomfortably in his chair.

"That's a good idea. One of us could go in my car to the north end of the park and pick him up. The other can stay here and keep in touch through the phone in my car. At least we'll know if he's alone."

"He knows me, so I'll go pick him up. You and Cat can stay here. But, you must promise me that this evening we go to the police. I think if we make it that far we've wound off all the string we have. Okay? Surely, you don't want any more of this?" Julio asked with a look of concern.

"Okay. I agree. I think you're right. We're way out of our league."

Cat brought the coffee out and they relayed their conclusions and plans to her. "There's one other person who knew we were with Julio," Cat said.

"Who?" Jeff and Julio said at once.

"Hector Rodriguez. Claudio called him for me. Don't you remember? I'm sure he called him at the club."

"Shit! When Hector is at the club, he talks to a lot of people. I'm sure he's told someone that he knew Cat was safe, and probably that she was with me. With the Fabriza contacts, it wouldn't be all that hard to come up with the phone number and address of my rental apartment. There might have even been someone there who had crashed before at my place. I'm sure that's how those guys found out where we were," Julio said.

"Well, it's done. I'm going to take a nap. It's probably going to be a very long day," Jeff said. He looked at Julio with a smirk. "Stand up and let me look at your ass again. It's probably time to change your bandage."

Julio stood up and went in the living room and dropped his pants. Jeff took off the old bandages and after washing the wound again with disinfectant, put on new bandages. Julio looked over his shoulder and laughed, "I knew about getting gut-shot, but never heard of getting butt-shot. You certainly have soft hands, Jeffrey, you fool," he said with an affected lisp.

Jeff smiled and slapped his ass hard enough to cause a little pain, and then went to lie down. Cat joined him. "Hold me, Jeff," she said as she put her arms around him. He was asleep in seconds.

Jeff woke up to the sound of the phone at 6:30 a.m., having completely slept through his normal 4 a.m. ritual. He ran to the living room just as Julio was starting to pick it up.

"Let the answering machine get it! We're not supposed to be here, remember?" Jeff said.

After four rings, the recorder clicked on. "Jeff, this is Jesse Castillo. News has reached me that you are now involved over your head, as I was afraid you would be. You must call me as soon as you can. It is most urgent that I speak with you."

Jeff picked up the phone before Castillo hung up. "Mayor Castillo, this is Jeff."

"Jeff, I'm glad I found you. You remember me mentioning a man named Herman Guerra. He called a few minutes ago regarding Catarina Contreras, the girlfriend of Raphael Fabriza, who was kidnapped yesterday. Guerra believes you were with her.

"He is afraid that a war will erupt unless the Fabriza family is assured that she is safe. He is willing to talk with you about the man Gaspar if you wish, as a gesture of goodwill. The city doesn't need problems between these two families. I would consider it a favor if you would advise Fabriza that the girl is safe. Julio can tell you how to contact him. Meeting with Guerra is up to you."

ROYAL REVENGE

"Why does he think it was me with her, unless he was responsible for the attack on her?" Jeff asked.

"These people have ways of knowing these things. I had heard already that you met Catarina Contreras at the *Casa de Liberacion*, and I assumed that the man seen by the police leaving her apartment was you, since the description of him was so similar. If I knew that, he certainly would. Please call Raphael Fabriza. It may help avoid further problems. Guerra can answer your other questions, if you still wish to see him."

"I need to come downtown late this afternoon. I'd like to meet with him then. Shall I come to your office?"

"You could meet in a restaurant near my office. It wouldn't be advisable for him to come here. There is a good place to meet just a block from my office, to the east on Flagler Street. I will have him meet you there at four. The name of the place is Cafe Havana. He will identify himself to you if you don't remember him. I'll call you later to confirm it."

"I'll wait for your call, Mayor," Jeff said as he hung up.

Jeff told Julio and Cat of his conversation. "Of course, I didn't tell him that Fabriza already knew Cat was safe. Or that she was here. I'm beginning to get paranoid about everyone."

At 8:45 they were back on the balcony. Just before nine a long black limousine pulled up and parked on Ocean Drive near the middle of Lummus Park.

Julio called the number in the car. "Claudio, this is Julio. Lock the car and walk to the north end of the park near 14th Street. I'll pick you up there."

"But Julio ..."

"We've had some problems, Claudio. Just do what I say, please," Julio said as he hung up.

"Call the car again, Julio. Let's see what happens this time," Jeff said. Julio quickly dialed the number again. This time it was busy. "What the fuck?" Julio said, skeptically.

"He's calling someone else. We're going to have to be very careful," Jeff said.

Moments later they watched as the young man locked the car and started walking north. "Try it again," Jeff said. This time there was no answer. "It's too hot for anyone else to stay in the car with it locked up like that. Let's see what happens when he reaches the north end of the park. Take my car and give me the keys to yours. Drive up Collins to where Ocean Drive cuts in. Then turn south. Don't stop unless I tell you to. There's a gun in the glove compartment. Put it in the pocket in the driver's door. You can get to it easily there if you need to."

"I've never even held a gun before. Besides, you can't think Claudio ..." Julio protested.

"I'd never killed anyone before, either, but I did this morning. I don't trust anyone now. You shouldn't either. I'll call you when I see you turn onto Ocean."

Cat and Jeff watched as the red Mercedes came slowly down Ocean Drive. Jeff called the limousine again. There was still no answer. Claudio was standing on the curb at the north end of the park, plainly ill at ease. The Mercedes continued down the street and Jeff called Julio. "He's standing on the curb near 14th Street and I'm pretty sure he's alone. I called the limo again and there's no answer. Stay on the phone while you pick him up. I'd like to know who he called. Then take Ocean Drive all the way south until you get on Collins again. Go nice and slow so I can watch you. Let's see if anyone follows you. If I tell you someone's following you, kick his ass out of the car and get out of there as fast as you can. Okay?"

"I feel like fucking Double-O-Seven. But I will follow your instructions to the letter, fearless leader," Julio said. "I see him now. Shall I pick him up?"

"You're in the clear, Julio. I don't see anyone following you. Stay on the line, though, until I tell you to hang up."

ROYAL REVENGE

Jeff heard Julio calling to Claudio over the noise of the traffic and the honking horns of the cars as Claudio ran across the street. "Hey, Julio. Nice car!" he said as he got in. "Why all the mysteries, man? What's happening? Whose car is this?"

"Hello, Claudio. Let me ask the questions first. Who did you call from the limo after we talked this morning?" Jeff heard Julio ask.

"I called Raphael's secretary. I have to call in if I ever leave the car. How'd you know I called anyone?"

"Let me ask the questions. Does Raphael know where you are, or that you were meeting me and Cat?"

"Sure. He's been scared to death about her. I had to tell him she was okay. He wants me to bring her to his father's place in Boca, until they find out who shot our place up. Why?"

"Jeff, I guess you heard all that. What do you want me to do now?" Julio asked into the phone.

"Go up Collins to 16th. Park by Flamingo Park. Walk in and find a bench to sit on. We'll meet you there. Stay on the phone 'til you get there. I can't see you anymore."

Minutes later Julio told Jeff he was leaving the car and hung up. Jeff and Cat hurried down to Julio's car and went to meet them. Cat hesitated and her eyes narrowed when Jeff put one of the pistols he'd acquired that morning in her purse, but she said nothing.

Jeff parked Julio's Mustang a few spaces down from the Mercedes. He and Cat walked into the park until they found Julio and Claudio sitting on a bench. Cat ran to Claudio and hugged him. She then introduced Jeff. They shook hands firmly. "Why don't you tell Claudio what's happened up to now, Cat, then maybe he'll understand all the intrigue," Jeff said.

They sat together at the base of one of the tall royal palms in the park as Cat related everything to Claudio. His eyes kept getting wider and wider as he realized what they had been through. When she had finished, Claudio caressed her cheek and looked at Jeff. He was very earnestly concerned about what Jeff thought, and it showed.

"Raphael and the Fabriza family have nothing to do with this. I am sure of that. The man Gaspar was a renegade. He left Miami because he killed one of the Fabriza people. Raphael thinks he worked for Espinoza," Claudio said the name with hate and disgust. "Raphael will meet with you and tell you these things himself. He would do nothing to hurt Cat, and he has no reason to hurt you or Julio. I suggest we call him and meet with him now. You will see that the Fabriza family is not your problem."

Jeff looked at Julio. Julio shrugged. They both believed Claudio. It was obvious to them that he cared very deeply for his sister and would not wish her harmed.

"Go back to my car and call him. We can meet back here in an hour. Do you need to pick him up?" Jeff asked.

"Yes. He doesn't drive. Do you want to meet here?"

"Why not? We'll get sandwiches across the street and eat in the park," Jeff said, somewhat at ease for the first time in the last twenty-four hours. "Might as well make a picnic out of it."

"I will call Raphael now. He will be happy to meet you. I am also happy for Cat. It is easy to see why she likes you," Claudio said as he shook Jeff's hand warmly.

13

An hour later, Jeff met Raphael Fabriza for the first time. They had left the limousine at Lummus Park again and had come in Julio's car to the spot where Jeff and Cat had arranged a picnic under the shade of the trees. It was hot, but a pleasant breeze from the ocean made it bearable. Jeff found Raphael to be as charming and urbane as Cat had pictured him. After pleasantries and lunch, Raphael spoke to Jeff.

"I would prefer to converse privately with you, in English. Some of what I tell you Cat and Claudio and Julio do not need to know, for their own safety. Do you object?"

"Not at all," Jeff said, and then he told Cat and Claudio in Spanish of Raphael's wishes. Jeff and Raphael moved a bit apart from Cat, Julio, and Claudio, who were happy to talk to each other after the events they had endured.

Raphael took a long pull on his beer and began speaking. "Claudio told me everything you told him about your situation as he drove me here. As you know, my family is involved in what you call the mob. It has been this way for all my life, and I cannot escape it. Someday, I will be forced to carry on as the head of this family. God will be my judge, so I do not apologize to you for anything. The reason I will tell you certain things today is because I want you to take Cat away from Miami, so she will be safe. This is very important to Claudio, and Claudio is very dear to me. I can protect Claudio, and I believe Julio's involvement is not of interest to the people who object to your investigation.

"Two years ago, my father told me that we had a traitor in our family. Many of the things we were doing without problems before were being sabotaged now. Shipments were intercepted, men were arrested, some were killed. The man Gaspar was part of it. Before we were able to catch and punish him, he disappeared. For a while things were normal. Then we found the same problems with our operation in Canada. Two of our best people were killed, probably by Gaspar. Our own people in Canada were the ones who turned Gaspar over to the police.

"Unfortunately, we still have a problem. There is one of the Espinoza family very high up in our organization. They have begun to invade our territories and are now doing very well in several places where our family once was in control. Especially in Canada. They are very smart. You probably think the most difficult part of the business is getting the merchandise into the United States. That has been solved for years.

"The biggest problem is storing the merchandise and moving it throughout the two countries without getting caught. The Espinoza family has found a way to do that in Canada. We are not sure how. In many cases, our normal methods have failed because information gets to the authorities or because our shipments are hijacked by the Espinoza family.

"We believe the attack on Cat's apartment was because of your inquiries about Gaspar. Miami is a very small community in our circles. It is well known that you believed my family responsible for your wife's death. The only person who would be bothered by your questions is the one in our midst who works for Espinoza. The fact that you were there in the apartment with Cat was coincidental. No one in the two families knows the true nature of the relationship I have with Cat. Many would think she has information she could give you. You can see that she does not. You must think of the people you have contacted about Gaspar. One of them has concern that you may somehow discover the traitor in our family. That is the only explanation for your difficulties in Miami."

"But why am I involved in the first place? The police in Canada say the problems at the company I purchased there have no relation to Gaspar," Jeff asked.

"The police know nothing. They are interested only in closing their files. They still would be looking for Gaspar if we hadn't told them where to find him. They told you he worked for us. That is untrue. I would say he was working for someone at the company in Canada. That is the only explanation."

"But, the troubles stopped. If Gaspar worked for the people up there ..."

"Gaspar is dead. You said the troubles stopped after you completed your purchase. Your wife was killed, and the troubles began before you completed the purchase. It is possible that Gaspar was a little slow in completing his contract. It is possible that the fact the purchase was completed made further action against you unprofitable for those who hired him.

"There is no question in my mind that the whole situation was related to your purchase of that company. Someone wanted it stopped, and killing your wife was their method. It failed, and it's over. I'm sorry for you, but I'm sure the people responsible for your wife's death are in Canada, not in Miami.

"I am very serious when I tell you that you must leave Miami. You endanger yourself and Cat, as well as your friend here," Raphael indicated Julio. "The second attempt means that you have been identified as a threat to these people. Please go home. There will be a great deal of trouble here soon. The reaction of my father will be swift and violent. He considers the attack on Cat as an attack on himself. He will react against the Espinoza people. There will be blood in the streets tomorrow or the next day. If you are here, you, and those with you, will be in great danger. I cannot help you further."

"But ..."

J. Trey Weeks

"There is nothing here for you. Accept that. The connection to your wife's death is in Canada. In Miami, you are simply in the middle of our problems. You can do nothing here except get yourself killed. And maybe Cat and Julio. Leave Miami. Leave immediately."

"I still don't know why someone tried to kill us twice. It doesn't make sense."

"Someone tried to kill or scare Cat to keep her away from you. The second time the target could as well have been you, or Cat, or even Julio. They want to make your questions stop."

Jeff still wasn't convinced but realized that Raphael had told him everything he was going to. "We will leave tomorrow. You have been most kind to see me and tell me these things, Raphael. We'll take you back to your car now, and call Claudio tomorrow before we leave. I will take very good care of Cat," Jeff said as he rose. They shook hands warmly.

The others had disposed of the litter from their picnic and were ready to leave. Jeff handed Julio his car keys and retrieved his own. "I'll take Cat with me, Julio, if you'll take Raphael and Claudio back to their car," Jeff said.

A few minutes later, Jeff and Cat were going up the stairs to the condo when they heard, and felt, an immense explosion. Jeff burst through the door and ran to the balcony. Raphael's limousine, what was left of it, was across the street. It was burning furiously, and bits and pieces of it were scattered up and down Ocean Drive. He could see Julio's car parked on the street, about fifty yards further south. Julio and Raphael were crouched behind it.

Raphael and Julio began walking rapidly toward the condo as the sound of sirens became louder. They were staring down at the street and Julio was supporting Raphael with an arm around his waist.

"Claudio! Where is Claudio? Where is he?" Cat demanded as she stared in shock across the street and realized what the burning hulk represented. Jeff took her in his arms. She slapped him hard across the face. "*Bastardo*! They have killed Claudio. He is dead because of you and your damn questions. He is dead, he is dead," she sobbed as she fell against Jeff, her body limp and wracked with grief.

Julio and Raphael came in moments later. Raphael had tears running down his cheeks. He looked at Jeff and shook his head silently. He came over to Cat and embraced her. They held each other up, silently grieving.

Jeff and Julio gently moved them into the bedroom, and Jeff closed the bedroom door. He then went across the room and closed the door and curtains to the balcony. Julio was sitting on the couch, his head in his hands.

"What happened?" Jeff asked softly as he sat beside Julio.

Julio looked up, tears running down his cheeks. "We parked at the first available spot. Claudio wanted to start the engine in the car and get the inside cool for Raphael. We were sitting in my car, talking, when Claudio walked down to the limo and he opened the door and got in. Then the fucking thing just blew up. With poor Claudio in it. It literally exploded in a million pieces. There were big chunks of it flying everywhere. The rest was just a big ball of fire.

"Raphael went into shock. I had to run around the car and hold him down to keep him away from his car. I thought we'd better come up here before the cops came. I'm pretty sure there was an old couple killed beside the limo. They were just walking by, Jeff. Just out for a fucking walk and they get blown to eternity. Where in God's name does this end? Have you had enough yet, Jeff? Are you finally convinced that you ought to get out? Raphael told me that he wanted you to take Cat and get out of Miami. I want you to do the same. Get away from here before you get us all killed."

"I told Raphael I would leave tomorrow and take Cat with me. I honestly don't know if she'll still want to go. She blames me for what happened to Claudio. I'm afraid she's right. I never thought it would go this far."

"I've told you and told you. Everyone has told you. This group lives in a different world with different rules. You're not a player. I'm not either."

The sound of sirens was very loud, and then suddenly they were silent. Jeff pulled back the curtain slightly and looked out into the street. The street was blocked entirely with police cars, a fire engine, and ambulances, lights flashing. There were various service people milling around the remains of Raphael's car, which was still exuding wisps of steam and smoke.

Jeff let the curtains drop back as Raphael and Cat emerged from the bedroom. Raphael was completely composed. He was calm and very cold. In fact, he had assumed a completely different personality. He politely asked Jeff for permission to use the phone.

Cat sat wearily on the couch and put her head in her hands. She was still crying softly. She avoided looking at Jeff. Julio went to her and put his arms around her. She put her head on his shoulder and sobbed. Jeff wanted to go to her but resisted. He was miserable for her but realized that he could give her no comfort.

Raphael was apparently talking with his father. "You have heard? My driver, Claudio, was killed when the car blew up. It could well have been me, also. Cat is safe. She is leaving Miami temporarily. Yes, it has started. I will be in Flamingo Park in Miami Beach in fifteen minutes, on the north corner. Please have someone that I know pick me up there. We will make our plans tonight."

He listened intently for a long time, and then continued, "I don't believe I am in danger at the moment. Anyone would think I was with Claudio in the car, unless they were watching, and I don't believe they were or we would have seen them. I am sure it was people from Espinoza. If it had been the man I met I would have been killed. He is leaving tomorrow. I am sure he is not involved. I will see you soon."

Raphael turned to Jeff after hanging up. "I am leaving now. The police will be everywhere around here soon. I am sure they will come to the apartment to ask questions. I think it best that I walk up to the park alone. I will leave through the alley."

He went over to Cat and took her hands and helped her rise from the couch. He hugged her closely and said in a very soft voice, "Go with Jeff to his home in Atlanta. Leave Miami as soon as you can. Claudio was a victim of my family's problems with Espinoza, not of Jeff's questions. You know where to reach me if you need me. We will plan services for Claudio as soon as we can. I will call you through Julio."

He shook hands with Julio and Jeff and left without another word.

Cat came to Jeff and put her arms around him. "I am sorry for hitting you," she said as she put her face into his chest. He was holding her when the phone rang. Jeff let it ring until the answering machine clicked on.

"Jeff. this is Jesse Castillo ..."

Jeff picked up the phone. Cat went to sit on the couch as he said, "The war has already begun, Mayor. A little while ago, Raphael Fabriza's driver, who was his girlfriend's brother, was killed when their car exploded. There is nothing to be done now. Will Guerra still meet with me?"

Julio looked at Jeff with a look of total disbelief.

"My God. I hoped we could avoid this. I do not know about Guerra, Jeff. I will call him now. Hold on while I call him on the other line," the Mayor said. He came back on the line moments later. "He will meet with you. He says he knows nothing of the matter with Fabriza's car. Are you sure you still want to do this? I cannot say that I trust him. You may be in greater danger than before."

"I want to see him," Jeff said.

"You are crazy, but ... Do you remember where to go?"

"Yes, Cafe Havana at four o'clock," Jeff answered as he said good-bye and hung up.

"Now I know you've lost it! You're fucking crazy! What in the hell do you intend to accomplish by meeting the number two man in the Espinoza family? Do you still think this is a fucking chess match?" Julio asked, incredulous.

"That's exactly what it is, and I'm tired of the three of us being used as pawns," Jeff said. "Think about it, Julio. So far, the dead people are my wife and Cat's brother. When do some of the bad guys lose? I propose we change the game. We go on the offense. Guerra is second in command, so he's a real key. As long as we have him, there's no war and we're safe. It's so unlikely that we can probably pull it off."

"What's this 'we' shit? Count me out of this, *Kemo Sabe*. You have lost your mind for sure. Jeff, for God's sake, quit! You're way over your fucking head," Julio said in disgust.

Since they were speaking English, Cat was having trouble following the conversation. She looked from one to the other in bewilderment.

Jeff ignored his objections and continued rapidly, "Here's how I do it, Julio. I'm meeting Guerra. You and Cat are staying here. There will be enough cops around here for the next twenty-four hours that it's the safest place in Miami. Guerra's an accountant. I'm a civilian. He won't expect anything. When I get Guerra, I'll take him to your place in Coral Gables and tie him up and leave him.

"Then, I come back here and we work out the trade. Guerra for no war. Raphael's family will agree to it, because then he'll have Guerra. Espinoza will agree because he loses either way and he loses less by agreeing to no war. I get any information Guerra has, and we have safe passage out of here from both families. It's not checkmate, but at this point, I'll settle for a stalemate."

ROYAL REVENGE

Julio moaned with frustration. Cat looked at them both, and then asked in Spanish, "Will someone please explain to me what is happening?"

"Your boyfriend here has become mentally ill because of this tension. He has delusions of grandeur. He thinks he's a king instead of a pawn. He thinks he can capture the second most powerful man in the Espinoza family. He doesn't understand yet how stupid he is," Julio said to her.

"What does it mean, Jeff? When are we going to Atlanta? We must leave Miami soon. I don't want anymore to do with these people," Catarina said, pleading.

"We're leaving in the morning, Cat. Tonight, we're going to do some damage to these assholes. Maybe we'll even find out who killed Connie and Claudio. You will be safe here with Julio. Don't worry," he said as he took her face in his hands and kissed her.

"Don't worry, he's here from the government and he'll help you," Julio said wearily as he stood up. "I must be one of the inmates and certifiably insane. If I live through all this, I want to be committed to an institution for the rest of my life." Julio paused when he saw neither Cat or Jeff paying attention to him. "Okay, Jeff, what do you want me to do, other than helping you hold the gun to your own head and then to mine?"

"Stay here so I can call you if I need to. I'll be back here by six. Let the machine answer the phone. Take care of Cat. If I'm not back by six, take Cat to Raphael's place in Boca. Call me on my car phone if anything happens I need to know. I'll see you at six."

Julio rolled his eyes. "If everything goes greater than great, and if the whole fucking bunch surrenders when they see you riding in on your silver stallion, you won't be here by six without a shiny new helicopter. Miami traffic is the worst in the world. You won't be at the frigging causeway by six. Jesus, I can't believe you're going to take on the whole Miami Mob single-handed when you can't plan beyond the fucking five o'clock rush hour."

Jeff was obviously irritated as he said, "Okay, Julio, I'll call you at or slightly before six and tell you where I am. If I don't call, leave. Okay? And thanks. I know you think I'm crazy, but I'm sure that I can pull this off. We can't just wait for their next move against us."

"I'm as crazy as he is. Why am I doing this?" Julio asked no one, throwing his hands up in a gesture of total futility.

Cat kissed Jeff passionately and said, "I don't want you to do this, but I know I cannot stop you. You cannot trust them. You must be very careful, Jeff. Come back to me. I've lost Claudio to these people already. I don't want to lose you to them also."

"I will," he said. "I promise you. They'll never know what happened."

"We probably won't either. I hope we don't all die laughing, waiting to see the fucking ending of this comedy," Julio muttered as Jeff went out the door quietly, stuffing one of the guns acquired that morning into the waist of his pants at his back, covering it with his coat.

Julio went to the small bar and held up a bottle of vodka and a bottle of rum. In English, he said, "Catarina, I'm having several drinks, maybe as many as ten. Would you like to continue sober, knowing what's happening, or in a complete drunken stupor, so if by chance you should survive, you survive in relative sanity?"

She looked at him, not understanding a word he said other than her name.

In Spanish, with a great deal of compassion, he said, "Cat, may I make you a drink? I think we both could use one. Then we must get ready to pack up our things and to help Jeff."

ROYAL REVENGE

14

It was well before three o'clock, but it seemed as if Miami's rush hour had already started. Jeff crept forward in the snarled traffic as he made his way downtown to the Royal Floors office. The office was in a building on a side street only a few blocks from Cafe Havana, so he passed the office and parked his car in a garage next to the restaurant. He went inside the restaurant briefly to look around.

Cafe Havana was a remodeled diner, done in Miami's Art Deco rage. The counter was white, with ten bright green and pink chrome-trimmed stools attached to the floor in front of it. The wall behind was covered with a mirror and shelves full of glasses. The booths were also white, with matching pink and green seat cushions. There was an old-fashioned miniature jukebox in each booth. There were only three people at the counter, all young Hispanics, engaged in lively conversation with the young, good-looking Hispanic waitress. Jeff turned and went back through the revolving door. He walked the few blocks back to his company's office.

The Royal Floors receptionist was new and had never met Jeff before. She was polite, but not talkative. The papers from Giuseppe were there with her in a sealed envelope. Jeff sat in the small reception area and scanned the papers. He shook his head in disbelief as he scribbled his signature, agreeing to pay the bank and the Canadians over five million dollars, twenty-one months before the either note was due. He sealed the envelope and handed it back to the receptionist who was busy directing incoming calls. She raised her finger to indicate that he should wait until she finished her call. As soon as she was free, she said, "I'm sorry, Mr. Royal. This is to go by FedEx back to Mr. Portales, correct?" Jeff agreed by nodding. "Is there anything else I can do for you, Mr. Royal?"

As she was talking, he noticed a stack of padded express envelopes beside her. Pointing at the envelopes, Jeff said, "I'd like several of those, please, and some of that wrapping tape, the real strong stuff." She smiled and handed him a few of the envelopes. She then reached below her desk and gave him two rolls of strapping tape. Jeff left after thanking her and walked to his car.

He still had about thirty minutes before Guerra was due to meet him. Jeff took the time to combine three envelopes, putting one within the other, until they were quite heavy and thick. He then checked the ammunition on the silenced pistol with which Julio had almost been killed that morning. He had four bullets left. He checked the Mauser in the driver's door panel. It still had nine bullets left. He put it down under the passenger's seat, along with the strapping tape. He put the other pistol in his express mail package, lightly sealing the outside envelope. Satisfied that the package looked innocuous, he waited until five minutes before four to start walking back toward the restaurant, the package under his arm. He looked around cautiously, to see only average people hurrying to their cars or into the shops and office buildings lining the street. He walked up to a women's store and looked casually into the window. This allowed him to watch the front door of the Cafe Havana without being overly conspicuous.

At exactly four o'clock, Herman Guerra went into the Cafe without a backward glance. Jeff recognized him from their previous meeting almost twelve years before. Herman Guerra was very short, almost tiny, but had a purposeful air about him because of his control of vast money and power. Jeff waited about three minutes to see if he could spot anyone following

Guerra. He didn't, so he entered the cafe. Herman looked like a prosperous banker, well dressed and business-like in a dark pinstriped suit, with a white shirt and bright red tie.

When Jeff approached the booth Herman had occupied, Guerra looked at him momentarily without recognition. Then, a smile spread across his dark face, and he reached across the table and shook hands vigorously with Jeff. "You look quite different, but you look very healthy and well, Jeff. Of course, it has been twelve years since we last met," Guerra said. "I am sorry about your wife. I wish we could meet sometime under more pleasant circumstances. Even last time was unpleasant because of your troubles at the paper."

"I agree," Jeff said as he slid into the seat opposite Guerra. "I'd like the circumstances to be better sometime. But they aren't, so we have to make the best of them." The waitress interrupted him before he could say anything else, asking for their order. They each ordered coffee and returned to their conversation.

"I've just learned to speak Spanish," Jeff said in that language. "and I like to practice. But if you prefer we could speak English."

"It would be much more private if we spoke English here," Guerra said.

"You are aware of the background of my wife's death in Canada and the reason why I'm here?" Jeff asked in English.

Guerra nodded.

"I suggest we get right to the point. What can you tell me about the connection between the killer Gaspar and the Espinoza family?"

Guerra responded in an aloof tone as if holding a press conference. "There is no connection between him and the Espinoza family. Gaspar has worked for the Fabriza family for many years. Over a year ago, he left the country as a result of a killing he did for them. It is possible he still worked for Fabriza during the time he was in Canada. If there were any connection, it would be with Fabriza. However, I do not think there is any connection. In my opinion, Gaspar was working independently, probably for someone in Canada."

They were interrupted briefly while the waitress served the coffee.

"You're saying that your family had no knowledge or influence on Gaspar while he was in Canada?"

"Absolutely not," Guerra said. "Gaspar has never been connected to us."

"Then what about the drug-related killings up there? The Fabrizas and the Espinozas are the primary players in the drug business in Quebec. What did those killings have to do with Gaspar? He did kill two others, didn't he? Fabriza says he was working for you then. You're saying that he was working independently or for them. Who's lying? Who was he working for?"

"I can't answer that, Jeff. I can just say he wasn't working for us. We have had very little to do with Canada in any case, and certainly had no part in your wife's death."

At that moment Jeff was distracted by the door revolving and turned around to see two men in dark suits enter the cafe. They looked strangely out of place in Cafe Havana. They looked directly at him and Guerra before the waitress seated them in the first booth. Jeff thought he saw a brief flash of recognition on Herman's face when he looked at them. He put the express envelope up on the table and loosened the seal, putting his hand in the open end, pointing the other end directly at Herman's chest.

"Are those two guys in the suits that just came in yours, Herman?" he asked, ominously.

"No, Jeff, of course not. I think they are just regular customers, like us," Herman said, smiling weakly.

ROYAL REVENGE

Jeff smiled warmly, but his eyes were cold as ice. "Herman, in this envelope is a gun. It has plenty of bullets in it, and I know how to use it. It belonged to a guy who tried to kill me this morning. I think you might have known him. The gun has a silencer, so I think I could probably kill you and those two up front and still get away without any problem. You would be the third guy I've killed today, so I will have absolutely no problem shooting all three of you. Do you understand me?"

Herman's face was very calm, but a mist of sweat glazed his forehead and upper lip as he nodded and said, "I understand."

"You must do everything I ask, exactly as I tell you. I'm very nervous and I have nothing to lose. Okay?" Jeff asked.

Herman nodded silently and sipped his coffee. It took both his hands to hold the cup still.

"First, call the waitress over and pay the check. Leave her a big tip. Then we will leave. You will go in front of me, walking very slowly, and you will stay very close. If you get more than one foot in front of me, I will shoot you in the back, hopefully in the spine. We will go through the door together. After we get through the door, we will turn to the left and go into the parking garage there. Do not say or do anything else or I'll shoot you first and then I'll worry about what to do next. Now start by paying off the waitress. Understood?"

Guerra nodded, licking his lips nervously. "*Señorita, por favor,*" he called to the waitress as he made the motion of writing in the air. She brought the check totaling three dollars and Guerra left a twenty-dollar bill.

Jeff nodded at him and he stood up and they headed for the front door, walking casually. Neither of the two men seemed to notice them. Jeff's skin crawled up his back and he could feel his testicles shrink up into his body as he and Herman passed their booth, and his back was to them. Sweat trickled in a river down his sides. He and Guerra went rather awkwardly through the revolving front door together and entered the parking garage. Jeff moved closer to Herman, to his side. "Walk up to the next floor. It's a red Mercedes with a black top. On the left side toward the back. You'll be driving," Jeff said as if they were discussing the weather. His hand was still in the express package, but now the barrel of the gun was only inches from Guerra's ribs.

They got to the car and Jeff went to the driver's side and unlocked it. He motioned for Guerra to get in, closed the door and went around and got in the passenger's side. He put the keys in the ignition and said, "We're going to Coral Gables. It's three dollars to get out of the garage. Get your money ready now. Drive very carefully and don't try anything."

"I will have your goddamn balls for this," Guerra hissed.

"I suggest you worry about your own balls right now, Herman. If you keep up with your bad attitude you may make me leave you alive without them," Jeff said as he shoved the barrel of the gun so hard into Guerra's crotch the man's face turned white with pain. "Now do what I tell you, and don't give me any more of your crap. Just drive, very slowly and very carefully."

As they emerged from the garage the two men in suits were leaving the cafe. They both stopped and stared at the car as Herman drove slowly out. Jeff looked out the back window as Guerra drove further down the block. The men conversed briefly, still staring at the car, and then turned and walked very rapidly into the parking garage.

Jeff picked up the car's phone and dialed his condo. The machine answered. After the tone, Jeff said, "Julio, this is Jeff ..."

Julio came on the line. "Jeff, we've been worried about you."

"You shouldn't be, I'm ahead of schedule, Julio. So far there are no problems, except that he's a little irritated with me. Some of his people may be following us, but I'm sure we can lose them. He's driving me to your place now. We're not far and I'll call you from there. Any problems on your end?"

"No. The police visited the apartment. I knew one of them. They wanted to search the place, but I convinced them it wasn't necessary. They never saw Cat. I told them I rented this place for a visit from a friend. They think I'm shacked up. They won't give us any problems, in fact, they'll be around the area all night and that makes me feel safer. Everything else is quiet. Oh, I forgot. Giuseppe called and left a message for you to call him. He said it was important."

"Okay, I'll call you in about ten minutes," Jeff said and then hung up.

"Julio Pozo?" asked Guerra.

Jeff ignored the question.

"He will also be dead as a result of this. So will Miss Contreras. I hope you know what you're doing."

"I know that you are going to do everything I ask, and cause me no problems, or you will be the dead one. That's all either of us needs to know. Now shut up and drive. Turn right at the next corner and pull over into a parking space as soon as you can."

Guerra found a space as soon as he turned the corner. After he parked, Jeff turned off the motor and removed the key. He used some of the tape to tie Guerra's right hand to the gearshift, almost completely covering his expensive Rolex with the sticky tape. As he worked, he kept looking back to see if they had been followed. Satisfied that they had not, he said, "Okay, Herman, now you can drive us to Coral Gables. We're going to Julio's apartment there. I'm sure you know how to get there, right?"

Herman looked at Jeff with undisguised hate. "Pablo Espinoza will never forgive this treatment of me, Jeff. If you let me go now, I will try to ..."

"Shut up, Herman. I don't want you to try anything for me. I think you've done just about all for me that I could ever want.

Just drive the fucking car. If you say one thing more, I'll use the tape to gag you."

A few minutes later Jeff and Guerra arrived at Julio's apartment. Herman had repeatedly denied that he knew where they were going so Jeff had given him directions. Jeff marveled that it had been only twelve hours since he had killed two men in that place. He motioned Herman to park the car in the back and warned him to remain quiet. Jeff put the Mauser in his belt and the other pistol back into the express envelope, with all of the remaining tape. He then took the keys and released Guerra by unwinding the tape. He locked the car after they had gotten out.

Holding the small man's arm very tightly, so tightly Guerra winced with pain, Jeff propelled him up the stairs, and let them into the apartment with the key from the potted plant beside the door. The rusty smell of blood and the chemical smell of the bleach used to clean up the place hit them as they entered. He locked and chained the door and emptied the express envelope, putting the Mauser and the tape down on the floor.

With the silenced pistol he wordlessly motioned Herman to sit on the end of the old-fashioned couch. Using all of one roll of tape, Jeff taped Herman's left arm very securely to the wooden frame of the couch back, taped his right arm to the wooden arm of the couch, and tied his feet together. For good measure, he then tied his bound feet to the coffee table. Guerra was virtually immobile, rather uncomfortable, and plainly furious. He glared silently at Jeff.

"Now, Herman, sit quietly while I call in, then we'll talk," Jeff said as he dialed his condo. The machine answered, but Julio picked up as soon as Jeff identified himself. "We're in your apartment, Julio. If I don't call in thirty minutes, call and tell Raphael where to find him, and get out of there."

Jeff hung up the phone and went to sit on the coffee table in front of Herman Guerra. He casually pointed the silenced pistol at him. Guerra was starting to show slight signs of panic in addition to his discomfort, as a bead of sweat rolled down the side of his face. Jeff smiled at him without warmth. "I'm going to ask you some questions, Herman, and you're going to answer every one of them. If you don't, we'll call Raphael Fabriza and tell him where you are. I'm sure he'll take very good care of you.

"If you cooperate with me, we won't call anyone. You can probably get out of that tape in a few hours or days if you really work at it. On the other hand, if you really piss me off, I can't tell you what I'll do."

"Go fuck yourself, *bastardo*! If you shoot me, you will be the next to die. I will tell you nothing," Guerra said, his eyes blazing, his body rigid.

Without answering, Jeff calmly walked into the kitchen and came back with the biggest knife he could find. He sat down again and pushed the point of it through the pant leg of Guerra's expensive suit, and then with a not-too-gentle sawing motion, cut away the material up to his crotch. Jeff then did the same to the other pant leg. Herman's eyes got bigger and bigger as he watched, partly in fascination, partly in horror. Jeff cut away the entire front of his pants.

As he cut through the first part of Guerra's underwear, Jeff said very coldly, but almost in a whisper, "I will stuff your *cajones* in your ears if you don't answer my next question. Please don't make me get mad, Herman. I have nothing to lose at this point."

Truly afraid now, Guerra's entire body went limp. "What do you want to know? You must understand that I don't concern myself with the day to day operations. Some of what you want I will not know. I will tell you what I can. Just get that knife away from me!"

Jeff put the knife down on the floor beside the coffee table. "That's better, Herman. First, you can tell me what Gaspar was doing in Canada for Espinoza. I will warn you that I know some things already, like the fact that you have a man in the Fabriza family, so don't try to tell me any lies."

Guerra was totally subdued as he began talking. "Gaspar came to us about two years ago. He said he knew we had a man placed in the Fabriza organization and that he wanted to work with us, since he thought that we would soon have the advantage. At first, we thought it was a trap set by Fabriza, so we gave him a couple of very dirty jobs to do. He was very efficient and carried them out in a way that we knew we could trust him. Unfortunately, the police almost got him, so we got him out of the country, first to the Bahamas, and then to Canada.

"Up there, he started to work for us against the Fabriza family. His goal was to take control of the distribution system they had in Quebec. He removed and then replaced several of their most important people. But he was often on drugs and out of control and in the process, he destroyed what remained of their network.

"After that, we began using a legitimate business like we have started doing here, one with lots of trucks moving around the country. The business we used was Dominion Distributors. The network was just established last summer. Gaspar set up a ring of workers at Dominion to move merchandise from Quebec to the western provinces. Your personal involvement when you began the purchase was regarded as a threat to what he had set up. The thing with your wife was just to scare you away. Then it became a simple case of Gaspar getting out of control."

Jeff looked at him with total disbelief. "A simple case? I ought to cut your throat right now, you fucking son of a bitch. How can you ...?"

At that moment Jeff heard a slight scratching noise outside the door. With a threatening motion of the gun, he indicated for Guerra to remain silent. Jeff picked up the Mauser and the knife and moved rapidly in a crouch toward the kitchen. The scratching noise stopped, and then, seconds later, the door burst inward, ripping the frame from the wall and breaking the chain in half.

Guerra's eyes were wide with terror as one of the men from the restaurant followed the door inward and aimed a pistol at him. Jeff shot the man twice with the silenced pistol. As he died with a spasm his pistol discharged into Guerra's stomach with a quiet "pop". Guerra screamed in agony and fright. Jeff lay on the floor behind the divider to the kitchen as the second man entered in a crouch with his gun held in front of him in the "shooter's stance".

In a split second, he glanced at Guerra and the dead man on the floor, then saw Jeff and fired at him, splintering the wood inches above his head. Jeff shot twice. The man cursed with pain as he dropped and rolled across the floor of the living room. The man shot again, hitting the lamp above the kitchen table, which exploded in shards of glass. Jeff pulled the trigger again but realized as the gun failed to discharge that he was out of ammunition.

The gunman fired as Jeff grabbed for the Mauser. Jeff felt a flash of pain and then a burning sensation in his leg as the Mauser discharged with an incredible ear-splitting roar, and the top of the man's head exploded in a pink-misted cloud. He fell forward and was silent in the thick pool of blood forming on the carpet under his face.

Jeff's ears were ringing from the sound of the Mauser as he looked at his leg to try to gauge the degree of his wound. It was very painful but appeared to have just broken through the skin on the fleshy part of his calf and exited on the other side, without severe damage. Jeff tied his handkerchief around his leg, shut the door as best he could, and limped over to look at Herman Guerra.

The man was sweating profusely, and his face was very pale and drawn. Blood pulsed and bubbled through his shirtfront onto his exposed underwear where Jeff had cut away his pants. He opened his mouth to speak and a pink bubble of saliva and blood formed and then burst as he exhaled. Jeff leaned forward as Guerra whispered with his dying breath, " ... at Fabriza ... Paul Carmona ... Canada network ... controlled by Caa ..." And then he died.

Jeff worked frantically with the butcher knife to remove the tape binding Guerra and put the remnants of the tape and the knife in the express envelope along with the cartridge expelled from the Mauser. He wiped the silenced pistol off with a towel and placed it in Guerra's hand. He put the towel in the envelope and looked out the door.

Miraculously, no one appeared to be in the courtyard. He shoved the Mauser into the waistband at the back of his pants and took a last look at the carnage in the apartment. He closed the damaged door as best he could behind him and walked as quickly as he could to his car. He got in, sat for a few moments, breathed deeply, and drove from the parking lot. He was two blocks away when he picked up the car phone and dialed the Miami Beach condo.

His hand was shaking so badly it took two attempts to dial the number. On the fourth ring, the machine answered. Jeff listened with impatience to the recorded message. Julio picked up as soon as Jeff identified himself.

"Julio, call Raphael and tell him that Guerra is at your place. He's dead along with two others. Raphael should try to remove them immediately, so you won't be involved. Tell him it's possible someone around there heard something, so his people must be very careful. He can keep Guerra's death quiet and avoid the war. I also know the name of a man that he wants very badly. I'll tell him who it is when we're all safe. I want you

ROYAL REVENGE

and Cat to meet me somewhere else. I'm pretty sure I know who's behind all this."

Julio sighed with total resignation. "I knew it. They're going to kill us all. I knew you would make it worse. I knew it."

"Julio, calm down and think! Go get your car and take it to the back. Pack up our stuff again and bring it with you. We need a place to meet." Jeff thought rapidly and then said, "Twelve years ago, we celebrated my demise from the newspaper in a particular place. It had a U-shaped bar and the waitress spilled a pitcher of beer on you. Is it still there?"

"Oh, you mean ..."

"Don't say the name. Is it still there?"

"Yes."

"I'll meet you and Cat there in what, a half-hour?"

"Okay, Jeff. But this is the end. After this I'm going away. I don't want any more of this crap."

"Just call Raphael and tell him what I told you. Don't forget to mention that I have the name he wants. Then get to the meeting place as fast as you can. Drive around a bit to make sure you're not followed. Cat and I are leaving tonight. Oh, and bring some bandages and the medical kit," Jeff said.

"Jeff, what happened? Are you hurt?"

"Just a little. It's no worse than yours. Hurry, Julio. I think we need to move very quickly," Jeff said as he hung up.

15

T. J. Murphy's was an old-style bar that had existed on the edge of downtown Miami since long before anyone remembered. It was a favorite watering hole for established executives working in downtown. Many of them had been regular Murphy's clients all their working lives.

The huge old U-shaped bar of polished wood was unusual in that it attracted most of the patrons. Certainly most of the regulars preferred it to the battered and scarred tables scattered in haphazard fashion around the remaining floor space. A towering center island held almost every kind of liquor available, in addition to twelve different beers on tap at the bar. The walls were almost obscured with pictures, letters, newspaper articles, and other memorabilia arranged with total disorder, many stuck to the wall with tape now turned brown with age. The wooden floor was generally cleaned only often enough to satisfy the health department.

The only entertainment was an ancient and deteriorating dartboard, which no one ever used, and two ancient color TV's on the wall at each end of the bar. Drinks were generous and strong, and the beer pitchers were huge, heavy glass, served very cold. The solid glass mugs of beer were so large that most women, those who strayed by mistake into this male haven, needed both hands to lift them.

The bartenders were well trained to be old-fashioned philosophers, great listeners, amateur psychologists, and professional drink mixers. They were very popular with the clientele, and most had been there for years. Murphy's proprietor, Thomas John O'Brian Murphy, was the third generation to run the bar. His success at finding and keeping bartenders did not extend to his staff of waitresses. Most of them were "Tommy's" ex-wives or ex-girlfriends, hired only because of his own soft heart, and their incompetence and clumsiness were well known.

It was to Murphy's that Julio and Jeff had retreated many years before to drink away the pain of Jeff's firing from the Star. They had decided to sit at one of the tables, so they could commiserate in private. It was typical of Murphy's waitress staff that the second pitcher of beer they ordered ended upside down in Julio's lap. It was also typical of Tommy that the rest of their drinks for the evening were on the house. They had taken full advantage of Murphy's hospitality that evening. It was to Murphy's that Jeff drove this evening to meet Julio and Cat.

The neighborhood in which Murphy's was located had gone through several changes since Jeff had last been there. For one, virtually all the signs around the bar were now in Spanish. In addition, almost all the storefronts had heavy bars on the windows. Jeff was disappointed to see that the once-bright and colorful windows at Murphy's had been almost obscured by the same heavy bars. But inside, absolutely nothing had changed. He recognized the faces of several of the barkeeps and even some of the customers, although all of the waitresses were different.

With his express package, now containing only the Mauser under his arm, Jeff walked in. He did his best to conceal his slight limp and to ignore the pain in his leg as he moved to a table in a corner facing the door. A cheerful waitress with hair of glaring gold straw and lips obscured by a wide stripe of bright red took his order for a pitcher of beer with a frozen mug.

Julio and Cat came in about five minutes later. Jeff signaled to them and they came to his table. Every male head in the room turned to watch Cat with appreciation as she glided to the table. They returned to their conversation and drink only when she was seated, many with obvious reluctance. She kissed Jeff and caressed his cheek with her hand when he stood up to hold her chair. "Thank God you are safe," she whispered. "Julio said you were hurt. I know a doctor who will see you tonight."

"I'm okay, Cat. I'm not hurt badly. I have a deep scratch on my leg kind of like the one on Julio's butt. I'll wash it out and bandage it later. I don't think I need a doctor."

"The first aid stuff is in the car. We can fix you up when we leave. What happened with Guerra? Who killed him?" Julio asked.

"After I got to your place, the guys I thought I'd lost, that I'm sure I lost, came after us. One of them shot Guerra. I shot both of them."

"Holy shit! You've got to be a real pain in the ass for these people. Were they from Espinoza? Did they follow you?"

"I don't think they were protecting Guerra at that point. They seemed to be after both of us. And I don't think they followed us because I was very careful to watch for them. They apparently knew we were meeting at Cafe Havana. And then they seemed to know where I was taking Guerra. I just can't figure how. Did you tell anyone where we were?"

"Of course not! No one but Cat and I knew you were there, and we didn't know that until you called us."

"What did Raphael say when you called him?" Jeff asked Julio after the waitress finally returned with two more frozen mugs.

"He sent some people to clean my apartment, again. He wants us to come to Boca tonight. He assures us we will be safe there. I think we should go. Raphael will contact Espinoza. He thinks everything will be quiet for a day or two. Of course, he is also very interested in the name that you know. What's all that about?"

"You don't want to know, Julio. Have you got all our stuff?"

"It's in the car. What do you mean, I don't want to know? You got me in this thing up to my fucking eyeballs. I'd prefer to know everything."

"Trust me a little longer, Julio. You don't want to know this. Cat and I are going to Atlanta from here. You should go to Boca. I'll call Raphael from Atlanta tomorrow and tell him everything I found out. In the meantime, the less you know, the safer you are. Okay?"

"I guess so, but I still don't like it. How are you going to get to Atlanta?"

"As fast as I can, in a way I hope they'll never figure. You don't want to know that either." Turning to Cat, he asked, "Do you still want to go with me?"

"Of course," she said without hesitation, looking directly into his eyes.

"Okay, let's drink up and get moving. I want you to take a cab up to Boca, Julio. It's best if you leave your car here."

"You're crazy. After one night down here, there won't be enough left for them to tow away. Besides, cab fare to Boca will be almost a hundred dollars. That's if I can find one who wants to go that far."

"They know the car. A lot of the time they know where we are. They have to assume you'll go to Boca. Leave the car. If it's damaged, I'll pay whatever the insurance won't. Here's cab fare," Jeff said as he handed Julio a hundred-dollar bill.

"I'm getting real tired of this cloak and dagger stuff. Will we ever be normal people again?" Julio asked earnestly.

"After tomorrow, Julio. I promise. Do you still have the phone number of my car?" Julio nodded, and Jeff continued, "I'll want you to call me when you get to Boca. I'll feel better knowing you're safe. We might as well get going. We'll put the stuff in my car and Cat can sit in your lap while we find you a cab. Let's go."

Jeff put twenty dollars on the table and they left Murphy's, to the delight of the patrons, who got to watch Cat cross the room again. After transferring, with some difficulty, the garbage bags full of their belongings from Julio's car to the small Mercedes, Julio bandaged Jeff's leg, as best he could, while they stood in the street. Jeff secured the Mauser in the driver's door pocket, and then drove around until they found a cab for Julio nearby. After embracing both of them, and telling them to be careful, Julio got in the cab and left. Jeff locked the doors and started driving. Leaving Miami on I-95, after a while he turned west on I-575.

"Where are you going, Jeff? This isn't the way to Atlanta. You should have gone north, up the Interstate to the Turnpike," Cat said.

He patted her leg and smiled affectionately as he said, "We're going to fool them this time, Cat. We're headed for Alligator Alley, the Everglades and Naples. We'll catch a plane there for Atlanta. I'm afraid to use any of the airports around here. They always seem to know where we are. Your seat will recline all the way back. Relax, and sleep if you can. It's a long drive."

She hesitated briefly before she said, "Okay, Jeff. I can drive some of the way if you want." And then she closed her eyes and was asleep moments later.

The Mercedes was quiet and purred with power as Jeff accelerated onto the freeway. Thirty minutes later, after negotiating through the never-ending construction in Fort Lauderdale at the start of the Everglades Parkway, he turned west and increased his speed effortlessly. Turning on his radar detector, he set the cruise control at 100. The car wasn't even breathing hard. Jeff allowed himself a few minutes to enjoy the power and luxury of the car before he picked up the phone and dialed information. Cat stirred softly but did not wake.

After getting the number and asking the operator to connect him, Jeff called a charter air service in Naples that Royal Floors had used before. They confirmed they had a small jet available for charter and could be ready to leave when he arrived in Naples later that evening. Jeff agreed to pay cash and they agreed that the destination, as long as it was within the U.S., could be determined, and the flight plan filed, after he arrived.

The phone buzzed softly just after he hung up. It was Julio. "I'm safe and sound, Jeff. They're treating me like royalty. Jesus, you ought to see this place. They must have torn down the fucking Taj Mahal to furnish it. Raphael says everything's cool for a day or two. They cleaned my apartment with no problems, apparently. I'm even getting new carpet tomorrow. He asked that you call him with that name as soon as possible."

"Tell him I'll call him tomorrow, probably just after lunch. I'm glad you're safe, Julio. I hope this will be all over and we'll get back to normal by the end of the day. I'll call you. *Adios, mi amigo*, and thanks for all your help."

"Be careful and take care of Cat. I'll be by the pool, reducing my tension level, most of it due to you, by the way. I'll be waiting for your call. Raphael won't relax until he knows that name. He's not going to be happy that you won't tell him until tomorrow. He will blame me for not having it. Please don't leave me hanging around here like an ignorant fuck all day, Jeff," Julio said as he hung up.

Jeff turned into the executive terminal at the Naples Airport just over ninety minutes later. The manager of Gator Charter came out of the small office to help him unload his car. His eyebrows raised very slightly when the only luggage consisted of garbage bags, but he recognized Jeff and asked no questions. He obviously enjoyed watching Cat stretch as she got out of the car.

Jeff parked his car and went into the office, carrying his express envelope. He made arrangements to fly to the same small private airport he had flown into when returning from Canada seven months before. He wrote a check for the entire cost, reserving the plane for two extra days.

"Mr. Royal, you could save a lot of money if you'd let us pick up another charter instead of sitting on the ground in Atlanta," the manager said.

"I may need the plane quickly. This deal depends on speed. I'd rather have it immediately available so I can get back here if I need to. It's also important that no one know. If the wrong people found out, it could blow the whole deal," Jeff said.

"It's your money, Mr. Royal. You're the boss. And don't worry. No one will hear anything from us. Are you ready to leave?"

Jeff looked at Cat and asked her in Spanish. She nodded, and they walked out on the tarmac and were in the air a few minutes later.

The plane leveled off after climbing smoothly to the assigned altitude. One of the young pilots came back to show them where the tiny bar and the ice were located. He offered to fix them a drink. They both declined, and he went forward. Jeff sat facing Cat, a foldout table between their two seats. He smiled at her, and then took her hand in his. "I'm sorry for what I've put you through, Cat. If I had known, I wouldn't ..."

"It eventually had to happen. I told Claudio that someone could kill him trying to get to Raphael. I knew that it was possible that someone would also kill me. It's not your fault that this thing happened. We knew the risks of being around the Fabriza family and Raphael. We knew the kind of people they were, and about their enemies. We accepted it."

"But ..."

"I want to tell you why I did it. Why I decided to live that way. Even though Raphael never touched me, I was still his

ROYAL REVENGE

puta, his whore. You must understand my reasons. Maybe then you will respect me. I want you to respect me, and to understand. It is very important to me that you understand.

"When I was thirteen, my father introduced me to the knowledge of sex. He held me down and raped me, and then made me do other things to him. I couldn't tell my mother, but I had to tell someone, so I told my sister. Gloria was nineteen then, and when I went to her about it she became furious. The things he had done to me were the same as he had done with my sister. My father had promised her that he would leave me alone if she would continue to be with him whenever he required it. She stayed at home to protect me from him. Then she confronted him and he just laughed at her. He laughed as if it was a joke. He called her his '*puta pequeña*', and he told her that he would do anything he wanted with both of us. She hit him, and then he hit her so hard he broke her jaw.

My mother ran into the room. She had a knife. She knew about him with my sister, but never had the courage to do anything about it. I think something snapped when she heard him hit my sister. She told him to leave Gloria alone. He just laughed at her. Then he told her to leave the room, that it was not her concern. He was a very big man and we had never thought to challenge him before. He grabbed the knife, and ..."

Cat shook visibly while she brought herself under control. Tears formed in her eyes, and she wiped them away with her hand.

"Cat, you don't need ..."

"I must finish. He stabbed my mother with the knife. He didn't mean to, but she fought him when he grabbed it, and it just happened. Claudio and I heard all of this. Claudio was only twelve, and my father came out of the room with blood all over him. I was crying, my sister was on the floor of the bedroom, moaning. We could see my mother on the floor, the blood all over the place. My father dropped the knife and went to the kitchen to wash. Claudio picked up the knife and ran to the kitchen and stabbed him with it. He fell backward and it went all the way into his back. He died very quickly.

"The police came with the ambulance and the doctor. My father had friends who were influential in the government, so they were very careful. The police knew about everything, about why Claudio had killed him, but they called my father's death an auto accident.

"My mother got over her injury eventually, but she was never the same. She has not spoken to any of us in a long time. She blames us all for the death of my father. She has denied to herself that he did anything to deserve it. Gloria left as soon as my mother came home from the hospital. She has not seen my mother since she left. She still has many problems as a result of my father breaking her jaw. Her face is, well, still not right.

"After my mother got out of the hospital, when she got strong enough to do things for herself, she told Claudio and me to leave her house. We had no place to go. We went to live with Gloria in her apartment. It was only one room for the three of us. She barely made enough money to feed us all. But she shared everything with us. She made our clothes. She helped us study. She worked very hard to see that we could finish school. Gloria is the one who helped us come to live with Hector and Maria. She gave us the money to get here. She encouraged us to leave and to leave her there.

"No one knows of this, except Julio. Hector and Maria think that my mother sacrificed everything to have us come here. They think my father died in an accident with an automobile. She tells them that Gloria is a bad seed, that Gloria abandoned the family without reason. But Gloria saved Claudio and me. She was like an angel to us. She gave us everything she had.

"Claudio and I send her money every month. My mother gives her nothing, even though my father left some money.

ROYAL REVENGE

Raphael gave us enough money to buy Gloria a house, so she could leave her apartment. She lived by herself, and she finally had to quit work, because of very bad headaches.

"Before Raphael, we could only send Gloria enough for her to live. Now she can live a good life, as good as it can be. At least she doesn't have to suffer because of no money. She won't come here, because she doesn't want anyone to know about these things. She is in very poor health, and the doctor has told her that the headaches will get worse. So now she must take drugs every day to relieve her pain. Because of Raphael, we were able to pay for a lady to live with her now. Only with the money from Raphael could we do that.

"So you see, living as Raphael's mistress was worth it to me. I think of him as a brother, and Claudio truly loved him. He has been very generous to us. Gloria saved my life, and probably Claudio's. Whatever I have to do to help her now, I will do. And that is why I lived that way. I did not ever think I could be with a man, until Raphael, because he was so kind and so considerate of me. But that was not what he wanted. I think Claudio became the way he was because of my parents. It is terrible to kill your own father. Claudio thought he was protecting us, my mother and Gloria and me. For that he has been rejected by my mother. He hates my mother. I hate her also, for what she has done to all of us, especially to Gloria.

"I have never willingly been with a man until you. The reason I could love you is because of the way you were about your wife. You loved her and you are fighting very hard for her. People must fight for those in their family. That is one reason I was attracted to you. Most of the men I have met love only themselves."

Tears were falling freely down her cheeks, staining her blouse. She seemed to be unaware of them. She sat erect, dignified and proud, her eyes almost daring Jeff to reject her. Jeff sat quietly, shocked by what he had heard. He didn't know what to say to her. The enormity of her suffering reminded him of the stories Giuseppe had told him about his childhood in Ecuador.

"So now you know everything about me. Only Julio Pozo knows as much. Can you understand why I lived as I did? Can you respect me now?" she asked as she wiped the tears from her face.

"Yes. But I didn't need to understand. I loved you and respected you anyway. It doesn't make any difference to me why you lived like that."

"It must make a difference. I know men think I am beautiful. But men soon tire of a woman who is only beautiful and nothing else. Beauty is very quick to disappear. I am also intelligent and curious, very, very strong, and completely loyal to my friends and my family. You must be concerned about those things also."

"I never thought ..."

"You thought with this," she said, as she gently caressed his crotch. She smiled broadly, her eyes softening. "That is okay, because I think I thought the same way. You call it 'love at first sight'? I needed you in that way. It was enough at the time. And you needed me for the same reasons. But we have known each other only two days, although it certainly seems much longer with everything that has happened to us. When this is over, you must come to know me, and I must learn to know you. Only then can we decide whether this is truly love, and not just an attraction of our bodies. I am not interested in being anyone's *puta* again. The only man to have me will have only me, for what I am and what I represent, not for what I look like or what I appear to be."

"I want you, and only you," Jeff said as he took both of her hands in his.

Cat smiled and gave his hands a gentle squeeze. "We will decide that later, when we have time to know each other, instead of just trying to stay alive." She became calm, and fully composed, shaking her head slightly as if to forget what she had told him. Then she asked, "What are we going to do here in Atlanta, Jeff? How are you going to stop all these people from killing us?"

"We'll be safe in Atlanta. Tomorrow we will meet with my partner. I think he can help us finish the whole thing. I have some information for Raphael that will help him against the Espinoza family. I also think I know who is behind Connie's death and all the attempts against us. That's probably related to the Espinoza family too. I want to review all of this with Giuseppe and then I'll go to the FBI with what I know. You will like him. He's been my partner for many years. His background is much like yours. I think you will have much in common."

"I'm sure I will like him. I hope he likes me also, since he is so important to you."

They sat quietly, looking into each other's eyes, when a bell rang and the seat light went on. The young co-pilot came back through the door to make sure they had their belts fastened. "We'll be landing in about fifteen minutes, folks. It will be a little bumpy, so buckle up," he said with a smile as he left the cabin to go forward. Jeff translated the pilot's comments into Spanish, and Cat buckled her seat belt in compliance. After another long glance of intimacy between them, they looked out the window, each lost in their own thoughts until the plane touched down and taxied to the small terminal.

16

Atlanta

Jeff ordered a cab for Cat and himself and one for the pilots while they made arrangements for lodging. They gave him their hotel's number and he agreed to call when he needed the plane. When the first cab arrived, they helped him load the now well-worn garbage bags into it and said good night.

Jeff and Cat settled back in the seat. After Jeff had instructed his driver where to go, he looked at Cat with sudden concern.

"One of the things I forgot to do was to tell Rena we were coming. She'll be scared to death if we just drive up and ring the bell. We'd better call her. I guess I also better tell her I have a guest. That will be a surprise, too. She doesn't speak Spanish, so I'm not sure how you two will communicate. I'm also don't know just how she will feel about you." The concern in his voice was obvious.

"She was fond of Connie? She will resent me?" Cat asked, with equal concern.

"I don't think she'll resent you. She loved Connie like her own daughter, but she recognizes that Connie is gone forever. She said goodbye to her long before I did. She's old enough to be able to deal with things like that. I think Rena will just be surprised that I found someone. Don't worry, you'll like her and she will like you." He made the last statement very confidently, but inside, Jeff was quite unsure as to Rena's reaction. He reflected with mild amusement that Rena's opinion was very important to him.

Jeff instructed the driver to pull over, so he could call, but the driver handed back the headset to his car phone. "You can use this one for three dollars. I just add it to the meter."

Jeff gave the cabbie his number and the cabbie dialed his house. It seemed like he had been gone for months. In fact, he had only been gone four nights. Rena answered the phone on the first ring.

"Mr. Royal's residence."

"Hello, Rena, this is Jeff. I ..."

"Oh, Mr. Royal. I've been so worried. You can't do that to me! You never even called! I've been out of my mind with worrying about you. Where are you?"

"I'm on the way home, Rena. I should be there in a few minutes. Didn't Olivia call you and tell you I was in Miami?"

"Of course she did. But that's all she told me. She didn't tell me anything else. Then all that stuff was on the news about that man that killed Mrs. Royal and about all the troubles in Miami and I ... Never mind about all that. Have you eaten? Shall I fix you something to eat for when you get here?"

Jeff suddenly realized he hadn't eaten since lunch. "That would be wonderful, Rena. I have someone with me. I met her in Miami. She'll be staying with us for a while. Can you fix something for both of us?"

"Sure. I'll fix some sandwiches for you both. I'll also get the guest room ready."

"Uh, Rena, um ... you don't need to fix up the guest room. She'll be staying in my room."

"Oh. Well ... a ... I'll have the sandwiches made then. And I'll turn down your bed. I just changed the linens in there. What is the lady's name?"

"Catarina Contreras. She's very nice and I'm sure you'll like her, but she doesn't speak much English. So it will be hard for you to get to know her as well as I do, I mean ..."

"Oh Mr. Royal, I know what you mean. I'll look forward to meeting Miss Contreras." She pronounced it CAN-TRAY-RUZ. "And I'll make sure she feels welcome in your home. I had better get to work on those sandwiches, or you'll be here and there won't be anything to eat, and I'll be the one who's worried about her welcome," she laughed. "I'll see you and the lady in a little bit. Goodbye, Mr. Royal," she said cheerfully.

When the cab arrived at Jeff's house about fifteen minutes later, Rena opened the door and rushed out to meet them. She put her arms around Jeff and hugged him fondly, almost fiercely, and then took both of Cat's hands in hers. "Welcome to Atlanta, Miss Contreras. We are happy to have you. I have a little food inside. Let me help you with your things."

"Thank you, Rena," Jeff said warmly, and then he translated Rena's comments in Spanish for Cat.

"Thank you, Rena. I am happy to know you, also," Cat said in halting English. The two women went into the house, arm in arm, while Jeff and the driver put the garbage bags and the express envelope in the entry. Jeff paid him and shut and locked the front door with a sigh of relief. It was good to be safe at home.

Rena had prepared a virtual feast of sandwiches, soup, and salad, and had two places set in the kitchen. She bustled about until they were seated, and she was sure they had begun eating. "I'm going to get your things now and put them in the bedroom, Mr. Royal. I'll lay out towels and so forth. Just call if you need anything," she said as she glanced at the back of Cat's head, and then with a smile, nodded her approval to Jeff.

ROYAL REVENGE

When they had finished, Cat began clearing away the dishes, but was shooed into the bedroom by Rena. "You must be tired, I'll do all that. Go on to bed, now, both of you."

Rena had put all their things into the closet or folded them and put them in bureau drawers, and had laid out towels and a bathrobe for both of them. Jeff started taking off his clothes when Cat asked, "Is this Connie's robe?"

"Yes, it was," Jeff said, suddenly unsure of his feelings about Cat wearing something that belonged to Connie, especially something as intimate as a bathrobe.

"I don't think I should wear this. Maybe when we have known each other a long time. But, not now. I hope that does not bother you?"

Jeff felt a flood of relief. He hadn't anticipated how strangely he would feel with Cat staying in what was really Connie's house, sleeping in Connie's bed. Rena's attitude had helped a great deal, but Cat's concern and respect for Connie made him feel far less guilty, although he knew there was no reason for him to feel guilty at all. He and Connie had talked at length about what they would do if either of them died, when she had gotten sick several years before. Connie was very specific and serious, because at the time she was in the hospital, with her illness undiagnosed, and they both expected the worst. Jeff remembered her words very clearly.

"I want you to mourn me and to miss me, and to remember my birthday in your thoughts. But I want you to go on living. Find someone to love you, someone that you can love. I wouldn't be happy unless I knew you were happy, Jeff. On the other hand, I would feel the same if our roles were reversed. I would mourn you and miss you, but I would go on about my life, and hopefully find someone else. This wouldn't be someone to replace you, but someone to love me and be with me."

Jeff suddenly realized that he hadn't answered Cat. He went toward her and took the robe. "No, that won't bother me. In fact, I think it's very kind of you to be so considerate. I'll hang this in the closet." And suddenly all the guilt feelings fell away. Jeff stood in the closet for a few moments with his eyes closed and finally accepted the fact that Connie was dead. He mentally said goodbye and returned to the bedroom with a sigh of relief. Cat was in Connie's bathroom getting ready for bed. Jeff washed and then slid between the cold sheets with a groan of content. Cat came out a few minutes later and got in the bed beside him. Jeff turned out the light and put his arms around her.

She moved away slightly and said in almost a whisper, "Connie made a beautiful home for you. I am sure she was proud of it. I know you have some feelings that are hard for you about me being here. I will not be offended if you would like me to sleep in another room. I know this is difficult."

"It's okay now. Connie would approve. I want you here."

She moved back toward him and put her arms around him. "Okay, I will stay. Now we must sleep," she said, as she caressed the back of his neck. Jeff was sound asleep in an instant.

The digital clock beside the bed showed 4:15 when Jeff woke up with a start. He started to switch on the light until he remembered that Cat was sleeping beside him. He put on his shorts and running shoes and slipped out quietly. Usually Colleen Schaeffer would be ringing the doorbell about now, impatient that he had overslept, but Rena had told her to take the week off. Jeff picked up his sweatbands and dumbbells, disarmed and then reset the burglar alarm, and left through the front door. As he was going out, he noticed the express package containing the Mauser still lying on the entry floor where Rena had left it. It was sealed, so he decided to leave it there.

It was still and warm and foggy, and a light mist fell sporadically as he ran through the neighborhood. Because of

ROYAL REVENGE

the familiar, safe, surroundings, Jeff ran automatically, his mind moving rapidly in a thousand different directions, independent of his body. His leg was a bit stiff and hurt a little, but he was grateful for the time to think, as the past two days had been so hectic that he hadn't been able to do much more than survive.

Jeff was still very unsure of his next move. He felt that he was very close to uncovering the reasons for Connie's death. But he couldn't seem to connect all the information that he had together in a rational sequence.

As his mind moved rapidly from one scenario to the other, he unconsciously ran faster and faster, until the first signs of fatigue, and a stinging, cramping sensation in his injured calf made him slow down abruptly. Forcing himself into a slow jog, he reached the end of his usual route and turned back towards his house. He began the process of review and analysis of the information he had, and his mind started moving faster and faster, driving his body back into an unconscious symmetry. A while later, he again was forced by the pain in his leg to clear his mind and slow down.

It still just didn't make any sense. What threat could he or Connie have been to these people? What possible advantage would anyone get by forcing him out of the Dominion acquisition? Was Dominion even part of the equation? There were so many unanswered questions. But there were also a lot of clues. He just didn't seem to be able to tie them all together.

Jeff had turned down his street and was now about a hundred yards from the entrance to his driveway. He jogged slowly, deciding to finish his workout with his mind as blank as possible. He heard the car before he saw it.

He looked over his shoulder at the source of the roaring sound. Through the mist, he saw a flash of red lights, and then a dark shape moving very rapidly toward him. The headlights came on full, and for an instant Jeff stopped and stood still, transfixed like a scared rabbit in the road, hypnotized by the bright lights from the car.

Jeff threw his body into the trees at the side of the narrow road a split second before the car rushed by him. He lay in the wet pine needles and grass and watched in slow motion as the car skidded to a stop, the driver nearly losing control on the slick street.

The door on the passenger's side opened and a man got out quickly, looking back toward Jeff. The beam of a powerful flashlight cut through the mist, searching the trees just above the point where Jeff lay. The light bobbed up and down as the man began walking rapidly toward him.

Jeff crawled on his belly toward the wall around his property, frantically removing the fluorescent wrist and head bands he wore, burying them in the clumps of wet pine needles as he passed. He dug down below the ground cover and took handfuls of moist black dirt, which he rubbed on his face, legs, arms, and chest, hoping to be less visible to the man with the light. The man passed scant yards from where he lay, and Jeff could hear his heavy breathing as he walked past him. With some regret he left behind one of the chrome dumbbells he carried, unable to crawl with both in one hand, afraid the sound of them knocking together would betray him to the man who was now behind him, flashing the light through the trees in a searching pattern.

"We know you're there, Royal. Come out to the road. We need to talk to you."

Jeff was startled by the voice of another man, probably the driver, not more than twenty yards in front of him. He had forgotten about the driver. His heart was pounding. He was sure they could hear the sound of it thumping in the pre- dawn quiet.

"Put out the light, Frank. He's between us. Walk slowly toward me. There's no place for him to go," the driver said.

ROYAL REVENGE

"Mr. Royal, you can make this easier on everyone if you come out. We're not going to hurt you, we just want to talk."

Jeff heard the driver move off the road into the trees and walk slowly toward him. Then he heard a heavy "thud" and a groan as the man behind him fell to the ground. The mist was heavier now, and suddenly turned into rain, the drops plopping into the pine needles and leaves slowly and steadily, and then there was a rush as the sky opened with a downpour.

"Shit! I think I broke my fucking ankle!" the man behind him cried. Jeff turned and looked as the flashlight went on again, this time held low and pointing toward the ground.

"What happened, Frank?" the driver yelled over the sound of the rain, much closer to Jeff than before.

"I stepped on a fucking dumbbell. I twisted my ankle really bad. I think I broke it!"

"Can you get up?"

"Hell no. It hurts like a bitch. I swear I'll kill that fucking son of a bitch when I get my hands on him."

Jeff felt the nearby presence of the driver. He couldn't see or hear him, but he felt his nearness in the form of a cold slither of fear going up his spine. It was raining more slowly now, and the mud he had rubbed over his body made his hands slippery. He washed off the handle of his remaining dumbbell as best he could and raised himself into a crouch.

"Frank, shine your light down here toward the wall. I think I see him," the driver called out. Jeff moved in a slow running crouch from tree to tree in advance of the light's beam, toward the last position of the driver's voice. Suddenly he saw him, about twenty feet behind where Jeff crouched by the wall. Jeff was now between his gate and the two gunmen. He started to move into a run toward the gate just as the driver turned and saw him. Jeff hit the ground as he heard a bullet sing over his head, smack into the stone wall, and ricochet away. He scrabbled rapidly behind a big oak tree as the driver ran towards where he had just been. The man was now only a few feet from him, looking toward the wall. Jeff raised up just as the driver turned toward him. The driver fired again, the bullet drilling into a tree inches behind him.

Jeff threw the dumbbell at him as hard as he could and pushed his body off the ground and hurled himself toward the driver with the same movement. The five pounds of polished steel hit the man in the chest with a dull thud, knocking him to the ground a split second before Jeff's body fell on top of him. He smelled the man's foul breath as it left his lungs with a rush at the impact.

Jeff felt a terrible stab of pain as the man hit him hard in his back with the butt of the gun. He grabbed for the man's wrist as he brought the gun up to hit him again. The driver's other hand went around Jeff's neck, the fingers digging into his throat viciously. Jeff hit him in the face with his free elbow, as hard as he could. The man groaned with pain, and in the dim light he saw a spurt of blood from his nose. Jeff was now looking directly into his eyes, and the picture of Gaspar filled his mind. A sudden rage gave him new strength, and he twisted the man's arm toward the ground as he hit him in the face again with his elbow.

The driver moaned in agony and the gun fired again, and Jeff saw the flash from the muzzle. He heard the loud pop and felt the thump of the bullet as it went into the man's ribs. Jeff now lay on top of him, breathing in great gulps of air, the gun between them. The metallic smell of blood and the stench of the man's voiding bowels filled the air around him. He rolled off the inert body beneath him and sat up, trying to draw a fresh breath.

Suddenly the light hit him and the other man called, "Carlos, did you get him...? Shit!" He saw Jeff and raised his gun and fired. Jeff desperately threw himself away from the man beside him as he saw a bright flash and he heard a loud bang as the other man's gun exploded in his face, the barrel clogged with mud from his fall.

Jeff felt the driver's neck. There was no pulse. He ran back to the other man, finding him easily by the now still flashlight lying on the ground beside his body. The gun, a twisted, smoking mass of metal, lay beside the light. The explosion of its barrel had virtually taken the man's head off his body, and the remnants of his brains and part of his head lay beside his body in a mound of pink and red.

Jeff felt his stomach heave at the sight and vomited until there was nothing left to come up. He was shivering uncontrollably from the cold and shock and fear. His emotions overloaded as the combination of terror, relief, pain, cold, and fury fought for control of his brain. He fell to the ground. Jeff sat in a puddle of mud and vomit in the rain, shivering, his arms around his knees like a small child, rocking back and forth, feeling totally alone and vulnerable, feeling sorry for himself and wondering what he should do next.

He was tired and scared, and he struggled to hold on to his resolve as he fought back waves of fear and terror. He consciously sought to bring memories of Connie's suffering to the front of his mind, pushing the fear backward. Soon, he got control and forced up the face of Gaspar, willing it to fill his mind, and his anger grew and grew. He allowed the anger to grow into hate until it threatened to overcome him. Then, he forced himself to breathe deeply and slowly.

Finally, he was calm and controlled. He had sat there for what seemed a long time, but it was no more than a few minutes. Jeff got to his feet and stood in the heavy rain, allowing it to wash his body. He picked up the flashlight and his dumbbell. He looked around in the trees until he found his sweatbands.

The men's dark car was still sitting in the middle of the quiet street with its lights off. Jeff started toward the gate, the flashlight in one hand, his dumbbell in the other. He found the other dumbbell and put both of them and his sweatbands on the ground just inside the gate to his house. He was walking quickly back to the car with the flashlight off when he heard another car coming.

Jeff dove for the shelter of the ground as the car came rapidly around the curve, its beams on high, flashing in a bright reflection off the car in the road. The speeding car stopped quickly and expertly, skidding to the side of the road, without hitting the men's car in the middle. The rain suddenly slowed and became light drizzle. The resulting quiet was eerie. The only sound was the idling engine of the second car.

Jeff resisted the urge to rise up and look at the car that had just stopped. A few seconds passed before a very powerful searchlight beam pierced the drizzle and fog. It swept the entire length of the gunmen's car. Immediately after that it started at the gate and swept across the wall behind him, searching the entire length of it slowly and carefully, casting ominous shadows from the trees onto the wall.

Jeff cursed the fact that he hadn't taken the driver's gun when he picked up his dumbbell. It hadn't occurred to him that there would be more of them. He buried his face in the pine needles and mud when the searchlight passed over him. His heart started pounding again, and he began to shake. He had to force himself to calm down enough to think of the best way to escape.

His body tensed all over as he tried to gauge the distance to the gate and his chance of making it that far without feeling a bullet in the back. He got his legs under him and was poised to run to the gate and its fragile safety just as he heard the rasping sound of a two-way radio and the top of the second car erupted in the flashing blue lights of the Atlanta police.

ROYAL REVENGE

17

The police left the house three hours later. About the same time, it finally stopped raining. Even the bright sunshine was not enough to brighten the atmosphere in the house after they left.

Sergeant Stephen Yates had been a patrol cop in Atlanta for twenty-four years. He thought he had seen everything. But, he had never before seen a half-naked millionaire who was built like Adonis, covered from head to foot with mud, vomit, blood, pine needles and leaves, wandering around in the rain at five o'clock in the morning with two gunshot victims lying in the woods. One was almost headless, for crying out loud, lying dead outside Royal's fence. Glad the case was now the problem of Homicide, Yates finished his report at the same time he used the last drops in the large bottle of correction fluid he carried with him at all times.

Sergeant Yates had come around the corner a little too fast that morning when his headlights had picked up the car sitting dead in the middle of the road. He had stopped, barely, and then shined his spotlight over the car. It was empty. He then pointed the spot at the wall to see if anyone was trying to get over it or something.

Yates couldn't think of any reason for someone to abandon their car in the middle of a narrow city street at five in the morning. Suddenly, it occurred to him that he hadn't turned on the rooftop flashers. The next car around the corner could wipe him out. Just after the blue flashers lit up this guy who looked like a fifty-year-old with a teenager's body, in expensive jogging shorts and shoes, came walking out of the woods with his hands up.

Yates put Jeff Royal in the car and handed him a blanket while he radioed in. He then moved the two cars off the road and into Royal's driveway. Royal walked with him into the strip of woods between the road and the fence around that castle he called his house. He showed the sergeant both bodies.

Yates took pictures of each of them and called for backup. Royal took him into the house. There the maid served him coffee from a silver tray that had to be worth as much as his car while Royal cleaned himself up. Newbern came with his entourage from Homicide about thirty minutes later and took over. That was fine with Sergeant Yates except that he had to start over with a new report since Newbern wanted more detail about the crime scene.

Homicide Detective Rick Newbern was not nearly as happy as Sergeant Yates. It was into his already full hands that this crazy case had been pushed. When he left the house that morning, Newbern had told his wife that he had a feeling the day would turn to shit. Hell, the day had <u>started</u> as shit. He already had three unsolved murders to investigate that were going nowhere. And, from that terrific start it had gotten worse quickly.

This guy Royal took the cake. The I.D. on the two bodies outside his fence indicated that they were the types who were there for one reason. Someone wanted Royal dead. They were there to do the job. One would think that Royal would want to give out any information he could. Yet, all they could get from him were the basic facts about what had happened this morning. He acted almost like a suspect. His lawyer was worse. What an asshole!

Newbern knew nobody but their mothers (and probably not them) would grieve for either of the two thugs in the body bags in the driveway. He couldn't understand why Royal was being such a royal pain in the ass. Maybe it went with the name, he thought, with a chuckle and a sigh of resignation.

Newbern's time at the scene went from bad to worse. The reporters showed up about seven o'clock. Newbern had to post a man at the gate to hold them at bay. Then, the damn lawyer got involved. According to him, Royal would answer only those questions about the events of the morning. He did not have to give his opinion about why anyone wanted to kill him, even if the whole point was to protect him from further attempts. Royal had already hired his own security from Pinkerton. He preferred that the police finish their investigation as soon as possible, and then leave.

After three hours, they had two black bags full of known thugs, one with pulp for a head. They had no motive and little information beyond that. Judging from the size of the throng of reporters gathered at the gate, every politico in the Atlanta Police Department would want a piece of Newbern's hide when they read the report. It hadn't helped that Royal was so influential, rich, and well connected. Newbern could only ask, he couldn't push since the guy had done nothing wrong. Jeez, he loved this job.

The two men were not in Atlanta on vacation. Newbern was sure of that. Frank Albert Taylor was on parole in Florida and had twice done hard time for manslaughter and a host of other stuff. According to Florida, Taylor was a cheap thug who should have been on death row long before. The Florida police were sure he'd killed at least two more people in the last year. Who knew how many others had met their death at the hands of that bag of shit? All that mud plugging up the muzzle of his gun had saved both states a lot of time and money.

Carlos Jaime Avila was another story. He was a very expensive professional who worked out of Miami. Never indicted, never even arrested, but always a suspect, he was one of those very smart pieces of slime who existed very successfully outside the law. A naturalized Cuban, his stock in trade was the elimination of anyone, anywhere, generally done to look accidental. The two states weren't going to miss him either.

The main problem was that these two were only "weapons", the means to an end. The end was Royal's demise. Their deaths only gave Jeff Royal a little time to wait for the next attempt. The motive and those who paid these two were still out there, probably in Florida. Florida meant drugs. Drugs meant money. Avila was professional, very expensive. It followed that those who paid him had good connections and lots of money, the kind that came from an active drug business. Newbern was sure they would try again soon to put Jeff Royal away.

The detective tried to convince Jeff Royal of that but got nowhere. Newbern knew that this was the guy whose wife was killed in Canada and who had received pieces of her delivered to his hotel several months before. It was plain to see that there was a lot more to that case than had ever come out. Someone didn't like Mr. Royal at all. Newbern knew that whoever that someone was would try again to kill him. And, they probably wouldn't miss the next time. Royal had been lucky this morning. Newbern's experience was that everyone's luck ran out eventually.

But, the thing that really amazed Newbern was how a regular, respectable businessman like Royal could be so fucking <u>calm</u> about an attempt on his life. He had found Royal to be courteous, very agreeable, and cooperative when telling of the events of the morning. He went over the whole story in detail several times.

Newbern was sure that Royal was telling the truth. His courtesy ended, however, when Newbern had started prying into the possible motives behind it. Royal's lawyer repeatedly advised Royal to answer no further questions. Newbern knew that this fancy lawyer would be the first to scream about the ineptitude of the police after the next attempt. The Chief would really fry his ass on this one, especially if another attempt was made on Royal. But what else could he do?

As Newbern drove down the driveway and through the gate, he wondered just how much time Lieutenant Harrison would want him to spend on this case. After all, the prospective victim didn't seem to want to help. He could probably expect the heat on his ass to be directly proportionate to how much publicity the thing got, he concluded. Since there were no less than thirty reporters at the gate, that would be plenty. Newbern groaned inwardly and fought the urge to run over one of the more aggressive reporters as he drove away.

After the police left, it took Jeff another thirty minutes to get rid of his lawyer, Arthur Malman. Arthur had handled Jeff's business affairs since the inception of Royal Distributors, and he had become a close friend. Arthur wasn't very happy either.

"Forget that you're not cooperating with the police. That's bad enough. What concerns me is that someone is trying to kill you. They've hired professionals who would have killed you this morning if you hadn't been extremely lucky. They're damned serious. They probably won't quit until you're dead. What the hell are you involved in? What are you hiding?" he asked.

"Arthur, most of this you don't want to know. It will be finished today and then, I'll go to the police and tell them everything I know. I appreciate your concern, but I can handle this. The security guards are already at the gate now. They'll be here until I don't need them anymore.

"Can you wait a few more minutes? I have something I want to give you. I'll be right back," Jeff said as he left Malman sitting in the den. Jeff came back about fifteen minutes later with a large envelope, which he handed to Malman.

"I'll call you later, Arthur. I want you to take this. Keep it safe for me." Jeff handed him the envelope. "Inside there's a brief hand-written will. Please look it over today. You'll need to rewrite it in legalese. I'll sign whatever you come up with tomorrow. Also, there's a letter to be opened if something happens to me. It's very important that no one sees it or knows that you have it. But, if anything happens to me, open it right away and follow the instructions, okay?" Malman nodded reluctantly, a look of very serious concern on his face.

"Thanks again, Arthur. I'll be all right, I'm sure," Jeff said as he tried to usher his attorney out the door.

"I'd appreciate knowing what you've got yourself into, Jeff. Normal people don't have two men trying to kill them in the wee hours of the morning, and then hand their lawyer a handwritten will to process. As your lawyer, I advise you to cooperate fully with the police. As your friend, I urge you to!" he said earnestly.

"I'll call you later, Arthur, probably tomorrow. Don't worry," Jeff said as he virtually pushed Malman out the door.

Jeff went into the bedroom. Cat was sitting in one of the lounge chairs, staring aimlessly out the window at the garden. When he had left Sergeant Yates to clean up and change clothes, he had told Cat very briefly about the events of the morning. She had stayed in the bedroom in seclusion for the entire time the police were at the house. Jeff smiled at her and moved toward her. She rose from the chair and put her arms around him.

They embraced with the fierceness of two people who weren't sure of the time they would have to spend together. Cat's eyes glistened with the tears that manifested her conflicting emotions of love, relief, and fear. She pushed him away, reluctantly, tenderly. "I am so afraid for you. These people will not stop. What did you say to the police?" she asked.

"I told them very little. They know nothing of what happened in Miami. They were upset, but I don't think they can help us now. Maybe later ..."

ROYAL REVENGE

"Later you will be dead! I will be dead! Rena will be dead! You cannot do this on your own, Jeff. You must decide now that you can no longer risk yourself, or us. I have lost my brother. You have lost your wife. They have tried to kill you more than once. You have even killed a man outside your own house! End this now, or you must continue with it alone."

She was crying, now. Jeff tried to take her back into his arms, but she pushed him away. "No. I mean what I say. I think I love you. I want to be with you. But, I will not be a part of whatever you are doing with these people. I am too afraid. Why won't you tell the police everything? Let them get your revenge."

"It's not revenge I want, Cat. This is more than a gang war in Miami. It's more than a madman killing my wife. All those things are related. It started in Miami, not in Canada. I am sure of it. But, I have no proof, yet. I must talk to Giuseppe before I tell the police what I think. He can help me finish this. He's the only one who can. Please go with me to meet him. I promise I will go to the police this afternoon. I will tell them everything and leave the rest to them."

"We are going to have lunch with Giuseppe? You will go to the police afterward? You promise me?"

"Yes. Whatever happens, I will go to the police as soon as we leave Giuseppe."

"If you do not do this, I will leave tonight. That I promise you. Nothing will change my mind," Cat said with a look of determination.

"I don't want you to leave. I will go to the police," Jeff said, as he took her in his arms again, hoping he could keep his promise.

Arthur Malman shook his head in wonder as he got in his car. Jeff was very nervous, almost irrational. And, yet, he was calm at the same time. He certainly knew how much danger he was in or he wouldn't write out a will. What in the world was in the letter? He picked up his car phone as he drove out of the driveway. Malman dialed Royal Floors. He asked for Giuseppe Portales. The Pinkerton guards moved the reporters away so he could leave.

"Giuseppe, this is Arthur Malman. I'm just leaving Jeff's house. Two men tried to kill him this morning. What the hell is he involved in?"

"Oh, shit!" Giuseppe exclaimed. "Is he okay?"

"He has some scratches and bruises, but other than that he's not hurt. I'm worried, though. He's very nervous, and yet, he acts like the whole thing is just a minor inconvenience. The police have left. He wouldn't tell them anything about why these people went after him. He called me so I could help him with the police. He got Pinkerton guards at the house right away. I think he's in some real trouble.

"What about the guys who tried to kill him? Have the police got them?"

"They're both dead. Jeff killed one of them and the other one's gun exploded in his face. They're professional killers from Florida, according to the police. What the hell is going on?"

"I really don't know, Arthur. Jeff is getting ... Well, you know how he's been since the thing with Connie. Then the police caught the guy that killed her. This week Jeff went to Canada to talk to the police. He also went to Miami and started asking a lot questions about the guy who killed her.

"For some reason Jeff's convinced that the mob in Miami had her killed. I told him to stay out of it. I tried to get him to leave it all to the police. You know how hardheaded he gets sometimes. The police have told him that the guy in Canada worked for someone up there. But Jeff won't stop with that. He's obsessed with connecting the killer to the mob in Miami. I don't know why. It's almost as if he's lost his mind. I don't know what to do about him. He really stirred up some shit down there."

ROYAL REVENGE

"Someone better do something, soon. He was real lucky this morning. Try to convince him to work with the police, will you? I'm really worried. He could end up dead. He's in way over his head."

"I'll talk to him again, Arthur. I'll do everything I can. Thanks for calling me. I'll call you later," Giuseppe said as he hung up.

Giuseppe leaned back in his chair and rubbed his temples. He knew he could talk to Jeff until hell froze over. But when he was on a crusade like this nothing would change Jeff's mind. The guy was impossible to convince when he thought he was right, regardless of evidence to the contrary. It was a great quality sometimes, but it had caused them problems over the years. Several times Jeff had given up great deals when he didn't like the people involved. Even when Giuseppe proved him wrong, he wouldn't bend.

"Sometimes you must play by your instincts, by what your guts tell you, Giuseppe. Facts and figures don't always tell you everything you need to know. The people behind the figures are more important. I feel funny about this deal. My instincts have been good. I have to listen to them," he'd said as he rejected a proposal for them to buy a competitor.

As it turned out, Jeff was partially right. The guys had cooked the books. But, they still could have made a good deal out of it. It would have made them a lot of money.

Giuseppe got up and closed his office door. He needed time to think. Jeff and his fucking instincts. Why wouldn't he leave well enough alone? It was very unfortunate, but Connie was dead. The guy who killed her was dead. That should have been the end of it. Now he was involved in who knows what with all that bullshit in Miami. If Jeff got himself killed, it wouldn't bring Connie back.

But without him, the suppliers would start looking for other people to sell. They'd all start looking at Royal's credit lines. The banks would get even more uptight, and if they needed lines of credit they wouldn't get them. The sales force would eventually get nervous. Some would probably leave. They'd be covered up with auditors. Hell, the company would probably go down the tubes.

What in the world did Jeff think he was going to prove? All he was going to do was screw up everything. The worst part was that the whole thing was out of control now. Jeff had really stirred things up in Miami. Giuseppe was afraid that his friend and partner had really gotten them into deep shit this time.

ROYAL REVENGE

18

Giuseppe Portales was born thirty-five years before in Quito, Ecuador. He had a sister who was born when Giuseppe was four. She was a beautiful little girl with black curly hair, dimples, and black eyes. Giuseppe had loved her more than anything in the world. He spent most of the money he had earned by carrying bricks to his father for toys, clothes, and pretty things for his sister.

Giuseppe's father was a skilled brick mason like his father before him. Alfredo Portales' skill was well known in Quito and he made a very good living for someone who worked with his hands and back in that city.

Giuseppe remembered his father fondly. He was very strong and handsome and, yet, so very gentle with his children. They lived in a small, no, tiny, house but it had a tile floor, and water in the kitchen. And, the *baño* was in the back yard, unlike some in the neighborhood. Giuseppe and his sister were content. They enjoyed school and life in general.

Giuseppe's mother, Angelina, was born into an old-line Portuguese family in Rio. When she was in a good mood, which wasn't often, she would tell the children of her own childhood in Rio. Her father was a very wealthy contractor. Angelina was his only daughter. Her mother died in childbirth. Angelina's father spared her no luxury. He tolerated her every whim. She had the best clothes, her own servants, and the best private schools.

When her father decided to spend a year on a building project in Quito, he brought Angelina with him as part of her education. The luxury she had left in Rio was difficult to match in the dirty, poor environment of Quito. She was one of the most beautiful women in Quito, but her beauty was wasted on the poor excuse for high society there. Angelina soon tired of the few friends she met and began to visit her father's work.

It was there that she first saw the handsome brick mason who worked for her father. More out of boredom and spite than any real attraction, Angelina had seduced Alfredo into her own father's bed. Her passion was quickly forgotten when she realized that she was pregnant with Giuseppe.

Totally enraged at the news, Angelina's father halted his building project and moved back to Rio, disowning his daughter and leaving her to the fate she had chosen. Alfredo and Angelina were married at the age of nineteen. She never saw her father again. Even naming Giuseppe after him hadn't softened her father's heart.

Angelina did not adjust well to the hard life of a poor Quito housewife. She had a fiery temper and was very hard on the children. After Giuseppe's sister was born, Angelina regressed to a dream world and often stayed in bed for days at a time. Alfredo did everything he could to make a good living for her and his children, to keep the house clean, and to see that the children were clothed and fed. He was very much in love with his beautiful wife. But, the more he tried, the more difficult and reclusive Angelina became.

When Giuseppe was ten, his father caught Angelina in bed with a bartender from a nearby restaurant. Enraged, Alfredo beat them both to death with his bare hands, and then threw their bodies in the garbage bin behind his house. A little over an hour later, Alfredo jumped to his own death from a brick scaffold, four stories up.

Giuseppe and his sister went to live with his paternal grandfather, Alphonso, and his second wife, Maria, a woman who was even younger than Angelina. Maria had married the old widower the year before, shortly after meeting him. She had preferred the comparatively luxurious life of a brick mason's wife, even a very old one, to the abject poverty of a farm girl. She was young and pretty and very kind and loving to the children.

Giuseppe quickly became a happy child once again. His grandfather still worked most days on various building projects. Giuseppe often worked with him after school, carrying bricks to earn a little money. He was also learning the trade.

At the age of thirteen, Giuseppe had grown into a young man. He had passed puberty at the age of twelve and was very handsome. His dark hair and flashing eyes combined with the good looks he had acquired from his parents made him look much older than he was. His body was hard and muscular from carrying bricks. His skin was darkly tanned from the hot sun. He was smart, clever, and inquisitive. He did very well in school and was a favorite with his teachers.

One day after school Giuseppe came home and began to change clothes to go to work with his grandfather. Maria had sent his sister out to play. She came into their room as Giuseppe was getting ready to go to work.

"Give those to me, Giuseppe, so I can wash them," she said as he took off his school clothes. He stood in his underwear as she looked fondly at him, "Your grandfather doesn't need you to work with him today. I want you to help me with some things around here, Giuseppe."

He was a little embarrassed that she'd look so directly at him in just his underwear. She took his clothes from him and laid them on the floor beside the bed he shared with his sister.

"You're turning into a handsome young man, Giuseppe," she said with a strange, husky whisper as she moved toward him and put her hands on his shoulders.

Giuseppe had noticed that Maria had been hugging him more and more and closer and closer lately. He was ashamed that the feel of her soft body and firm breasts against him excited him so. He always tried to move away so she couldn't feel his erection, but she usually hugged him closer.

This time he felt her soft breath on his neck and felt her lips brush his skin and he didn't want to move away. Her hands traveled softly down his back and then up his arms to his shoulders. "Your back is very strong, but your muscles are tight. Lay down here and I will rub your back. Then, you can do the things I need done," she said quietly, her breath coming in rapid little gasps.

Giuseppe sat down on the bed. His penis was sticking up out of the top of his shorts. He tried to cover himself with his hand. Maria took his hand in hers, and began to rub the muscles there, all the time looking at his erection. She moved slowly up his arm, kneading, caressing, never taking her gaze from his crotch.

Giuseppe's heart was pounding. His mind was flooded with conflict. He was embarrassed to have her look at him. Her hands felt so good he didn't want her to stop touching him. Her smell was intoxicating, and he was getting very excited. But, he knew this shouldn't be happening.

"Does that feel good, Giuseppe?" she asked, as her hands rubbed his shoulder.

"Yes. It feels very good, Maria, but ..."

"Shh. Just lie down and close your eyes, Giuseppe. Let yourself relax."

He lay back on the bed and closed his eyes. Maria continued to rub his shoulders, and then, his chest and stomach. Giuseppe felt the first signals that he was about to ejaculate. He was breathing rapidly. "Maria, I..."

"Shh. Relax."

He felt her soft hands move down his stomach, touch his penis, and then, go around the waist of his shorts, gently tugging them down. Instinctively he raised his body so that she could take his underwear off. His heart felt like it would break out of his chest. And, then, one of her hands went around his penis while the other cupped his testicles and seconds later he came with a flood on his stomach and chest.

Giuseppe opened his eyes and saw her smiling tenderly at him. Maria took his shorts and gently wiped off his stomach and chest. Then she stood up and took off the dress she was wearing. She wore nothing under it.

Giuseppe had never seen a woman naked before, except for the few seconds he had glimpsed his mother or Maria before they were dressed. Her body was lush and full with a dark triangle of hair between her legs.

She lay beside him on the bed and stroked his forehead. "Relax, Giuseppe. Close your eyes and just relax," she said as her hand moved from his forehead down his face, gently closing his eyes before moving to his chest and, then, down to his penis.

Maria twisted on the bed until her head hovered over his crotch and he could feel her long, black, silky hair shimmering across his legs and stomach. Giuseppe almost fainted when her soft breath tickled him. Then, her mouth closed around his now, again, erect penis. She sucked him briefly but soon got up on her knees and mounted him.

He had never before felt such exquisite pleasure. He opened his eyes halfway and saw a very sultry-looking Maria smiling down at him as she rode him up and down. Her firm round breasts crowned by black nipples jiggled up and down with the rhythmic movement of her body. Her smile became a grimace as she bit her own lip in pleasure.

Soon Giuseppe matched her rhythm. He raised his hips as she came down with her body. He took her breasts in his hands, feeling the hard nipples, squeezing them between his thumb and forefinger, and finally raising up and taking one in his mouth.

Maria moaned with ecstasy. They kissed, her tongue frantically searching within his mouth. She pushed him back down on the bed and moved up and down on his shaft faster and faster. Giuseppe moved with her. She cried out, and then bit her lip, and then cried out again. Her hands fluttered over his chest, his shoulders, frantically kneading and caressing, touching every part of his torso. Her breath came faster and faster until she was panting furiously. A drop of sweat rolled down her neck, between her breasts.

He moved harder and harder, his only thought to go ever deeper, his mind focused only on his rising passion. It was if he were trying to fold up his entire body and insert it into her. Suddenly, she cried out with a long wailing moan and sunk her nails into his shoulders as tears rolled down her cheeks.

At first Giuseppe thought he had hurt her. But, then, he felt her contractions and he closed his eyes and with a moan of his own he came like he had never come before.

With Maria's urging his grandfather readily agreed that Giuseppe should stay home two days a week after school to help Maria around the house. He was glad that Giuseppe and Maria had become so close. He noticed only that his young wife was more beautiful than ever, and that she seemed very, very happy. Besides, on the two days Giuseppe stayed home, the dinners she served on the meager budget he gave her were absolute works of art.

And, then, one day about a year later, Giuseppe's grandfather was hit in the head with a falling brick. When he regained consciousness, he had a terrible headache. Finally, he decided to leave work and go home. One of his workers came with him on the bus to the little house so the old man wouldn't have any problems.

The rest of the day was still a blur in Giuseppe's mind. This was his day to "help Maria". He and Maria had been in the bed for over an hour, having sex in every possible fashion Maria's now very active mind could create. She was just enjoying her second orgasm on top of him when the door to the bedroom abruptly opened.

His grandfather stood there, a look of complete shock on his face, a look that quickly turned to fury. The worker who had come on the bus with his grandfather literally ran from the house. The old man roared with rage and grabbed Maria by the arm and dragged her to the front door. He threw her out the door and then came back into their room and pulled her clothes from the closet and threw them out the door after her. He had yet to speak until he said in Spanish, "If I ever see you again I will kill you, *puta*!" Giuseppe curled up in fright on the bed as his grandfather moved toward him.

Suddenly the old man stood straight up, both hands clutching the sides of his head. His body trembled violently. His face was already dark red from anger, but it then turned even darker, almost purple. Finally, his eyes rolled back in his head and he fell to the floor. His tongue stuck out of his mouth like a limp purple rag. His body shuddered violently and, then, he was still. Giuseppe cried silently as he lifted his dead grandfather to the bed. Within an hour, the police had come with a doctor. The doctor said Giuseppe's grandfather had died from the blow to the head which caused bleeding in his brain.

The coroner came shortly after and took his grandfather's body away. All of the neighbors had witnessed Maria's embarrassing exit and she had scurried away before the old man had returned to the bedroom. Soon the priest came to the house and talked with Giuseppe and then with several of the neighbors. The people from the church orphanage took his sister away immediately. Giuseppe didn't see her again until many years had passed.

The next day, Giuseppe was sent to a home for teenage boys. It was more like a prison, a reform school, than a home. Giuseppe shared a cell-like room with five other boys. There was a total of thirty boys in the home. The regimen was very hard and absolutely rigid.

The beds were made of rough wood and covered with a thin mattress of rags and straw. The windows had no screens. The boys wore uniforms of rough blue cotton, which they were allowed to wash once a week. All the classes were in English. They were never allowed to speak Spanish in the presence of the teachers.

Six days a week they were up at five o'clock for work in the pitiful little garden. Breakfast of bread and coffee was served to them outside. Then they stripped in the yard under the watchful eye of the headmaster. They washed with lye soap and the cold water from the well, before dressing in the same clothes for school. Their classes were taught by monks and lasted from eight until one. Lunch consisted of weak soup. Forced siesta until three. Cleaning chores until six. Dinner of stew and bread. Study in absolute silence until nine. Lights out at nine. Three hours of church, two hours of study, and then forced exercise or chores for the rest of the day on Sunday.

The menu and the schedule never changed. There were no free periods, no recreation, nothing to read beyond the material given them in class. They were never allowed outside the grounds of the school. Giuseppe became a virtual robot, his only diversion the imaginary travels he took to the countries they studied in school.

He often lay on his hard bed after the lights went out and thought about how things would be in the future. He would go to the United States and work. He would be very rich. His bathroom would be inside and have hot water. He would have books to read and beautiful women around him. He would never again eat stew. He would never again wear dirty clothes. He would never again work in a garden. And he would never ever again depend on anyone else, only himself.

ROYAL REVENGE

Giuseppe accepted this life as appropriate punishment for his behavior. For the three years he was in the boy's home he was a model of obedience. He did all the work asked of him with energy and without complaint. He had learned English so well he spoke with little accent. He did very well in school, especially in math. There was no privacy, but he was very aloof from the other boys. Giuseppe was alone in the world, and no one would ever get close to him again.

The old monk who taught the math courses and the headmaster of the home were so impressed with Giuseppe's abilities that they began to groom him for entrance to Quito's University. Giuseppe didn't like either one of them, but he worked harder than ever, anxious to please. He knew a good education was his only chance to leave Ecuador. Giuseppe began to feel that his life was on track again, that he had some control, and that he could have a future.

He had been accepted into the university at 17, and a local scholarship fund agreed to pay his expenses because of his good grades and excellent conduct. He was excited beyond belief. He had visited the university with his math teacher. The living conditions in the university dormitory were luxurious compared to those at the boy's home. He had talked with several of the other students there. They were from much better backgrounds than the boys he had lived with for the last three years. Some of them had even been to the United States. He would have a great deal of freedom compared to his isolation at the home.

Finally, he would have a chance to make something good happen in his life. Finally, he would have a future. Finally, his hard work would pay off.

That good feeling ended the day before his confirmation and graduation from the boy's school. The headmaster called Giuseppe into his office at precisely nine o'clock that evening, as the boys left the study hall to go to their rooms for the night. He walked down the long hallway with a feeling of curiosity but sure that he had done nothing wrong, and therefor had nothing to worry about.

Headmaster Flanagan was a prissy Englishman who had started the school years before. He was a tall, thin, bird-like man with a protruding Adam's apple, sparse red hair, and a perpetual whine for a voice. He ruled the school, and its youthful inmates, with total control. His stern, inflexible discipline was liberally enforced with a thin switch he cut weekly and polished with perverse care.

Giuseppe had never been called to Mr. Flanagan's office before, as he had never misbehaved or made anything but good grades. The other boys had told stories about the cruel penalties the Headmaster dealt out within the confines of his office, and often had welts across their backsides to prove it. Some of them had hinted at other punishment too awful to discuss, and a call to Flanagan's office was generally viewed with abject terror.

In his current good mood, however, Giuseppe assumed that Flanagan just wanted to talk with him about his move to the university the next week. Besides, he had never done anything to require discipline. He knocked on the door and entered when Flanagan whined for him to come in.

"You wish to see me, Mr. Flanagan?" Giuseppe asked as he entered the office and closed the door softly.

"Yes, Giuseppe. Come in and sit. I am very concerned about something. Have we not done everything we possibly could do for you? You are going to the university. Very few of the boys have ever had this chance. Is there some reason you are so ungrateful?"

"But Mr. Flanagan, I am very grateful. I know how very lucky I am to have this chance. Why would you think that I am not grateful?"

Flanagan imperiously crooked his bony hand, indication that Giuseppe come to the side of the desk. "If you are so grateful for what we have done for you, why would we find something like this under your mattress, Giuseppe?" he asked with a loud accusing whine as he shoved a well-worn magazine under Giuseppe's nose.

Giuseppe looked at the magazine with horror and disbelief. It was cheap pornography, the kind he had sometimes seen when a new boy came into the home and brought it with him. Pornography was totally forbidden, of course. The teachers always seemed to find it quickly, and the penalties for possessing it were terrible.

Fighting cold waves of terror that threatened to overcome him, Giuseppe stammered, "But Mr. Flanagan, this book is not mine. I did not put it there. I have never seen this before. I swear it!"

"I want you to look at this filth. You must see how bad it is. Look!" Flanagan forced Giuseppe to look at the open pages, and then he began to leaf slowly through the book, watching Giuseppe's reaction as he turned to each new page.

Giuseppe had not seen a woman since the day Maria had left and his grandfather had died. There had been no outlet for his natural sexual urges in the home. The only privacy they had was the privy, and then only if someone else wasn't in it at the same time you were. Masturbation was a very serious offense. Any sexual contact between the boys was tantamount to murder. The pictures were dark and fuzzy, but very explicit. Giuseppe felt himself get erect.

"I can see that this kind of filth appeals to you. I am very disappointed, Giuseppe. I didn't think you were an animal like some of the others. I am terribly disappointed in you. I am afraid that you will not be a good candidate for the university."

Tears fell down Giuseppe's face. His gut heaved. The ache in his chest was almost overwhelming. "Mr. Flanagan, I swear that book is not mine. I never saw it before. Please, I swear it ..."

"But you must be punished for this, Giuseppe. We can not have this kind of thing here at the home go unpunished. It was in your bed, under your mattress. You must have known it was there. What can I do, besides ..?"

"Please, Mr. Flanagan. I must go to the university. I must!"

Flanagan looked at the handsome young man standing in front of him with tears still streaming down his face. His face turned a dark pink and his breathing became rapid. He picked up his dreaded switch, the one he had just cut that morning and polished with great care and pleasure. He stroked it unconsciously, with almost loving touches, as he spoke.

"Because you've never caused any problems before, I'll be easy on you. You will still be punished tonight, but you will be confirmed tomorrow, and you can move to the university next week. But you must never tell anyone how kind I was to you by punishing you tonight, or you will be removed from the university. Do you understand? Do I have your word?"

Giuseppe looked at Flanagan. His reedy voice had lowered to a hoarse whisper. His face had twisted into a demented leer, and he looked at Giuseppe with palpable hunger.

Giuseppe nodded meekly, with a horrible sinking feeling of resignation and disgust, suddenly knowing the stories he had heard from some of the other boys were true.

"Take off your clothes, now," Flanagan said, breathlessly.

Giuseppe stripped and stood naked before him.

"Now look at this filth. Look at it!" he rasped as he bent Giuseppe's head down, slowly turning the pages of the lurid magazine with trembling hands.

Giuseppe looked. In spite of himself, he got excited, thinking of his times with Maria.

Whack! The limber switch cut into the tender skin of his buttocks. Giuseppe winced. Flanagan grabbed his head and pushed it closer to the magazine. "Turn the pages yourself, Giuseppe. Look at each one of these people. Tell me what you see. Tell me what you like about these filthy pictures. Here. Look at this one. What is she doing to him? Tell me!" Flanagan was trembling all over. His face was florid and sweat dripped from his chin. He rubbed himself and wheezed with excitement.

Whack! Whack! Whack! The switch cut into Giuseppe's skin a dozen more times, across his buttocks, his back, his legs, across his genitals. The pain was intense. The scars were both physical and mental. He could remember it to this day.

The worst memory, however, was the sight of the perverted Flanagan. The old man dropped the switch and stood behind his desk, his pants around his ankles, masturbating. His leering eyes never left Giuseppe's body. Finally, Flanagan came in a high wheezing moan and collapsed in his chair. He sat for a long time with his eyes closed, breathing heavily.

Giuseppe stood mutely before him, embarrassed and ashamed. Tears fell down his face. His stomach churned. He struggled to keep from vomiting.

Flanagan opened his eyes and croaked, "Remember, Giuseppe. You must tell no one about this. I was very easy on you. Your punishment could have been much worse," Flanagan said as he sat wearily back in his chair. He put the magazine in his desk drawer. Then, he indicated with a feeble motion of his hand that Giuseppe was dismissed.

"I understand, Mr. Flanagan. No one will know. I promise. No one will ever know," Giuseppe said in a whisper as he put on his clothes. He was shaking and could not stop the tears from coming.

Giuseppe fought for control as he walked to his room. Someday he would kill this bastard. Someday he would be strong enough and rich enough so that people like this would have no control over him. Someday.

19

Giuseppe was startled back into the present when his intercom buzzed. "Jeff's on line one, Giuseppe," Olivia said.

He picked up the phone. "Jeff, I hear from Arthur Malman that you're back home. I also hear that you're alive only through the grace of God. What in hell have you gotten yourself into?"

"I got in town late last night, Giuseppe. I guess I didn't realize how serious those people were. Two guys tried to kill me this morning while I was out running. I was lucky they didn't, no question about it. I want to talk to you about what I found out in Miami. Can we have lunch today?"

"I'm not sure I want to know what you found out, Jeff. Someone tried to kill you, for Christ's sake. Why don't you just leave it with the police? Arthur said you wouldn't even cooperate with them. Why not? There's no way I want to be involved with those people."

"You are already involved, Giuseppe. We all are. The whole deal goes back to the company. I'm sure of it. We have a very serious problem. We need to talk it out. Meet me for lunch today. I'll explain it to you."

Giuseppe could feel his palms get sweaty and his heart began beating faster. He took a deep breath before he spoke. "Okay, Jeff. If you insist, I'll come over at noon. Carmen wanted to have lunch today, but ..."

"Don't come here. There is a bunch of reporters parked out by the gate again. Let's meet at the club. No one ever goes there for lunch, so we can talk in private. I'll shake these vultures and meet you there at 12:30. Bring Carmen if you want to. Okay?"

"I guess so. Is it safe? I mean, what makes you think they won't try again today? Jesus, you act like it's nothing."

"They'll have to recruit someone else, first. They may not even know these guys failed, yet. I don't think there were any more than these two here. I'm going to the police right after I see you and tell them everything I've discovered so far. That should finish it for them. I'm pretty sure we'll be safe. I'll have one of the Pinkerton guys follow us to the club and stay there while we have lunch."

"Okay. We'll see you at 12:30. Be careful, Jeff."

"I will, don't worry. See you later," Jeff said as he hung up.

Giuseppe stared at the wall for a long time after he finished talking to Jeff. He was frightened by Jeff's tone of voice. Jeff was way too calm. He talked about almost getting killed in the same casual way one would use when talking about the weather. He knew that tone of voice. In the past that had been one of the signs that Jeff was absolutely determined to finish what he had started, and damn the consequences.

It would be impossible to change his mind about all this. Now they were all involved? The company also? What in the world had he found out? Damn! Just when things were going so well. Why in the hell didn't Jeff just sit at home and write his fucking book? The guy could be a real pain in the ass when he got like this. Now they were really in the middle of a mess, and, it was all due to his fucking nosing around.

Giuseppe picked up the phone to call Carmen.

Jeff wasn't nearly as calm as Giuseppe thought he was. He had thought he would be safe in Atlanta. He was still shaky after the events of the morning. Someone was getting very nervous about Jeff's questions, and that wasn't good. His next call was to Raphael Fabriza at his father's home. A woman's voice answered in Spanish.

Jeff replied to her greeting in Spanish and then asked for Julio Pozo. He heard muffled conversation in the background as the woman held her hand over the phone. A moment later Raphael's voice came on the line. "Who is calling? There is no one by the name of ..."

"Raphael, this is Jeff Royal. I have a name for you, but I'd also like to talk to Julio. Can you put him on the line with us?"

"Certainly, Jeff, but ..." Raphael tried but could not conceal his impatience. "Just a moment. I will get Julio," he said after a brief pause. After a short wait, Jeff heard Julio pick up another extension.

"Jeff, this is Julio. I guess you're in Atlanta. How was your trip?"

"Fine, until this morning when two guys tried to kill me again while I was out running near my house." He heard Julio gasp. "I'm okay. They're not. They're both dead. Would you know anything about that, Raphael?"

Raphael stammered a moment and then said, "Jeff, I assure you! I ..."

Jeff was convinced that the surprise in Raphael's voice was genuine. "I believe you, Raphael. I think I know what's happening. I'm pretty sure that the people trying to kill me are hooked into the Espinoza family. This morning the people they hired weren't interested in anything but seeing me dead. Since you still didn't have the name you wanted, I'm sure it wasn't you or your people. Julio, is everything okay with you? Are you going to stay there?"

"Well, I guess I will now, Jeff. I can't believe this shit. I'm afraid to go back to Miami right now. Raphael says I can stay here as long as I want. Of course, I'll need to go back to work, sometime. Eventually."

"You can probably go back in a few days. I think this will be over today. Why don't you let me talk to Raphael now? You don't want to know about the rest of this. I'll call you later tonight."

"Dammit, Jeff, I'm not a fucking child. I'm getting tired of ..."

"He is right, Julio. I think there are some things you must not hear, for your own safety," Raphael interrupted. "Why don't you go back to the pool and see what the girls are doing?"

"Betrayed by my lowest instincts, again. I just want you both to know that someday soon I won't be so easily manipulated by money, booze, and sex. Goodbye, Jeff," Julio said with a hollow laugh that was obviously forced, as he hung up.

"We have introduced him to a very nice lady, Jeff. But he is still very upset by all this, as I'm sure you can tell. He is a reporter and he wants to know all of the details. That will be a problem for us, eventually. He has gone outside. I think we can talk now," Raphael said. "You have the name I want for me?

"Yes. But first, you should know that everything you've told me has been written down. Also, there are some other things I've found out. Believe me, you don't want any of this made public. If anything happens to Julio, Cat, or me it all goes to the newspapers. I'm sorry, but ..."

"I understand that you must protect yourself. We will protect Julio as long as we need to. We have no reason to hurt you, and you know how I feel about Cat. And now, the name. Please." Raphael's voice was very hard, very impatient.

"Who is Paul Carmona?"

There was a very long silence. It lasted so long that Jeff wasn't sure the connection hadn't been broken. Then Raphael's voice came back on, this time in a tone so low it was almost a whisper. "Jeff, there must be a mistake. Where did you get that name? Paul is ..."

"That's the name that Herman Guerra gave me as he died. I'm sure he wasn't lying. He had no reason to at that point. He was so far gone he just barely got it out. So, who is this guy?"

"He is ... He is my cousin, my father's nephew. He has lived with us since we were little boys. My parents have treated him as they would their own child. I can hardly believe he is the traitor. I will kill the son of a bitch!" The rage in Raphael's whispering voice was palpable.

"I'm sorry, Raphael. This must be painful for you. But I am also sure there's no mistake. Guerra said, 'the man at Fabriza is Paul Carmona.' I'd like to know what you find out from him. I still have some questions that I want answered."

"I will call you later. We will talk to him at once. Please give me your number," Raphael said with a flat tone devoid of emotion.

As Jeff gave him his number, a cold shiver went up his spine. He could feel Raphael's rage. He was glad he wasn't *Señor* Carmona.

Jeff looked at his watch. It was almost noon. He hadn't spent any time with Rena. Jeff went into the kitchen to see her. She was sitting at the table, trying to converse with Cat. Cat looked beautiful in a dark blue pantsuit. It was plain they liked each other a great deal.

"I'm sorry about all this, Rena. I thought I left all of this in Miami. I didn't think these people would do anything to us here. We'll keep the guards on duty until things settle down again. Do you want to continue to stay here? You know I'll do whatever you want. If you want to go to a hotel or go visit your family in Macon, I understand."

"That's all right, Mr. Royal. We'll be safe with the guards here. I'm just worried about you. Are you going to be all right?"

"Yes, Rena. I'm going to be fine. Cat and I will have lunch with Giuseppe at the club today. After lunch I'm going back to talk with the police. I'm pretty sure that I know everything I need to know, now. Finally."

Then in Spanish, he said to Cat, "We're going out to lunch with Giuseppe. Can you be ready to go in fifteen minutes?"

"Will this be okay to wear? If so, I am ready now."

"It's perfect. You're beautiful!"

She smiled at him, one of those dazzling smiles that he knew he would never tire of seeing. "One more call, and then we can go." As answer to the unspoken question on her face, he said, "To the police. I want to make an appointment to see them."

He was rewarded by a smile that almost melted him. He smiled back, and then turned to go into his study.

Jeff sat at his desk. He started several times to pick up the phone and call the number on the card Detective Newbern had given him. He closed his eyes. He still couldn't put all the pieces together. Could Giuseppe have known about the drugs at Dominion?

He felt himself take a sharp breath. Jeff couldn't believe such a thing could occur. It was something he had repeatedly pushed to the back of his mind. It had lingered there for some time, ever since he had talked to Guerra. Now it had surfaced, almost against his will. He shook his head. Surely not. The drugs were going through Dominion before either of them had ever seen the place. Besides, Giuseppe wouldn't do that. Period.

Jeff put the Detective's card in his wallet. He'd call him after lunch with Giuseppe. First, he had to talk to Giuseppe.

Cat came into the study. "Jeff, it's been almost thirty minutes. Shouldn't we leave?"

He had lost track of the time. He picked up the express envelope from the entry hall as they went out the door and got in Jeff's car. Cat looked at the envelope with an expression of dismay.

"Fortunately, Giuseppe's almost always late, so we'll probably get there about the same time he does. This is just in case someone wants to spoil our lunch," Jeff said as he stuck the envelope into the glove compartment.

Buckhead Country Club was only about five minutes from Jeff's house. It took longer today because Jeff wanted to make sure he wasn't followed. One of the reporters jumped into a car and tried to follow him as Jeff roared out the drive. Jeff was pretty sure he lost him. In his haste to leave he had forgotten to get one of the guards to come with them. Oh well, it was only lunch.

The club had a long winding drive that ran past the 18th hole of the golf course. There was valet parking at the entrance. Jeff was impatient because the minivan that turned into the drive in front of him was moving at about ten miles per hour. He was separated by the car in front from the club's entrance when he saw Giuseppe and Carmen leave their car and go into the club.

"That's Giuseppe and Carmen, getting out of that blue car," he said to Cat. He turned his head toward her when he heard her gasp. Her face was chalky white. She was very upset.

"What's wrong?"

"That woman. I know her."

Jeff hit the brakes. Fortunately, there was no one behind him. "How do you know her? What ...?"

"She used to go to the *Casa de Liberacion*. She was always with Raphael's cousin."

Jeff felt his heart hammering. "What is the cousin's name, Cat?" he asked with a dreadful, sinking feeling that he already knew the answer.

"Paul Carmona."

20

Jeff waited until Giuseppe and Carmen had disappeared inside before he drove around the valet's stand and headed out the driveway. His mind was reeling with indecision and unanswered questions.

Should he confront Giuseppe and Carmen? Should he now go to the police? Did this mean Giuseppe was involved? Did it mean anything? Could it just be a coincidence? He knew Giuseppe had met Carmen in Miami. Maybe Cat was mistaken. Maybe Carmen just looked like someone she knew. Although, Jeff reflected, Carmen was a very striking woman. There wasn't a mistake in identity.

He stopped by the side of the drive, on the grass where the club's pro would probably murder him if he saw the car. Jeff looked at Cat. She was still white and shaken. "You are sure?"

She nodded with determination. "I have not seen her for over two years, but I am very sure it is the same woman. Her name is Carmen Saez?"

Jeff nodded.

"Then it is her. I do not like her. She is one of those women who manipulate men. She led Paul around like a small dog."

Jeff picked up the car phone and called the hotel where the pilots were staying. After a brief wait he was put through to their room. "This is Jeff Royal. Can you have the plane ready to leave in thirty minutes?"

"You'd better give us an hour. We need to check out and file a flight plan, Mr. Royal. Where are we going and how many passengers?"

"I want to go to Boca Raton. Two people. Which airport will you use?"

"I'd prefer Pompano Beach. It's small, but we'll avoid the traffic at ..."

"That's fine with me. Don't check out of the hotel. We'll be back late tonight. I'll meet you at the airport within an hour, sooner if you can. Thanks," Jeff said as he hung up. He turned to Cat. "I'm going to have to break my promise to you. Carmen changes everything. Will you go with me to see Raphael? When we get back tonight I will go to the police."

"... I suppose. But only if you tell me what we are doing. Why are you going to see Raphael?"

"Just a moment, I need to make a few more calls, and then I will tell you everything. Better still, let's get on the plane. Then we won't be interrupted. It will take some time to tell you all of it."

Next, he dialed Raphael. After a very long wait, he came to the phone. He sounded very weary. "Jeff, I'm sorry. I've been very busy. What do you want?"

"I'd like to come to see you this afternoon. I want to talk to Paul Carmona."

"... That will be difficult, Jeff. *Señor* Carmona is in seclusion. I don't believe ..."

"I know it will be difficult, Raphael. But I believe I have some more information you will want, about the movement of merchandise. I will give you all of it after I talk to him. It's very important."

"I ... I will let you see him, Jeff. When can you be here?"

"I'll arrive at Pompano Beach Airport at about three o'clock. Can you meet us? Cat will be with me."

ROYAL REVENGE

"Julio will come with someone else to pick you up. They will bring Cat here and then take you to the place where *Señor* Carmona is resting. I will see you there."

The next call was to the country club. Jeff asked them to notify Mr. Portales, with his apologies, that he was unavoidably delayed and would not be able to meet him. Jeff hung up before they were able to ask any further questions.

Then Jeff called his home. Rena answered. "Rena, this is Jeff. Something's come up and we're going to be gone until rather late this evening. I'm not sure about you staying there alone. Wouldn't you like to go to a hotel?"

"Mr. Royal, I'm fine. Nobody's going to do anything to me. You just call me if there's anything you need," she answered.

Reluctantly, Jeff agreed but asked to speak to the Pinkerton man in charge. He waited while Rena went to get him. After the man identified himself, Jeff said, "I want you to have six men there at all times. I want all of them armed, two of them in the house. That lady is very important to me. Any problems?"

"No sir. I'll get some more people out here within the hour. Are you expecting any visitors?"

"No. But I didn't expect any this morning either. Keep everyone very alert. And I don't want you to let anyone in that house until I return. Understood? I'll be back after midnight. Let me speak with Rena again, please."

Rena came back on the line. "Yes, Mr. Royal?"

"Rena, we'll be back late tonight. There will be two guards in the house with you. I've told them to let no one in. I just wanted you to know. Also, Mr. Portales might call. If he does, just tell him you don't know where I am, or when you expect me to return. Okay?"

"Well I don't, do I? Don't worry, I'll be fine, Mr. Royal. You and the lady be careful, now. I'll have sandwiches ready when you get back. Goodbye," she said cheerfully.

Just after Jeff hung up the phone, it buzzed. Cat looked at him with a questioning look when he failed to pick it up. "I'm sure that's Giuseppe. He won't be happy that I didn't meet him." After it buzzed a few more times, it was silent. It rang twice more before they reached the airport.

A few minutes later, Jeff turned into the airport. The pilots were already there, going through the motions of getting ready to leave. They put sandwiches on board, and Jeff and Cat went to their seats. Jeff stuffed the express envelope under the seat. They buckled up, and after a brief wait, they taxied out and took off. As they left the ground, Jeff wondered what Giuseppe really knew.

21

Giuseppe was quite disturbed when the waiter delivered Jeff's message. Jeff had never failed to meet him before, for any appointment, unless he was sick. And the message was ominously vague. He threw his napkin down on the table and said to Carmen, "Let's go back to the apartment. Jeff isn't coming, and I don't know where he is. We have to decide what to do very quickly. I'm pretty sure the shit's going to hit the fan now."

Carmen smiled, "Don't worry, Giuseppe. I can ..."

"You can do what? You can just get in the goddamn car. Let's go," he muttered, his eyes narrowing with fury.

They rode without speaking to the apartment they shared. Giuseppe tried Jeff's car phone several times. There was no answer. He called Jeff's home just before they left the car. Rena told him she didn't know where Jeff was. He slammed the phone down. "Damn! He's onto something, Carmen. This isn't like him. He knows something. I can feel it."

"Relax, Giuseppe. You're in control, not Jeff. Everything's going to be fine. Let's just go inside. We'll get you settled down, first. Then we can decide what to do next." Her hand stroked him softly. She could feel him get excited. Carmen knew how to handle Giuseppe.

Giuseppe opened the door of the luxurious apartment and went straight to his desk, leaving Carmen to close and lock the door. The little ebony box was in the top drawer. He took it out and placed it on the desk in front of him. He opened the little latch and raised the lid and took out the mirror and laid it on his desk. In his haste, he spilled some of the precious white powder on the desk. He dipped his fingers in it and rubbed them on his gums. Giuseppe poured more of the powder onto the shining surface of the mirror, which lay on his desk. His reflection looked back at him. It disturbed him. Staring back was a face that reminded him of someone else. Someone he didn't like. But he couldn't remember who it was. His face was florid and dark and sweaty. He had huge dark circles under his eyes.

He made three lines of the powder and snorted it forcefully up his nose. Moments later, a rush of well being spread across his body, then shot through his brain. He leaned back in the chair and closed his eyes and let the drug course through his body. He felt himself relax.

His eyes were half-open when Carmen emerged from the bedroom. She was naked except for a man's blue cotton shirt. Her face had a wanton smile, and she carried a limber switch in her hand. She walked slowly, enticing and exciting him.

She stood in front of the desk, watching his eyes. One button at a time, she slowly and seductively took off the shirt. She pinched her nipples until they were hard and erect. She dipped her fingers between the lips of her vagina, and then sucked on them slowly. She ran her hands down her body, her motions inviting, erotic. She plainly enjoyed the effect she was having on Giuseppe. Carmen put the switch to her mouth, and then licked it up and down and sucked on it. Giuseppe watched with growing expectation. She rubbed the switch on her breasts, then slowly, lasciviously, up and down between her legs. It glistened with her moisture. Her eyes never left Giuseppe's.

Carmen came around the desk. She laid the switch down on it. She put her hands around Giuseppe's head and drew him to her breasts. He eagerly took one in his mouth and sucked fiercely as she unzipped his pants and fondled him.

ROYAL REVENGE

She pulled away from him. "Do you like to do that, Giuseppe? Do you like to suck on my breasts? Tell me you like them!"

Giuseppe nodded. He looked up at her. His face was pleading, almost pitiful. His eyes had a sleepy look, half-closed from the effects of the cocaine.

Carmen dipped her fingers into the cocaine and then inserted them in her vagina. Then with a sigh she moved the ebony box to the side and sat on the desk, facing Giuseppe. She spread her legs and placed them on his shoulders. She pulled his head down to her.

With a moan of pleasure, Giuseppe buried his head between her legs. His tongue entered her. Carmen threw her head back in ecstasy. Her hands were entwined in his hair. She held his head tightly against her. She began breathing faster. Soon, her body shook, and she moaned as she reached her first climax.

Giuseppe's efforts became more intense. His head and tongue moved faster and faster. Carmen's body bucked up and down on the desk with orgasm after orgasm. After a long time, she pushed his head away. She moved away from him and picked up the switch again.

"Take off your clothes, Giuseppe," she said as she rubbed the switch up and down the front of his pants. Her face was twisted in a sadistic grimace. Her voice was husky, low, almost a man's voice.

Carmen watched as Giuseppe obediently stood up and stripped off his clothes. He threw them in a mound on the floor. He took off the jewelry he wore and threw it on top of his clothes. He stood in front of her, naked. He was excited, but his body shook as if from being cold. Tears began to fall down his cheeks as he cried silently.

Carmen leaned across the desk and put a dash of the powder on the mirror and arranged it in a line. She snorted it up her nose and leaned back with a sigh as the drug took effect. She sat up and looked at Giuseppe with malicious desire. Suddenly she hit the desk very forcefully with the switch.

Whack!

"Come close to me, Giuseppe. Come here." She took hold of his penis and guided him to her side. He stood beside her. He was fully erect. Tears fell from his eyes, unabated.

Carmen stroked him, licking her lips with pleasure. She leaned down and took him into her mouth, licking, sucking, bringing him almost to the point of orgasm, and then pulling away.

Her breathing was rapid, her voice very husky, a low, rasping whisper. "Tell me what you were doing, Giuseppe. You know that was a filthy thing to do. What were you doing to me?" she asked as she fondled him with the switch.

"I was ..."

Whack! The switch cut across Giuseppe's buttocks. Giuseppe winced from the pain. "You must be punished for doing these things, Giuseppe," Carmen said as she raised the switch again and again.

Giuseppe woke three hours later. He was in their bed. His mind was very fuzzy. His head throbbed and throbbed. His body hurt from the many times Carmen had hit him with the switch. She was asleep beside him. The switch lay beside her. He looked at her sleeping body with hate and disgust. She was beautiful.

He couldn't remember most of what they had done. He usually couldn't. But, lately, it was worse. He went into the bathroom and looked at himself in the mirror. The reflection almost made him sick. His nose was red and running. His eyes were shot with blood and had black circles under them. There were big red welts across his skin, even on his stomach. He stuck out his tongue. It had a yellow, chalky coat on it. He took two aspirin. Then, he splashed cold water on his face, trying to clear his mind, trying to remember what he had to do.

Suddenly he remembered about Jeff. What did he know? Giuseppe was sure he knew something. Shit! What could they do, now? He put on his robe. He went to his desk and called the office. The operator put him through to Olivia.

"Olivia, this is Giuseppe. Have you heard from Jeff?"

"No, Giuseppe, I thought you were having lunch with him. He hasn't called. Have you tried the house? I'll be happy to ..."

"That's okay. He was supposed to call me after lunch. If he calls you, tell him I'm at home, will you?"

"I guess you're not coming back to the office, then. Did you forget that you had a meeting with George this afternoon? He's called about four times."

"Damn! I forgot. I ... I'm not feeling well. Tell George I'll meet with him first thing tomorrow, okay?"

"Well, okay. He won't be happy, Giuseppe. But I'll tell him. Goodbye."

Giuseppe could hear the irritation in her voice. She had practically hung up on him. Olivia didn't like to cover for him. That was getting more frequent, too. He knew he was pushing her. Tough shit. That was part of the job. If she didn't like it, she could take a hike. There were plenty of other secretaries to be found, especially for what they were paying her.

He released the latch and opened the ebony box. The mirror lay on top of the powder. A glance at the face in the mirror made him shut the box and put it aside. What in the hell had happened to him? How did he get so fucked up?

Giuseppe sat at his chair, his elbows on the desk, his head in his hands. What _had_ happened? At first, it was just a little high he wanted. The joints didn't have much effect any more. This stuff made sex so good. Then he found that he wanted it to help him relax, to think. Now he couldn't remember why he wanted it. He just wanted it. He didn't hear Carmen come into the room. He was startled when she spoke.

"What's wrong? You look like you've lost your best friend," she said, with just a hint of sarcasm.

"Maybe I have," Giuseppe said without looking up.

"If you mean Jeff, it's too late for remorse, Giuseppe. Get a grip on yourself. If you really think he knows something, we need to act. It's him or us, now. I think it's pretty obvious what we need to do. Jeff's been very lucky we've been so patient. But his luck's run out. We can't scare him off, so we have to get more serious."

Giuseppe looked up at her. She was stark naked. She was gorgeous. She stood there, meeting his gaze, smiling proudly, insolently, daring him to challenge her.

Suddenly his vision blurred. He saw a woman's body, perfect in every detail. She had beautiful, olive-colored skin. Giuseppe loved to touch her skin. It was sensuous and soft. Her stomach was flat and hard, almost boy-like. Her breasts were full and firm, and stood up proudly, with huge, dark, nipples. Her waist was tiny, but her hips were full and lush. Her long legs were slim and very shapely. Giuseppe stared at her thick patch of black pubic hair. He licked his lips. Her face was out of focus. He was suddenly excited, filled with an incredible desire to have her. He shook his head as if to rid himself of the thoughts.

"Carmen, we've discussed this before. It's gone too far already. I agree we need to cover our ass. But Jeff is off limits. Period!"

"Baby, you're not thinking. Look at what we've put together. Are you going to let someone like him take it apart?"

He looked at her beautiful face. Her mouth was set in a tiny, impudent smile. Her eyes were very sultry with undisguised hunger. Her black eyes sparkled. She licked her lips, inviting him, knowing he would get excited. But, in his befogged state, he only saw a sneer of disgust, of loathing. He closed his eyes and then opened them, hoping to clear his vision. And, then, in a flash, her entire face became distorted. Abruptly, Giuseppe was staring into the face of old Mr. Flanagan. Giuseppe was filled with hatred and rage. He blinked his eyes again. As suddenly as it appeared, the awful face was gone. He was looking at Carmen's beautiful face again.

"This is the end of it, Carmen. Jeff is off limits. Scaring him was one thing. That's bad enough. Trying to kill him is another. Everything's gone too far. I'm still sick over the thing with Connie. What if one of these apes gets out of hand again? We're finished. We'll have to pack up and leave, or take our chances," Giuseppe said with determination.

"The end! No way, Giuseppe. It may be the end for you, but not for me. I'm in control of this deal. I'm not packing up and leaving. I'm not going to let a selfish prick like Jeff mess up my life. He should have stayed out of it. We've done everything we can to scare him away. If he's too stupid to take the hint, it's his tough luck. The deal with Connie wasn't an accident. That's the only way it _could_ have worked, and he's _still_ nosing around. If you're so fucking weak ..."

Giuseppe's mind snapped. He stood up and grabbed the ebony box and flung it across the room. He took off the robe so violently he ripped the sleeve. Leaping forward, he grabbed her by the throat. She tried to scream but he choked her and the scream became more of a gurgle. He threw her down and fell on top of her. He entered her violently, hoping to hurt her. She cried out in pain. She scratched his face, trying to force him away. Giuseppe slapped her face so hard her lip split and began bleeding. Carmen's eyes were full of hate, and just a little fear.

"Stop it, Giuseppe, you son of a ...!"

She couldn't finish. He hit her in the face with his fist. He could feel her cheekbone crunch. She moaned with pain. Tears welled up in her eyes. She was terrified.

"Giuseppe, please."

Her face alternated in Giuseppe's vision with the awful face of Flanagan. He shook his head. His mind was still foggy. He couldn't keep the faces straight.

"You bastard-bitch! I'll show you who's in control."

Giuseppe turned her over and propped her legs up under her. Carmen helped him, thinking he would finish his anger in a bout of sex. He entered her anus so hard that he tore her flesh. She screamed with pain. He hit her in the side of the head with his fist, almost tearing her ear from her skull. Her body went limp. No longer sexually excited, he turned her over. Flanagan stared back at him. He hit her again and again, until she was completely still, and the uncontrolled rage had passed.

Giuseppe stood up. He looked at his bleeding hands, wondering what had happened to him. He looked at the body lying in front of him. He bent down and felt for a pulse. There was none. She was dead. Her face was a bleeding mess. Giuseppe didn't feel remorse. He didn't feel fear. He didn't feel anything, even the pain in his hands.

He went to the desk and sat, nude, his hands bleeding onto the leather top. He had betrayed his sister. He'd betrayed his grandfather. He'd betrayed Maritza. He'd betrayed Connie. He wouldn't betray Jeff any further. He picked up the phone and called Jeff's house. Rena answered.

"Rena, this is Giuseppe Portales. Is Jeff at home yet?"

"Well, no sir. I don't know when he'll be coming back, Mr. Portales. Can I give him a message for you?"

"Yes. Tell him that I have a very important package for him. I won't be able to bring it by, but I'll put it in my mailbox. He has the key. It's urgent. He should pick it up as soon as possible tonight, even if it's very late. It's very important. Tell him that."

ROYAL REVENGE

"Of course, Mr. Portales. There's an important package for Mr. Royal in your mailbox. He should pick it up at once, tonight, if possible. He has the key."

"That's right. Thanks, Rena. Remember, it's most important."

"I will. I'll tell Mr. Royal. Goodbye, Mr. Portales."

Giuseppe got out his cassette recorder and placed it on the desk. He went to the refrigerator and got a beer. He put on his torn robe, took a sip of the beer, and lit up a cigar.

With a casual glance at Carmen's body, he started dictating. It was difficult. He would start saying something and then erase it. For long periods of time, he couldn't think of what to say or the words to use. Two hours, three beers, and two cigars later, he had finished. He had used both sides of a cassette. Giuseppe labeled it side "A" & side "B" and put it in an envelope addressed to Jeff. He cinched up his torn robe and went to the mailbox and put the package there.

It was just before six o'clock, and a very nice evening. His neighbors were coming home from work, greeting their families. He had once had a family, but he had betrayed them. God, he had been stupid. Now he had nothing. Nothing.

Shaking his head, Giuseppe walked back inside. He locked the door and picked up the phone. He dialed. When someone answered, he said, "This is Giuseppe Portales. I've just told the police everything, and I mean everything. Killing Jeff Royal won't help you now. You'd better worry about protecting your own ass. Carmen's dead. You'll never touch me, you cocksucker." He left the phone off the hook. A man's voice was yelling at him.

Giuseppe went into the bathroom and flushed the key to the mailbox down the toilet. He got Carmen's makeup mirror and her bottle of sleeping pills and took them out to the desk. He picked up Carmen's body and threw it on the bed, and then covered it with the sheet. He felt nothing. Then, he gathered up his clothes and dressed. He took the switch and broke it in half and put the two pieces of it under the bed.

He went to the corner of the room and got the ebony box off the floor. The latch had held, and it was still well over half full. He poured the contents out on the large makeup mirror and methodically arranged it all in two-inch-long lines. There were fifteen of them when he finished.

He got a bottle of expensive brandy from the bar and poured a generous amount into a glass. He gulped it down, along with the half-full bottle of sleeping pills. The strong brandy made his eyes water and burned his throat. He lit another cigar. He poured another glass full of brandy, and gulped it down, also. He almost gagged as the second glassful collided in his stomach with the first.

He took a final turn through the bedroom for a last glance at Carmen. He still felt nothing. He sat at his desk and had a last satisfied puff on his cigar. Then, he snorted the lines of refined cocaine up his nose as fast as he could. He had finished seven lines when he lost consciousness and slumped forward. His diaphragm constricted his lungs and within ten minutes he stopped breathing. His heart stopped about two minutes later.

22

Atlanta, Boca Raton

As the plane leveled off, Jeff took both of Cat's hands in his. She smiled tenderly. Then, she released his hands, and leaned back in her chair. "Now you must tell me what this is all about, Jeff. What do you expect to do with Raphael?"

"I expect to find out who ordered Connie killed. She was killed because our company was taking over Dominion Distributors. Guerra told me she was kidnapped to scare me off. According to him, she was killed when Gaspar went out of control.

"I don't believe that. Guerra told me that Espinoza was running drugs across Canada using the Dominion trucks. Gaspar ran the ring for them. It couldn't have happened unless someone working for Dominion knew all about it. When we bought the company, that network was in danger. Connie was killed to take me out of the picture. That still left Giuseppe. I think he knew about it and was part of it. Giuseppe is the only one who could have known what effect Connie's death would have on me.

"Giuseppe couldn't have known anything when we started looking at Dominion. But he started getting serious with Carmen about the same time we began to get interested in the company in Canada. I think Carmen was behind his involvement. She was working with Paul Carmona, who was working for Espinoza."

"Espinoza! But Carmona works for Raphael! He is Raphael's cousin!"

"Just before Guerra died, he told me that Carmona was a traitor. Raphael told me that they knew someone in their organization worked for Espinoza. They didn't suspect Carmona. I told them. That was the name I had."

"But why Connie? Why didn't they do something to you? Why her?" Cat asked.

"Giuseppe would have known that we couldn't have purchased Dominion without me involved. I own 65% of the company. As far as the banks, suppliers, and the employees are concerned, I _am_ the company. He couldn't have pulled it off by himself with me dead. With me alive, but out of the way, he could do whatever he wanted. If I were dead, it would cause him lots of problems with banks and vendors. He had to make sure the company held together, so they could use it to move the drugs around Canada. I'm sure he also used it to wash all the money through. The amount of cash coming in has been enormous. He even paid off our bank loans to keep the auditors out."

"Then Giuseppe and Carmen tried to kill us that first day at my place?" she asked.

"I think that was meant either to scare me away or to scare you away from me. I've wondered why three thugs with machine guns could have missed killing us. I think they were told to miss, just to scare us. Giuseppe's gone bad, but I don't think he would kill me. At least, not then."

"What about at Julio's? They were the same people, weren't they?"

"Giuseppe knew I went out running every morning at exactly four a.m., and that I run for an hour. I've kept that schedule for five months. That morning I went out early and came back early. I think those people meant to kill Julio, maybe you. Again, probably to scare me off. I messed things up when I came back early."

"What about my brother. Who killed Claudio?" she asked this question in a tiny voice. The pain was evident.

"I'm sure things had gotten out of control by that time. Killing Raphael would have made Carmona stronger at Fabriza. It would also have ended my part in it. After Raphael, there's no where else I could have gone to look for information about Gaspar. If you think about it, Raphael should have been killed, along with Claudio. Claudio started the car without Raphael in it so he could cool it off. That's the only reason Raphael's still alive.

"Then, Guerra met with me to convince me that there was no point in going any further. He and Raphael both tried to convince me that everything that happened in Miami was between the two families. That it was not related to Connie or Gaspar. I think Raphael believed that. I think Guerra thought he could convince me of that. After all, I had met him before. He was smooth, and he probably could have pulled it off. I was pretty scared at that time."

"Then why did they kill Guerra? How did they know where you were?"

"Think back. The only time they didn't know where we were, was when we didn't talk about it over the phone at my condo. I think they bugged my phone. When we didn't give a location over my phone, they couldn't find us. As far as why they killed Guerra, I don't know. I'm sure those two worked for Espinoza. I'm not sure that killing Guerra wasn't an accident. I shot the guy with the gun. Then that guy shot Guerra as he died. It could have been simply a reflex.

"But this morning, they were out to kill me, period. I don't think those two were out just to scare me. I'm sure now that Carmona arranged that. He's the only one, besides Raphael, who could have known I was going back to Atlanta last night.

Raphael still wanted the name I had. He wouldn't have had me killed without that name. Carmona would have been very interested in making sure I never gave his name to Raphael. Giuseppe didn't know where I was. I was just lucky they missed."

"The real key is, who's behind Carmen and Giuseppe? As he died, Guerra tried to tell me who ran the network that moved all the drugs around. All he got out was 'CAA---'. I don't think Carmona could have done all this. He was sitting in the middle of the Fabriza family most of the time. It could have been Carmen, but I don't think Carmen had that kind of power. Who does that leave?" Jeff asked rhetorically.

"That's the person I want to find. That's the one who really killed Connie. *Señor* Carmona is the only one who can tell us that name. That's what I expect to find out from him. Hopefully that's what I will find out in Boca."

Jeff concluded with a look in his eyes that scared Cat. She hoped this thing would end soon. They had all suffered enough.

The pilot brought out the sandwiches. They ate them and then sat in silence for the rest of the trip.

The little jet circled out over the ocean, and then headed into the westerly wind for its landing in Pompano Beach. The tires screeched briefly as the pilot touched down. They taxied to the terminal. Jeff looked out the window and saw a gray limousine waiting. Julio stood beside it. He waved at the plane.

They walked down the stairs into the hot Florida sun. Julio and Cat embraced. He shook Jeff's hand, and then embraced him. There was a tense look on Julio's face.

"We're going to Raphael's father's house. There's been a change in plans. Raphael said he will explain when he sees you," Julio said.

Jeff was disturbed. This didn't look good. He had come to suspect changes and the people who made them. "Let me talk to the pilots before we leave. Then we'll go, Julio. Why don't you wait in the car with Cat?"

Jeff walked inside with the pilots. He got a piece of stationery from the office inside. He scribbled a brief note on it, and then sealed it in an envelope. He sat down with the pilots in the waiting lounge.

"I want to be able to leave for Atlanta at a moment's notice. It could be an hour; it could be three hours, even six hours from now. You'll need to stay here by the plane. Here is the number of a man named Arthur Malman." He wrote Malman's name and phone number on the front of the envelope. "If we're not back, or if I, personally, don't call you here within two hours, then you must call this number. When you reach Mr. Malman, open the envelope and read the letter inside to him. He will give you further instructions. Any questions?"

The two pilots looked at each other. It was plain they had lots of questions.

"I know it all sounds a little strange, but I assure you everything is legal and aboveboard. This is a just a very complicated deal. Mr. Malman is an attorney. He couldn't come with us. There's no reason to be concerned," Jeff assured them.

"Okay, Mr. Royal. We'll need to call the office and check in, though. We'll file a plan for Atlanta, leaving in two hours. We'll delay it if we need to. Same airport in Atlanta?"

"Yes. Two passengers for sure, maybe three. I'll see you or talk to you by, let's see, ... five o'clock. Okay?"

"Yes, sir." They stood up as Jeff left the lounge and climbed into the waiting limousine.

"This job gets stranger every day. You'd think they were fucking CIA, or the goddammed Mafia, or something," one of the pilots said to the other, who nodded his head in agreement.

While the limousine sped from Pompano Beach to Boca Raton, Jeff told Julio essentially the same things he had revealed to Cat on the plane. Julio was clearly pleased that Jeff would finally tell him what was going on although he was shocked at the same time.

"So now what? If you're right about Giuseppe, you go to the police. Raphael will take care of Carmona. What's left? Why are you here?" Julio asked.

"As I mentioned, there is someone behind all this. Someone at the top in Canada who pulled the strings. Back to our chess game analogy of yesterday, Giuseppe is a pawn. Carmen is a knight. Carmona is a bishop, for sure. But he's not the main character in our game. He's involved in another game. Someone set this distribution network at Dominion up for Espinoza. That someone worked directly under Guerra. That's who's ultimately responsible."

"And if Carmona can tell you who it is? Then what?"

"The police. I promised Cat. I promise you. From now on, I let the police handle it. By the way, Julio, why don't you come back to Atlanta with us? Call the paper and take off another week. You could tell them you're working on a story. You might as well get an exclusive on this one. It certainly will be sensational enough for the <u>Star</u>!"

"Only if you swear, again, that you will see the police this evening and let them handle everything from now on. My nerves are already shot to hell. I can't take any more of these people shooting at me and you and Cat. I don't like danger and intrigue. Hell, I don't see how James Bond can get it up. I'd be too scared all the time."

They laughed hilariously. After about twenty minutes, they arrived at the huge gate protecting the Fabriza estate. The limo driver rolled down his window, and a uniformed guard with a gun on his belt looked at the occupants of the car. He opened the gate and waved them through.

The estate of Carmino Fabriza was a virtual Garden of Eden. A winding drive took them through manicured grounds that were so perfect they looked almost natural, as only grounds in Florida or California can look. The limousine pulled up to the huge front doors of the palace-sized house, and the driver jumped out of the car and opened their door. Julio helped Cat out of the car.

"What did I tell you about the Taj Mahal? Just wait 'til you see the inside!" Julio said excitedly to Jeff.

They entered an elaborate marbled reception area and were greeted by Carmino Fabriza himself. The man, if one could ignore his profession, was as charming as Raphael. He was slightly shorter, heavier, and darker, but it was obvious that Raphael was his son. Carmino took Cat's arm and led her into the living room, where a tuxedoed butler was serving champagne. Carmino introduced Jeff to Raphael's mother. Consuela Fabriza was small, dark, and withered. She had spent most of her adult life in a wheelchair, a victim of a chronic respiratory illness. But she was alert and witty, and plainly doted on Cat. Cat embraced her fondly.

They each took a glass of champagne and made small talk for a few moments. Then Carmino excused Jeff and himself and took Jeff's arm and led him from the room. They walked down a hallway lined with beautiful paintings. Jeff was no expert, but the paintings seemed to be originals, framed perfectly, and very expensive. Eventually, Fabriza led him into a study. The walls were lined with books, from floor to ceiling. The floor was covered with an immense thick Oriental rug. A massive leather-topped desk occupied one corner. Leather couches and armchairs faced a huge marble fireplace, unusual in South Florida. Fabriza indicated a chair. Jeff sat, and the old man sat and faced him.

"My son has told me much about you, Mr. Royal. He has told me, also, of the loss of your wife. That is most unfortunate. Please accept my sympathies. You must know that we had nothing to do with her death. I hope you believe that?" He looked up at Jeff for confirmation. Jeff nodded. "Good. I also understand that you have been most helpful to us. We appreciate the kindness you have shown Cat. We are very fond of her. In fact, we had hoped ... Never mind. In return, we will try to help you."

"Thank you, Mr. Fabriza. I ..."

Jeff was interrupted as Raphael entered the room. Raphael greeted Jeff warmly and then sat down. He looked ten years older. His eyes were tired, and his face was very drawn. He had the look of a man who had just attended the funeral of a close relative. He smiled at Jeff and then leaned forward, his elbows on his knees, a very intent look on his face.

"I see you have met my father. I know you came because you want some information, so I will get right to the matter at hand.

"Unfortunately, *Señor* Carmona had a heart attack and died a little while ago. I will tell you what I know that concerns you."

He waited for a reaction from Jeff. There was none, and he continued.

" *Señor* Carmona, as you told us, worked for Espinoza, apparently for a long time. He had a girlfriend, who was actually his wife in secret, named Carmen Saez. She worked with him. Carmen was the one who convinced Paul to work for Espinoza. I know her. She had a hold on him that was almost unnatural.

"Some time ago, maybe as long as three years, she met Giuseppe Portales, the man that works for you. He is your partner, I believe. They became very close, the three of them. They met often in your condo in Miami Beach. I am told that the three engaged in, how do you say it, a *'menage a trois'*. Carmen developed the same strong hold on *Señor* Portales that she had on Paul. She also introduced Portales to the use of cocaine.

"A little after this, Gaspar was in Canada, working for Espinoza. His original mission was to take over our network there. The man was not easy to control, and he destroyed the network. Eventually, he set up a new network to move merchandise throughout the country, using the trucks of Dominion Distributors. Then you came on the scene to buy the company. Espinoza became alarmed that your purchase would undo what they had set up.

"Carmona, of course, became aware of this. He knew Portales was involved, with you, in Dominion Distributors. He convinced Espinoza to let Carmen run things, since her hold over Portales was so strong. Carmen is very greedy, and she jumped at the chance. With Paul's knowledge and agreement, she moved to Atlanta with *Señor* Portales. His cocaine usage was very heavy by this time. She quickly took total control of him.

"Portales knew that eventually you would find out. He was terrified by this. He was very concerned about you. Of course, he also knew you would not agree to what they were doing. Carmen suggested that your life be threatened. `Portales thought that would only make you mad and you would interfere with their plans. Then they decided to threaten your wife. Portales agreed, reluctantly. He knew you would retreat to protect your wife. He was told they would only hold her to scare you away. Maybe he truly believed that. I don't know.

"Gaspar was told to kidnap her. Gaspar was unmanageable, but he probably acted on orders from Carmen. In any event, he tortured and killed your wife. This removed you from the operation and made sure that Portales was in charge for good, and Portales was totally under Carmen's control.

"They had no problems for as long as you were out of the picture. Then you started asking questions. When you came to Miami, they tapped your phone, so they usually knew what progress you were making. To make you stop asking questions, they threatened you, first at Cat's apartment, then at Julio's. When you kept on, they became very worried. They decided to try one last time to discourage you. Guerra was told to meet with you and convince you to leave well enough alone.

"Before you met with Guerra, you met with me. That really worried them. Carmona and Espinoza decided that it would be a good time to eliminate me. They missed me. Unfortunately, Claudio was killed in the attempt."

Raphael paused. He closed his eyes very briefly, as if remembering Claudio, and then took a deep breath and continued.

"Now they had a new problem. We had become allies. At least, they thought we were. When you agreed to still meet with Guerra, they had another chance at you. They ignored Portales. This time they were to take you and kill you. It never occurred to them that you would take Guerra. That was a very bold and foolish move.

"Of course, as soon as Julio called me, they knew Guerra was dead, and that you probably knew about Carmona. At this point, they had to kill you before you could give me Carmona's name. I'm surprised you got out of Miami alive. I'm more surprised you survived them this morning.

"Tomorrow, they will be told that we have taken care of Carmona. They must know that very soon after that Portales and Carmen will be exposed. You should be out of danger then. Until then, I would be very careful.

"That is all I know. I'm sure it is all *Señor* Carmona knew. I have a list of names at your company in Canada that are involved. I will give you that. The others are, as you know, Carmen Saez and Giuseppe Portales."

Jeff sat in the comfortable chair. He looked at the two men in front of him. They could have been discussing a merger or acquisition with him. Instead, they discussed betrayal, drugs, death, loss of friendships, destruction of families, and greed.

He was stunned. He had convinced himself that Giuseppe was involved, but the confirmation of that fact hit him like a shot to the head. He sat in silence and composed himself. Raphael and his father did nothing to interrupt him. Finally, he turned to Raphael.

"There are still a few questions, Raphael. Who ran the network in Canada? Gaspar was a hired gun. Carmona couldn't have run it. He was too close to you, here. I don't think Carmen could do it. She was strong, but not that strong. Giuseppe wouldn't have known how. Who is it?"

"It must have been someone up there at your company in Canada. I have a list of people for you, as I said."

"But the list is of people at Dominion. This person had to be outside of Dominion. This is the person who worked with Gaspar in the first place, before the network was in place at Dominion."

The old man looked at Jeff, appraising him. He was impressed. He looked at his son. He was plainly irritated that Raphael had failed to think of this last unknown detail. He had done well, but he would definitely need added training.

Raphael looked at his father, apologetically. "Jeff is right. There must be someone else." Then he addressed Jeff. "That name could come only from Carmen, Giuseppe, or Espinoza himself. Guerra would have known also. Did he say anything?"

"He died before he finished. He said, 'the network is controlled by CAA---.' Then he died. Would this person have been here, or in Canada?"

"Either place I think. The contacts are what would have been important," Raphael answered. He looked at his father. His father nodded his agreement.

"I guess I'll have to ask Giuseppe," Jeff said. His eyes were very cold. His voice was threatening. Carmino Fabriza looked at him with higher admiration.

Raphael said, "Jeff, we could ..."

"No, Raphael, this one's up to me. I'll call you when I find out anything."

Jeff stood up and shook hands. "Thank you for telling me everything. That almost finishes it. You know I'm going to the police?"

"We expected that. You know nothing that leads to us. Destroying Espinoza in Canada will not hurt us. I do suggest you have someone protect you for the next few days, though. Carmen is obviously very dangerous. Giuseppe will be totally desperate now. We can help protect you. We know people in Atlanta that..."

"Thanks Raphael. I know you mean well, but, I have to do this my way. Julio has decided to go back to Atlanta with us. Can you have the car take us back to the airport?"

"Of course." They stood and shook hands.

"Mr. Royal, it was a pleasure to meet you. Please call us if we can help in any way," Carmino Fabriza said, as he shook his hand firmly.

"And you, sir. I am glad I met you. I appreciate your help."

Raphael handed Jeff a folded piece of paper as they left the study and walked down the hall. It had several names of Dominion employees on it.

Julio and Cat were still talking with Consuela Fabriza. Julio's belongings were in the entry, this time in a very expensive borrowed suitcase. They said goodbye all around one last time and got in the car and left at once.

They had been gone just over ninety minutes when they arrived back at the airport. The pilots were relieved to see them. The older one handed the envelope he had been given back to Jeff, as if glad to get rid of it. They took off minutes later.

They had traveled back to the airport in silence. Jeff told them what he had learned from Raphael while they flew back to Charlie Brown Field.

"So, you really didn't do anything but confirm what you already knew. You didn't get anything new. You could have saved the trip, although I'm glad you didn't. I've never been in a private plane, before," Julio said.

"I'm glad I came. Now I know for sure."

"So it is finished, then. You will go to the police, now?" Cat asked.

"Yes, Cat. I will call Detective Newbern from the car. It is up to him now. He can talk to Giuseppe and Carmen. I am finished."

She got up from her seat and threw her arms around him. Tears brimmed in her eyes and fell down her cheeks. "I am so glad. Now we worry about other things, normal things. Yes?"

"Yes. Normal things," he said as he kissed her, tenderly, then passionately. But, he wondered if his life would ever be normal again. So much had happened to him. To both of them. Was the nightmare really over? God, he hoped it was.

"Hey! Remember that I've got one of those normal things. And, it's getting excited watching you two carry on. Do you know any horny women in Atlanta, Jeff?" Julio asked seriously.

The rest of the trip was spent laughing at Julio's antics. They landed in Fulton County without delay. The pilots called a cab and went to their hotel. Jeff told them he would call them in the morning if he needed them.

As they drove away, Jeff picked up the car phone and called Detective Newbern. Newbern was surprised to hear from him, but readily agreed to meet at Jeff's house in an hour. Next, Jeff called Arthur Malman. Malman, very relieved that Jeff was coming to his senses, agreed to meet him at his home within the hour also.

He dialed his home. Rena answered.

"Hi, Rena. This is Jeff. We're on our way home. What's for dinner?"

"Well, what a nice surprise! I didn't expect you back so early, Mr. Royal. You'll have to take potluck for dinner, but I'll have it ready in a little while. Will it be just you and the lady?"

"No, Julio Pozo is with me. You'll remember him when you see him. You'll need to get the guestroom ready. Also, we'll have two visitors in about an hour, Mr. Malman and Detective Newbern. Will you have enough for them, too?"

"Of course. I'll get everything ready. By the way, Mr. Royal, Mr. Portales called about two hours ago. He said it was urgent. He left a very important package in his mailbox for you. He said you have the key. He insisted that you pick it up tonight. He sounded a little ... well, ... drunk. But he said, over and over, that the package was very important. I looked for a key, but ..."

"I have the key in my dresser. I'll swing by his place later. We'll see you in a few minutes. Goodbye, Rena."

Jeff frowned as he hung up. Now what? He felt a horrible premonition. And then, an abrupt tremor of fear clutched his heart like a giant fist. He was suddenly very worried about Giuseppe. He was sure something very bad had happened to him.

About ten minutes later, at twenty after six, he entered his driveway.

23

Atlanta

Jeff Royal met with Detective Newbern and Arthur Malman in his study. Cat and Julio were in the kitchen with Rena.

Jeff outlined what he had learned. Newbern was incredulous. "Why didn't you tell us all this stuff this morning? We could have questioned Portales."

"I had no proof. All I had were my own suspicions. I really didn't think Giuseppe was involved," Jeff answered.

"You still have no proof. Unless Portales or Carmen admit to all this, it will be very hard to prove anything."

"That reminds me. Giuseppe called Rena this afternoon. He left a package in his mailbox for me. He said it was urgent. I need to go pick it up. His place is only about five minutes from here."

"I'll go with you," Newbern said. "I assume Mr. Portales and Ms. Saez won't be there, but it's worth a try."

"There are several things we should do, at once, Jeff, to react to all this and secure the company's assets both here and in Canada. This will be a real mess. I'll wait here and jot down some notes," Arthur Malman said.

Jeff went to his bedroom and got the key to Giuseppe's apartment. Connie had often picked up Giuseppe's mail and checked on the place when Giuseppe and Jeff had been out of town. Of course, that was before Carmen moved in.

Newbern drove in his unmarked car. They went to the mailbox first. Inside was the envelope with Jeff's name on it. The apartment was dark, but Giuseppe's car was parked outside in his assigned space. Newbern knocked on the door. There was no answer.

"Open the package in the car. Maybe he bares his soul in it. I'll have to get more to go on before I can go any further."

Jeff felt the fear clutch his heart again as they sat in Newbern's car. He opened the package. Inside were a brief note and a cassette. Jeff read the note out loud.

"Dear Jeff. There's no way I can make up for what I've done. By the time you read this, I'll be dead. I prefer that to facing you. These tapes will tell you everything. You need to listen to them as soon as you can. Please forgive me. Giuseppe."

Newbern looked at Jeff's face. Jeff was white as a sheet. Newbern looked away briefly as Jeff fought for composure.

"We probably have cause to go in. Do you have a key?" Newbern asked softly.

"Yes, but ... I know what we'll find. I really don't think I can face that, now. Can we go back to my house and listen to these cassettes? A few more minutes aren't going to make much difference."

"Well ... You're probably right. I'll get an officer over here to secure the premises until we come back." After issuing orders over his radio Newbern started the car and drove back to Jeff's house.

They went into the study and Jeff inserted the first tape into his cassette player. Arthur Malman, Detective Newbern, and Jeff listened intently as Giuseppe's slightly slurred voice began. He talked in phrases, with gaps of time in between, often rather long gaps, where the only sound was the electronic hiss of the tape recorder or of Giuseppe's labored breathing.

ROYAL REVENGE

"This tape is being recorded on April 27 at four thirty p.m. Eastern Time, in Atlanta, Georgia, by Giuseppe Portales. I swear, so help me God, that everything in it is true and accurate to the best of my memory. Arthur Malman and Jeff Royal can attest that this is my voice. I have a little sister in Quito, Ecuador, named Angel. Mr. Malman and Mr. Royal will know that no one else could know that but me.

....

"Hello, Jeff. This is Giuseppe. I don't know how I got into this mess, Jeff. It just happened. It started in Miami just after we bought the company in Seattle. Maritza and I had been having big problems, you'll remember that, and I went to Miami Beach for two weeks to sort things out with myself. I met Carmen at a club there.

....

"At first, she was just another piece of ass. We'd drink and party and get high on grass. Then, I started going to Miami almost every weekend.

....

"Things were getting worse with Maritza. Maritza knew something was different, that I had changed. About two years ago, I moved out. You'll remember that, too. You were pissed, Connie was pissed. I wish I'd listened to you. Anyway, Maritza and I decided to get divorced. I didn't really care. I was going to Miami every weekend I could.

....

"One night, Carmen brought cocaine over. I tried it for the first time. Don't ever do it, Jeff. You'll never get that monkey off your back. I started to tell you all about this when we were in Acapulco. I wish I had. Maybe you could have helped me out.

....

"Carmen, of course, knew all about the company. She had started introducing me to her friends. One of them was a guy by the name of Paul Carmona. That's when things really started going to hell. Carmona had an unlimited supply of cocaine. At first, I was using it in Miami. Pretty soon, I began using it every day, even in Atlanta.

....

"One day I told Carmen about the potential deal in Canada. Since I was going to be up there so often, I wouldn't be able to come to Miami as much. The next week, she told me she would move to Atlanta and live with me. The thing with Maritza was over, anyway. Carmen came up a week later and moved in.

....

"Things heated up in Canada. We made the management deal, where we ran the place for ninety days. Carmen got very interested. You might remember that I took her up there a couple of times. All of a sudden, Carmen told me that Paul Carmona needed a favor. He wanted information about our agreement with Dominion. He was very interested in our deal there for some reason.

....

"Carmen, Paul and I were all together in Miami about a month before we closed the deal with Dominion. It had been a drugged-out weekend. You'd never believe the things we did. I guess I had gotten about as low as you could get.

....

"That's when they told me all about what they were doing there. They wanted me to help them. I was pretty strung out, but I refused. That's when they brought out the heavy guns. They had pictures of me doing things I didn't even remember. At the very least, I would have gone to jail on drug charges. Of course, they also told me I wouldn't get any more coke if I didn't work with them. I thought I was strong enough to kick it, but I wasn't. They also made it clear that we would be 'taken out' of the picture. They didn't want to lose control. I really didn't have a choice at that point. At least, I didn't think I did.

ROYAL REVENGE

....

"I told them you would find out. I knew you wouldn't allow any of this shit to go on. Carmen came up with the idea to scare you off. I knew that wouldn't work, and I told her why. That's when they, I guess we, came up with the idea of scaring you through Connie.

....

"I swear, Jeff, they were only going to take her and keep her for a few hours. When the first note came, I felt awful, really awful. Then, when the box came ...

....

"God, Jeff, I'm sorry. I loved Connie. I never wanted to hurt her. You know that. I couldn't believe what we had done. I didn't know what to do, then. At that point, it was all over for me. I wish I'd blown my fucking brains out then.

....

"Carmen told me today that they had planned to kill Connie all along. I swear I didn't know that until today. I thought that guy Gaspar just went overboard. I guess I wanted to think that. I know it doesn't help, but I killed Carmen today. At least I had enough courage to do that. Later on in this tape, I'll give you enough information to help hang everyone else. Maybe some day you'll be able to forgive me for what I've done. I hope so."

The tape stopped abruptly. The room was absolutely silent. Jeff stared at the machine on his desk. He was dazed. There were so many signs. And, he had missed them. Detective Newbern interrupted his thoughts.

"I should get some more people over there and go in. May I have your key, Mr. Royal?"

Jeff gave him the key without speaking. Newbern went out of the room, briefly, and then returned.

"A crew is on its way. They'll pick up the key. I left it with the guard at the front door."

Jeff didn't answer. He stared at nothing. Arthur Malman sat silently in his chair, his hands rubbing his temples. Newbern went to the machine and turned the cassette over.

After a moment, Giuseppe's voice filled the room again. It was getting more slurred than before.

"So now you know all of it with regard to Connie. Unfortunately, there's a lot more.

....

"You went off the deep end. That was what everyone wanted. Things went along great. Business was good. It was really good, you know. You may think now that a lot of the money that came in was from the drugs, but most of it was from the business. We built a great company, Jeff. And I almost ..."

....

There was a very long pause. The tape kept running, and they could hear Giuseppe sobbing softly.

"Sorry. Anyway, we were rocking along. The business was good, we didn't have any problems in Canada, things were fine.

....

"About a month ago, Carmen and the guy in Canada who was my contact, my boss, I guess you could say, started making noises about using Royal trucks to move shit around in the States. They wanted to expand. There was no end to what they wanted.

....

"I don't know how far it's gone down here, but they put a couple of people in the company here in Atlanta. Of course, I agreed to it. There's a file marked "Dominion Security" in my desk at the office with all the names you'll need to have. Give it to the police and let them take care of it. By the way, I'm sure Olivia Henson suspected something. She's very loyal to you, Jeff. I'm sure she was getting ready to tell you that I had some kind of problem. She probably thought I was drunk all the time.

....

ROYAL REVENGE

"When Gaspar was killed, and you went to Miami and started asking questions, I knew the shit would eventually hit the fan. We tried to scare you off, but you kept coming back. I'm almost glad you kept after it. I don't know what I would have done if they'd killed you, though. At least this way, I was forced to end it. I'm sorry, Jeff, really sorry.

....

"I don't know where I'll be from a money standpoint after this. Arthur Malman and Dick will have to sort all that out. I would appreciate it if you would let them hear this part of the tape. Everything I have left, if there's anything, I want to go half to Angel, half to Maritza. Arthur knows where to find Angel. Please tell Maritza I'm sorry and I still love her.

....

"Much of this, you may have already figured out. What will surprise you is the name of the son of a bitch that started all this. That is Lawrence Carter, the Vice-Consul for the U.S., in Montreal. He was Gaspar's boss. He ran the whole thing from day one. This guy is the most ruthless bastard I've ever met. He manipulated Carmen like she manipulated me. You wouldn't believe some of the shit he did. I will call him and tell him I've spilled my guts. Then, at least, he won't keep trying to have you killed. There's a couple of things in my Dominion file on him. One is a picture of him in bed with a twelve-year-old boy. Little boys were his specialty, although he had very few limits. Carmen took the picture. I found it in her stuff one day. The hilarious part is that the picture was taken in Miami. No diplomatic immunity. There's also enough about Canada so Inspector Roch can ask him a lot of embarrassing questions. I hope it's enough to fry the motherfucker. If I know him, he'll be on his way to Rio ten minutes after I call.

....

"I'm sorry we missed lunch today. I would have liked to see you one more time. Maybe I would have had the guts to thank you for everything you've done for me. Probably not. Maybe I could have apologized. Who knows? Anyway, I'm leaving now. I will put enough shit in my system to save the State the time and trouble to fry me. I'm sorry, Jeff, I'm really sorry. Please forgive me. I wish I'd been a better friend to you. Giuseppe."

....

The tape continued on, but there was no sound. The three men sat absolutely still. Newbern finally turned off the machine.

A phone rang in another part of the house. Rena came to the door of the study. "Mr. Newbern, there's a call for you. You can take it out here."

After Newbern left the room, Arthur Malman came over to Jeff's side. "We have a lot of things to do, but they'll wait until tomorrow or the next day. Why don't you call me when you're ready to see me? I'm really sorry, Jeff. It's plain that Giuseppe went beyond his ability to control himself. I'm very sorry, for him as well as for you." Malman waited a moment, and then left quietly.

Jeff was still sitting at his desk when Newbern came back into the room. "They were both dead. Carmen had been beaten to death. Giuseppe died from an overdose of just about everything. I hate to bother you now, but I need to get that file from his office desk. I also want to call that Inspector Roch in Montreal that you worked with. We need to get after the people on Mr. Portales' list as soon as possible. Can you get those things for me, now?"

Jeff nodded. At least it was finished. The nightmare was finally over.

24

Pablo Espinoza was really pissed off. He hit the seat of his opulent limousine with his meaty fist over and over. He hung up the phone again. He hated this goddam traffic. Eight o'clock on Friday night, and he still was sitting in this shit. He wanted to get home. He had a very special friend waiting. She was the youngest he'd had in months.

It was bad enough that Royal, that fucking amateur, had killed Herman Guerra. That son of a bitch had fucked up a beautiful deal. Guerra was truly a genius. He would be very hard to replace. And, now, Pablo couldn't get hold of Paul. Where the fuck was he? What had gone wrong, now? As soon as he was sure Paul was safe, he'd kill every fucking one of the Fabriza family. Surely Herman hadn't ...

The tinted windows of the big car shattered inward as the Teflon-tipped bullets from several machine guns raked its length. Pablo's head exploded all over the back seat. His fat body jerked up and down as another hundred bullets thudded into him. The bodyguard died before he ever got his gun out. Pablo's young driver's last thought before his own brain died was why anyone would want to do this to him. After all, he was just the driver.

***

The pilot revved the engines, preparatory to releasing the brakes and rolling down the runway. The roar of the big 767's engines abruptly ceased, and the captain's voice came on. "I'm sorry, ladies and gentlemen, but we have a slight mechanical problem that just developed. We'll have to return to the gate and have it looked at. We shouldn't be long at all." The French translation of that brief statement took up most of the short time that they needed to get back to the terminal.

The plane stopped at the gate. Almost immediately, the front door opened. The other first-class passengers of the Air Canada flight from Montreal to Lima were most surprised when four uniformed policemen came on the plane and arrested the man in 3-C. The plane left moments later without Lawrence Carter.

***

It was eleven o'clock p.m. in Montreal, eight o'clock in Vancouver. Fourteen homes across Canada were disrupted as Canadian police arrested the people who belonged to the names in Giuseppe's file. Several people were awakened. At least one came to the door with his dinner napkin around his neck. All of them were trusted employees of Dominion Distributors. Their neighbors were very upset. Their families were destroyed.

***

Atlanta police surrounded the homes of Pete Samuels and Gary Hoffman at midnight. Both surrendered without incident. Jeremiah Farley and Davey Hale were arrested at Royal Floors' distribution center.

***

Jeff met with his key Atlanta employees early Saturday morning. They were disturbed about Giuseppe. He had been an important part of the company since its inception. But, lately, Giuseppe had been acting strange. They were glad Jeff was back.

He scheduled a sales meeting for the following Friday, to inform every member of the sales force as to their ongoing direction, and to assure them of the continuing health of the company. Olivia Henson took charge of the project of removing Giuseppe's name from every office, bulletin board, and memo. Jeff hired their accountant, Dick Wortham, as Chief

ROYAL REVENGE

Financial Officer, and promoted the sales manager, George Hearne, to Executive Vice President. Jeff gave Olivia a fifty thousand-dollar bonus.

The <u>Atlanta Post</u> headline on Saturday read:

"LOCAL MILLIONAIRE ESCAPES DEATH: CFO COMMITS MURDER/SUICIDE"

"Atlanta, Georgia. Mr. Jeffrey Royal, president of Royal Distributors which is headquartered in Atlanta, narrowly escaped death at the hands of two gunmen early yesterday morning.

"Atlanta police report that the two gunmen, identified as Carlos Jaime Avila and Frank Albert Taylor, both of Miami, Florida, were killed in the attempt outside the grounds of Mr. Royal's Buckhead estate. Mr. Royal was unhurt.

"Mr. Royal was the husband of the late Connie Royal, also of Atlanta. Mrs. Royal was abducted, tortured, and brutally murdered last September while on a business trip to Montreal with her husband. The motive for the murder has not been determined. Mrs. Royal's killer is alleged to have been Jean-Claude Gaspar, 31, of Miami. Gaspar died in Montreal, Quebec, of multiple gunshot wounds suffered during his capture April 21 by Canadian police. Gaspar was alleged to be a longtime employee of the Miami Underworld.

"In an apparently unrelated event, Royal Distributors' Executive Vice President, Giuseppe Portales, was found dead in his home by Atlanta Police late last evening, an apparent suicide. Mr. Portales lived in the Buckhead apartment with Mrs. Carmen Saez Carmona, originally of Miami, Florida. Ms. Carmona was also found in the apartment. She had been brutally beaten to death, apparently at the hands of Mr. Portales. No further details were available from police at press time.

Royal Floors is headquartered in Atlanta and operates branches throughout the United States and Canada. It is privately held.

"Ms. Olivia Henson, a spokesperson at Royal Floors, declined comment. Mr. Royal has been unavailable for interview since the murder of his wife last September.

"Atlanta police said the two events seemed to be coincidental. No motive has been established in either of the incidents. Their investigation is continuing."

***

Arthur Malman sorted out the estate of Giuseppe Portales. His stock in Royal Floors went half to Maritza and half to Angel. Jeff Royal, by prior agreement, purchased the stock for the sum of two million dollars. Jeff paid that amount in cash. Arthur distributed it, one-half to Maritza Portales, and one-half to Angel Portales Sandera of Quito, Ecuador. The Federal Government confiscated everything else in Giuseppe's name pending its investigation of the sources of Giuseppe's cash.

Jeff kept the Pinkerton guards at the gate for three more weeks to discourage the growing hoard of reporters. The only visitor allowed to enter was Maritza Portales. Jeff had called her to tell her about Giuseppe's death. He let her listen to the last part of Giuseppe's tape. She had little emotion.

"Giuseppe died a long time ago, as far as I'm concerned, Jeff. I knew something was wrong with him. I thought it was alcohol. I didn't know enough about drugs to suspect anything. I knew for a long time he had other women in his life, but I thought that would pass. The last six months with him were truly hell on earth.

I'm sorry for him. I'm sure part of his problems had to do with his background in Quito. He wouldn't talk about it, his childhood. In fact, this is the first I've heard of a sister. You know how he felt about psychologists. They were for weaker people than Giuseppe.

"I did everything I knew to do for him, but, finally I had to go on about my own life. I gave up on him a long time ago. I'm sorry for the trouble he caused you. I hate him for his part in Connie's death."

Jeff couldn't think of anything to say.

25

Maritza stayed for dinner that evening and met Julio and Cat. They got along very well. Julio was very attracted to Maritza. Even after the first few days, as much to avoid the reporters as for any other reason, Julio and Cat stayed close to the house while Jeff was at work. Jeff always came directly home after work. They invited Maritza for dinner every night. She came, willingly. She and Cat seemed to have a very strong bond.

After a week, Julio went back to work in Miami. The <u>Star</u> soon published a sensational exclusive story about Giuseppe and his involvement in the Canadian drug ring. Neither Jeff, nor Royal Floors, was ever mentioned as a source. Julio came back to Atlanta to visit almost every weekend. Maritza always came over as soon as Julio came to town.

Rather quickly, Maritza and Cat became very close friends. Maritza often told Jeff that Connie would approve of Cat. Of course, the two women saw a lot less of each other eight months later, when Maritza moved to Miami to marry Julio.

But Jeff and Cat often went to visit them. While they were there, they stayed at their newly redecorated condo in Miami Beach.

Every day that they were in Atlanta, Cat took English lessons from Colleen Schaeffer. After a few months, Cat was totally fluent in her new language, although with a charming Spanish accent. Colleen continued with Jeff's exercise regimen, although Jeff gave up the Spanish lessons.

ROYAL REVENGE

Cat taught Rena enough Spanish for her to communicate with her in that language. Rena taught Cat how to cook "Southern style". They got along extremely well.

Royal Floors' business continued to thrive. About a year and a half after Giuseppe's death, Jeff sold Royal Floors to an investment group in the Midwest. He sold his house in Atlanta about the same time and he and Cat and Rena moved to a beautiful house in Coral Gables. Jeff sold the Miami Beach condo and bought a boat and went fishing frequently with Cat and Rena. He and Julio saw more and more of each other and Cat and Maritza became best friends. The two couples often got together for dinner and for weekend getaways. Avoiding full retirement, Jeff became a key and very public supporter of the drug education movement in Miami's schools.

After less than a week, the open warfare between the Espinosa and Fabriza families came to a close. After the deaths of Pablo Espinosa and Herman Guerra, the family was leaderless. The Espinosa family quickly ceased to exist, and Miami breathed a sigh of relief, although little changed regarding the drug business in Florida. The Cali and Medellín cartels, and eventually the Mexican cartels, just found new ways to distribute their products.

Raphael Fabriza died of AIDS exactly three years after Claudio's death. Shortly after, his father, Carmino, died of blood poisoning and other complications as the result of a bite by a Copperhead snake suffered while he was walking in his yard. Raphael's uncle, Alphonso, was killed in a raid by government troops near Medellin, Columbia.

Consuela Fabriza still lives in her huge house in Boca Raton and goes to Miami to visit Jeff and Cat quite often.

Jesse Castillo re-entered politics and is currently the Congressional Representative from Miami.

ABOUT THE AUTHOR

J. Trey Weeks has been a successful international businessman in his own right. Beyond that, he wishes to maintain his privacy, and let the story stand on its own merits. Good reading. Good fortune. And be careful where you vacation.

.
.
.